DIVIDED SKY

JEFF CARSON

CROSS ATLANTIC PUBLISHING

CHAPTER 1

"HE'S DRIVING a silver Jeep Rubicon, brand new."

Chief Detective David Wolf listened intently, cell phone at his ear, as he steered his department-issued Ford Explorer toward Williams Pass. "Got it."

MacLean read the license plate number, but Wolf caught only half of it.

"What was that? Reception just cut out."

The sheriff continued as if Wolf had said nothing. "Anyway, let me know what you find. And stay safe. Like I said, one dead, one missing. Sheriff Roll tells me that given the amount of blood they found, it's not looking too good for the missing. And then—"

The line cut out again. Cell reception never reached the zone Wolf had just driven into, and until somebody leveled the Rocky Points Ski Resort it never would. He hung up and put the phone in his center console.

Wolf drove up through the trees and past the newly renovated ski-base village, the cool summer breeze blowing through his open window. The resort parking lot was crowded for a mid-June Sunday afternoon, proving the town chamber of commerce advertising dollars were being put to good use.

The road passed the resort bustle and wound along the river, up a thickly wooded seam between the two mountains that delineated the ski area boundary. To the left, grass-carpeted ski runs cut through the pines; to the right, the well-to-do cleared their pieces of forest and erected homes.

Former sheriff Hal Burton's home came into view as Wolf drove out of the trees and into a wide meadow. Though Burton's neighbors were close by Colorado standards, the surrounding walls of forest gave the place a sense of isolation.

"I can take a leak off the back deck," Burton had once told him. The American Dream realized.

Wolf pulled into a dirt driveway, smoothed by a recent grading. The garage door was open, revealing only Burton's Ford SUV inside. His nephew Jesse Burton's Jeep Rubicon was nowhere to be seen.

He parked and stepped out into a warm sun, cooled by the ever-present breeze that persisted at ten thousand feet. A gust in the distance rolled down the mountain, swaying the trees.

His former boss's property was uncharacteristically unkempt. The grass surrounding the house was at least knee high, the riding lawnmower parked expectantly outside the garage door, warming in the sun.

He'd never known Burton to let the grass get that out of control. Or, more precisely, he'd never known Cheryl to let Burton let the grass get that out of control.

A plastic cup rolling in the wind drew his attention to the

shaded side of the house, where an upturned trash bin had been thoroughly destroyed by wildlife, leaving a refuse explosion with a blast radius that reached the far woods, over a football field away.

He put his hand on the seat of the riding lawnmower and pulled it back quickly as the heat seared his hand.

Cheryl's car was also missing from the garage. Judging by the array of power tools spread across her space, she'd been gone for a while. Probably on her annual vacation back east to visit her sister, which would explain the state of the house.

He opted to climb the steps to the front door rather than walk into the house through the garage. It was never a good idea to startle a bear, and especially when that bear was Hal Burton.

The sound of the doorbell chimed through the heavy wooden door. No other sound followed. Not a thump, nor a creak of wood.

He knocked, hard. Still nothing.

The door was locked, so he walked back down the stairs and made his way into the garage, where he knocked on the door leading inside.

No answer. He twisted the brass knob and pushed open the door.

"Hey! Burton! It's Wolf!"

Still no answer.

"Hal! It's Wolf! I'm coming in!"

He stepped inside, keeping his footfalls quiet as he waited for sounds of life that never came.

A dark line of logic snapped together in his mind, one involving Burton's nephew being a person of interest in a but they found a bunch of blood and now they're looking for Jesse for answers. The details are fuzzy. Roll's talking a mile a minute. Flustered. Sounds like he's medicating the stress with way too much coffee."

Burton shifted on the couch, still dead to the world.

"But they think Jesse's responsible," Wolf said.

"He's running, isn't he?" MacLean scoffed. "I don't know. Roll also said Jesse's girlfriend claims she was with him the whole night. So, it seems like he has an alibi. But ..."

"But he's running."

"Yeah."

"You want me to talk to Burton?" MacLean asked. "Explain the situation?"

"No need. I'll relay everything."

"All right. And as I was saying before our call cut out, we have to talk today. Me and you. Come to my office when you're back."

"What are you doing in the office on a Sunday?"

"I'll tell you when you get here."

Wolf hung up and stared at the wall. Why not let it wait until Monday?

He shook his head and stared down at Burton.

The man's face was still pressed into the couch, and his snoring seemed to come with more effort than it should have.

He remembered thinking the same thing while standing over Jack when he was a baby. Wolf had learned his lesson quickly by trying to roll his son over into what he deemed a more comfortable position. Jack had woken with a howl and had kept screaming for hours after that.

Wolf bent over, lifted his hand and smacked the side of Burton's face.

"Get up!"

Burton bounced. "The hell?"

"Hey!"

"What? What?" Burton sat upright, mouth hanging open and eyes fluttering. "Who the hell?"

"Wake up."

Burton squinted and pressed a hand to his temple. "What are you doing here?"

"They got a BOLO out on your nephew. Ouray County SD is looking for him in connection with a murder and a misper."

Burton smacked his mouth and rubbed his scalp in response. A dying animal wheeze came from his chest.

"Have you heard from him?"

No answer.

"Did you hear what I said?"

"No."

Wolf took a deep breath, hoping for patience, and repeated the whole spiel.

Burton stared at Wolf, incomprehension morphing to pain-laced concern. "Murder? Missing person? You have to start from the beginning."

Wolf explained how Sheriff Roll of Ouray County called MacLean, and told Burton about the man shot down in Ridgway two days ago, and how one of Jesse's friends had gone missing, leaving a trail of blood.

"And they think Jesse's responsible?"

"He's running, isn't he?" Wolf said, repeating MacLean's earlier words. "Have you heard from him?"

"No, I haven't heard from him."

"Where's your phone?"

"Go get him, where? He fled from law enforcement down in Ridgway. He's on the run."

Burton stood, and then his ample frame tipped back, and he landed heavily on the couch. That didn't stop him, though, and he bounced back hard to his feet. "Move."

Wolf stepped aside, letting the awakened bear march into the kitchen and down the hallway.

CHAPTER 2

"WHAT ARE YOU DOING?" Wolf called as he watched Burton disappear upstairs.

He hiked up after him, then choked as he stepped through a cloud of expelled gas hanging over the steps. "My God."

Burton was inside the master bedroom, passing the doorway with a duffle bag.

"Burton." Wolf followed the noise into the master closet. One side was empty, female clothing conspicuously amiss.

"Where's Cheryl?" he asked.

Burton grunted. He had the duffle bag on the ground and was stuffing it full. Satisfied with the debris he'd packed in, he got to one knee and then struggled to his feet.

Wolf watched him get up, aware the seventy-year-old was in worse shape than the last time they'd seen one another. As far back as Wolf could remember, Hal Burton had always been overweight and in less than optimal shape, but he had always moved with spry athleticism despite his bulk.

Without warning, he pulled down his sweatpants, revealing a bare, white, hairy rear end.

"Hey, come on." Wolf turned and stumbled out, glancing around for something to gouge out his eyeballs.

Burton emerged wearing a fresh pair of jeans, a flannel, and white socks, holding a pair of hiking shoes.

Wolf stepped into his path. "Where are you going?"

"You saw that text. I'm going to get my nephew." Burton pushed past and walked down the hall.

"Where is he?"

"South."

"He's not in Ridgway anymore. He fled. So, where do you think you're gonna go?"

The stairs sounded like boulders were being dropped onto them as Burton lumbered down.

Wolf followed. "Ruins. He said ruins, so which ruins? Mesa Verde? Canyon of the Ancients?"

Burton continued walking to the kitchen, sat on a wooden chair, and began lacing up his shoes.

"Hey, I'm talking to you."

Nothing.

"All right. Then I'll call Ridgway, let 'em know you just got a text from your nephew."

"No, you won't." Burton finished one shoe and slipped on the other.

Wolf pulled it off his foot and threw it over his shoulder down the hallway.

"What the hell?" Burton's bulging eyeballs were more marbled than a ribeye. "Go get my shoe."

"Burton. You're not driving anywhere. Five minutes ago, you were passed out drunk, dead to the world. There's no

14

way you're getting behind the wheel."

Burton gave him a smartass smile, which degraded into a sneer.

"And I will bring you into the station in cuffs if you try."

"Oh yeah. David Wolf, the sober saint."

Wolf said nothing.

"You're talking to the former sheriff, remember?"

"Join the club."

Burton leaned back hard. "I have to go get him, Wolf. You heard him, he didn't do it, and they even say he has an alibi."

"Then let the sheriff's department go get him."

Burton shook his head. "I have a bad feeling about this."

"Where is he?"

Burton shook his head. "I'm not going to tell you. You'll tell them."

"It's something to do with ruins, right? He used all caps the second time he said the word in that text."

Burton rubbed his face with both hands.

"Well?"

"Yes, it's something to do with ruins." The old man stared at him. "You can make a decision, I guess. You can either drive me down to where I need to go, or you can get your ass out of here and let me get on with my life."

"They have a BOLO out on your nephew, did I make that clear enough? Did you hear me the first time? He's wanted for the murder of that guy they're talking about in the papers, Alexander Guild."

"You said it yourself, he has an alibi."

"Your nephew is running from the cops. Guilty people run from the cops."

They stared at one another again.

"I could take your phone down to the station. Show MacLean. He lets Sheriff Roll know. They start looking down in the Canyon of the Ancients. There's another choice I could make."

The wind outside howled. The house creaked.

"That's where he is, right? Canyon of the Ancients is more remote. Not a pay-to-get-in type of place like Mesa Verde."

Burton shook his head. "They'd never find him. He's talking about some ruins me and him found a dozen years ago. It's off the beaten path. And if you did that, you'd be putting my nephew in danger, damn it. He says he's scared."

Wolf put his hands on his hips and looked out the sliding glass door. "Roll's been calling up here all morning. There're people looking for him. People on the clock, losing sleep. Away from their families."

Burton shook his head. "He's got an alibi and the text said he thinks somebody's after him. Kyle's family, whatever that means. I'm not willing to give up his position. And you know how shit could go down. You set loose a mob of men carrying guns on my nephew, and something bad could happen."

Wolf shook his head. "But why run? Why not just go to the sheriff's department if he's in so much trouble? Especially if he has an alibi? They could protect him."

"I'm not leaving him hanging when he asked for my help." Burton raised his voice. "You gonna leave me hanging when I'm asking you for help? After all we've been through?"

Wolf stared at him.

"Come on," Burton said. "You could drive me down. You don't even have to do anything."

Tears welled in Burton's eyes, and Wolf realized there

was a history at play in all of this. A past that had awakened the alcohol-sedated animal that lived inside the former sheriff.

"I know exactly where he is," Burton continued. "I'll get him. And then we'll bring him to Ouray. I'm not going to ... I *can't* let my brother's kid down on this, Wolf."

Wolf went to the door and looked out the glass. He checked his watch, thinking of Sheriff MacLean's request to come see him in his office, and the coming events of the next week.

Something big was going down behind the scenes, and he was pretty sure it was happening this Tuesday, when the County Council was set to have their monthly meeting. Something that involved him.

His mother used to tell him growing up, "Not everything's about you, honey," but he was getting the sense that this time his mother's advice was wrong.

Maybe his cop intuition was off, but he'd caught too many glances from MacLean and Undersheriff Wilson over the last two weeks and walked in on a few too many heated conversations that cut off the moment he entered the room.

And it wasn't just MacLean and Wilson. Something was bothering his entire detective squad—something that had all three of them—Rachette, Patterson, and Yates—avoiding eye contact the last week. Talking in huddles. And when they did look at him, they were the looks you gave a man after he accidentally drank a Coke tainted with Ebola.

And if that failed to inject him with doubt, there was the article in the Rocky Points Gazette that had come out right around the same time the strangeness began two weeks ago. Written by a hard-nosed young reporter named Marty

Jordan, the piece addressed the state of the Sheriff's Department.

Headlined "On Shaky Ground," the article focused on last summer's murder case, the investigation and prosecution of which had already spanned the last nine months, and threatened to go on for many more months if not longer, given the way the defense team was fighting tooth and nail against an under-budget, ragtag prosecution team led by DA Sawyer White.

Wolf had spent many hours on the stand over the last winter and spring, as he'd had an integral role in capturing the slime bag killer now trying to weasel his way out of jail with his team of high-priced lawyers.

Naturally, the topic of Wolf's collapse on the mountain during the investigation had been the big point on the stand, and in Marty Jordan's subsequent article. Wolf had cringed as he read the references to his episode as a panic attack.

Of course, technically it was the right term, and with the help of his wunderkind shrink, Dr. Hawkwood, he'd come to terms with it. But that article. He despised the pleasure that journalist took in raking him over the coals again.

"What do you say, Wolf?"

Wolf snapped out of his thoughts. "What are we talking here? Nine-hour drive? Fifteen?"

"Two. Three, tops."

"That doesn't make any sense. Takes three just to get to Ridgway. Canyon of the Ancients is west of there. I can't think of any closer ruins he's talking about."

"Okay, four. I don't know."

Wolf lifted his phone and checked the screen. With a

huff he put it in his pocket. "I need to tell MacLean about this."

Burton shrugged. "Tell him you're helping me out and you'll see him tomorrow morning at the office. Tell him I'm distraught and I need you to escort me down to Ridgway. Hell, tell him I'm drunk and you have to drive me, I don't care. He doesn't need to know we know where Jesse is."

"He's waiting to see me later today. Says he needs to talk to me."

Burton looked out the window.

"And you don't think there's going to be blowback for breaking procedure on this? You think we're going to be able to keep this hidden? I'm telling you, I'm already in hot water right now."

Burton's face crumpled. "For what?"

Wolf shook his head. "Where have you been, old man?"

Something akin to shame flashed in Burton's eyes. Wolf looked at the cluster of empty bottles on the counter and knew exactly where he had been.

"What happened between you and this kid?" Wolf asked.

Burton sat back and the chair creaked. He looked at the floor between them. "Nothing happened between me and this kid. That's the problem, okay? Don't you get it? My brother died, and I haven't seen this kid in years. Too many years."

"You said a dozen years."

Burton looked at him. "Yeah. Something like that."

Wolf sucked in a breath and watched a cloud skate past the top of Rocky Points Resort outside.

"Okay. Fine. But we go get him, and we bring—"

"And we bring him back into custody up in Ouray

County. I'm not looking to go on the run for the rest of my life with my nephew." He raised his arms and looked around. "And risk all this?"

They stared at each other again.

"I'm going to bring him in from the cold, Dave. I'm not gonna sic the dogs on him. I'm gonna be there for him."

Wolf let out his breath and nodded. "When's the last time you showered?"

"Who gives a shit."

"I do. The upholstery of my car does. Those jeans do."

"I'm not exactly certain."

"Get certain and get in the shower."

"We don't have time."

"Now."

CHAPTER 3

"I HEAR Wolf's on the chopping block."

Detective Heather Patterson was walking to her desk and skidded to a stop so fast her coffee spilled onto her hand. "Ah, crap."

Deputy Hanson turned from a conversation with Deputy Wilhelm. "Whoa, easy there, Patterson."

"What did you just say about Wolf?" She stepped close to Hanson.

"I..." Hanson straightened. "Sorry, I was just..."

"You were just saying you hear Wolf's on the chopping block?"

Hanson looked at Wilhelm. Wilhelm looked at his watch. "Gotta go." And he walked away to his desk.

"Why did you just say that to him? Why are you spreading that rumor?"

"That's what I heard."

"From whom?"

"Rachette."

"Bullshit."

Hanson raised his eyebrows. "He said you guys had to attend interviews with the council about his inability to lead."

"Ability." She wanted to reach up and knock him on the head. "Ability to lead, dumbass."

"Easy." Hanson walked to his desk and sat down.

She walked to her own desk, wiping her hand on her jeans.

Surrounded by idiots, she thought. And, then, as she sat in her chair, she wondered why her pulse was still thumping through her body.

It was just a real-life example of the telephone game they used to play in elementary school, when a person whispered something about a monkey in a tree in someone's ear, the next person added on a few new words, until the last person talked about shoving bananas up somebody's butt.

Or was it that Hanson had just said what she'd secretly been thinking for the last few days? Is that why she hadn't been sleeping?

And why was this the second time she'd heard somebody relaying the same rumor about Wolf today? Why now?

She thought back to the interview in the windowless room in the Town Hall building. The way the County Council sat behind those folding tables, looking at her, scrutinizing her every word, scribbling notes on their yellow legal pads.

Her heart rate went right back up.

"I believe David Wolf still exhibits all the traits necessary to be a good leader," she had told them.

A *good* leader? She remembered holding back from using the word great, hesitating for just a millisecond when she said it. At the time, she'd wondered why she'd hesitated, and couldn't come up with an answer for herself. A few of the council members had picked up on it, looking over the top rims of their eyeglasses, pausing their notes.

"I think he's a great leader," she had said, correcting herself.

Did it look like they didn't believe her at that point? She had been mulling over that moment for days now.

"On a scale of one to ten, can you please rate David Wolf's ability as Chief Detective?"

She'd rated him a nine. Then she'd spouted some drivel about how David Wolf was not a perfectionist, and how she admired that about the man. And that's why she'd given him a nine, because Wolf himself would disapprove of being rated a ten.

She shook her head, feeling she might puke from the memory.

"Shit," she said under her breath. She'd been trying, genuinely trying, to make him look good. Great! Damn it. But she may have undermined his chances.

Chances at what?

She sat back in her chair and stretched her protesting back.

She'd been assured by her aunt—and Rocky Points mayor —Margaret Hitchens that there was nothing to worry about. That the interviews—the confidential interviews—were standard procedure. She trusted her Aunt Margaret. But as rumors blazed through the department like wildfire, she wondered if she could trust Mayor Margaret.

Her phone rang, Rachette's name popping up on the display.

She pressed the button. "Have you been telling people Wolf's on the chopping block?"

"What?" Rachette huffed into the phone. "No. But I've heard the same thing today."

"Yeah? Well, Hanson seems to think he heard it from you. So..."

"What? Bullshit. I told him about my interview. I didn't say he was on the chopping block. Hanson said that?"

"You told him about the interview? They were supposed to be confidential."

"Confidential? I thought they meant they would keep our answers confidential. Not that I care. I told them what I told you I told them. That Wolf's the man."

She put a hand to her forehead and rubbed. "Whatever."

They sat in silence for a beat.

"MacLean told us it was just council procedure," Rachette said. "And that's it. I don't think we should worry about these rumors. Hanson's an idiot."

"Who else did you hear it from?" she asked, lowering her voice.

"Well, Yates said he heard it from somebody." She could hear Rachette speaking to someone else. "Who'd you hear it from? Yates says he heard it from Hanson." Rachette's voice faded slightly. "No, dude, I told him about the interview, not that he was getting fired."

She rolled her eyes.

Rachette came back on the phone. "Does Wolf know about these interviews yet?"

"I'm not sure. I didn't tell him because MacLean told us not to, but with all your blabbing, I'm sure he has audio files of all of us by now."

"Shit. Okay, my bad. We gotta tell him."

"You think?"

They said nothing to each other for a while, listening to the static.

"You guys on your way back from Carl and Minnie's?"

Today was Sunday and their entire detective squad was on patrol duty, something that happened every three weeks with their schedule. Earlier in the day, Rachette and Yates had been called to a domestic disturbance involving a crazy couple who lived in the woods northeast of town. Minnie Yorberg had apparently taken a baseball bat to the two home computers, and her husband, Carl had called 9-1-1, fearing for his life. With Wolf at Burton's house on the BOLO for Jesse Burton, it was more action in one day than they'd seen in the last month.

"Yeah, we're on our way back," Rachette said. "Got Minnie with us. Carl's following in his truck. He wants to press charges."

"Wait. You were talking about all this with Minnie in the car?"

Silence.

She gripped the phone harder. "Listen, first opportunity today, we're telling him about this whole thing. He has to hear it from us. And he has to hear it now."

"You're right. Actually, you know what? I've been calling him and he's not answering. You think he already knows and is avoiding my calls?"

She pictured Minnie Yorberg sitting the back seat of Rachette's vehicle, her ears wide open.

"I'll see you when you get back." She hung up and dropped the phone.

As she stared at her computer screen, Hanson's voice echoed in her mind. *I hear he's on the chopping block.* She picked up her cell again and scrolled for Wolf's number.

"Hey, what's going on?" MacLean's voice was right behind her.

"Hi." She swiveled in her chair and saw the sheriff sipping his coffee as if he had been there for a while.

"Was that Wolf?" MacLean walked to the side of her desk and took a coffee-commercial stance, cupping his mug with two hands, gazing into the mountains outside the window.

"No, sir. Rachette."

"How're things with Carl and Minnie Yorberg?"

"They're all coming in. Anyway, I was just going to call Wolf to see what happened at Burton's."

"His nephew wasn't there. Talked to him a few minutes ago."

"Oh." She set down her phone wondering now if Rachette was right, and Wolf had been ignoring his calls.

She felt for Wolf. The man had always been a rock in the department, but he'd shown his first cracks last year. The volatile situation with Lauren and Ella leaving, along with the stress of a murder investigation stringing him out, was all too much to take. And then there were the drawn-out court appearances that brought his condition into the spotlight and stripped it naked for all to see.

And now these interviews behind his back. She had a bad feeling. Not only because she could not fathom working in the department without the man, but also because she wondered if Wolf could take any more.

At least the birth this winter of Wolf's first grandchild,

Ryan, provided some joy. And he seemed to be taking the public scrutiny in stride. But he was always calm on the outside, wasn't he? He wasn't one to talk about things.

"You know," MacLean turned toward her and set down his coffee cup, "You do a great job."

"Thanks."

He started to say something, but then stopped himself and sipped his coffee.

"I think that Wolf does a great job, too," she said.

MacLean shot her a hard look. "I know you do, though you'd probably do better at his job than he does. He's attentive to details, but you're anal-retentive. And I mean that in a good way. Organized. People look up to you. You start things, and you finish them."

She opened her mouth to speak, but nothing came out. His nonchalance startled her. Her fears about the interviews solidified into a fist that punched her in the gut.

Before she could pull herself together and speak, he gave her a warm smile. It was such a strange, out of place gesture from the man, she was rendered mute.

"You don't need to fight for Wolf. It's not your job." He slapped her on the shoulder and walked away.

She stared as he receded into his glass-enclosed office at the head of the squad room and shut the door.

Turning back to her computer, she picked up her phone and dialed her aunt's number.

It went to voicemail after two rings, like she'd been screened. "You've reached Margaret Hitchens. I can't come to the phone right now, but if you leave a message, I'll get back to you as soon as possible. Mayoral office hours vary by day and week. If you'd like to make an appointment with me, please call—"

She hung up and dropped her phone on the table.

She had other ways of getting hold of her aunt, like showing up at her door and banging it down. And as for talking with Wolf, the second he set foot in the building, she was going to tell him everything.

CHAPTER 4

THE ROUTE to the southwestern part of the state led them straight south on 734 over Williams Pass, through Ashland, then west on 50 through Gunnison to Montrose, where they hooked up with 550.

Ironically the route took them through Ridgway, and twice Wolf had seen Ouray County Sheriff's Department cruisers, giving him a twist in his gut knowing they were passing through to go pick up their person of interest.

But they'd be back in Ridgway soon enough, Wolf would make sure of that, and he hoped the loyalty he was showing the old drunk sleeping next to him outweighed any blowback coming his way for their procedural detour.

As he passed yet another sheriff's department vehicle, Wolf thought back to the multiple times he'd met Sheriff Roll over the years. The man had been amiable enough, he remembered. Word was he was something of a ladies' man, too. He couldn't quite remember the details, but he did recall MacLean telling him that once.

Wolf looked over at Burton's sleeping form. He wondered

if the man would even remember what was going on when they reached their destination.

For now, Wolf had a waypoint of Dolores, Colorado to go on. Once they got there, Burton was going to have to tell him the rest of the route into Canyon of the Ancients. By Wolf's calculations they were looking at a four-hour drive, minimum, plus the time it would take to find Jesse, which was going to push them into around sunset.

Then, of course, they'd have to drive back up here to Ridgway and deliver their quarry. They had a long haul ahead of them and Wolf had already been up since before sunrise.

Mouth agape, head lolled against the window, Burton looked thinner than the last time Wolf had seen him. And not in a good way. Not by way of diet and exercise, but more like he was wasting away.

The last time they'd been together had been at Wolf's own surprise birthday party last summer. My God, had it been that long? Eleven months?

At that point Wolf had been several months into his attempt at living sober and recalled Burton had tipped back quite a few that night. He couldn't remember if Cheryl had been there. Burton had gotten a ride home with Margaret.

"Where are we?" Burton croaked without opening his eyes.

"Just passed through Ridgway."

"See Roll?"

"Saw some vehicles."

Burton sucked in a huge breath that sounded like metal on metal, then coughed, which sounded like rocks dropping on said metal. He straightened and blinked, rubbing his eyes.

"What time is it?"

"Just past three. You slept a couple of hours."

Burton checked his watch and Wolf saw the man's eyes glaze over.

"You sure you know exactly where he's going to be?"

Burton's gaze snapped back from somewhere else. "Yeah. There's a specific set of ruins he's talking about. Just..."

"Just what?"

"Just, I haven't been there since the last time I was there with him. Which was over ten years ago. I'm sure we'll find it, though. We weren't very far off the path, I remember that."

A stiff crosswind buffeted the car back and forth. Wolf had been flexing both forearms for the last thirty minutes, fighting to keep the tires between the lanes. Every few minutes a tumbleweed launched out of the sage and juniper and rolled across the asphalt.

Burton ironed his face with his hands. His beard was gone, quickly shaved with an electric trimmer before they'd left, leaving the old walrus mustache to dominate the area between his now sunken red cheeks.

"When's the last time you saw Jesse?" Wolf asked.

Burton eyed him. "I told you. It's been years."

"I'm just trying to get a sense of what this kid's like. How old is he?"

"Shit. I don't know. Twenty? Twenty-one? Somewhere around there."

"And is he dangerous?" Wolf asked.

Burton said nothing.

"Because they're saying to consider him armed and dangerous."

Burton shook his head, keeping his eyes out the window.

"Come on. I need something. Because right now we're just going out there blind."

"I don't know, all right?" Burton's face turned red. "I don't know. I used to spend time with him growing up. He was...troubled back then."

"Troubled?"

"He was a good kid. He was understandably troubled. His mother died giving birth to him, and after that his father wasn't in the picture."

Wolf waited for him to continue, but Burton settled into gazing out on the passing landscape again.

"Where did he grow up then? Foster system?"

"No. Family friend took care of him down in Ridgway. Look, he's a good kid. He wasn't my kid. I don't know..." Burton stopped talking.

"You don't know."

Burton's jaw clenched.

"I would expect never having a mother and his father not being in the picture would trouble the kid," Wolf said.

Burton said nothing.

"Who was this family friend?"

"Woman named Bertha. Look, I don't want to talk about it."

Wolf nodded. "Okay. Just know that I'll have my gun out when we are looking for your nephew."

Burton raised a thumb.

They were swerving and climbing up 145, just past the turnoff that led to Telluride. Wolf hadn't driven up that box canyon for years. He took his mind off Jesse Burton and let his thoughts drift back to when he'd skied with Sarah and her friends for three days at the resort that was now home to some of the richest people on the planet. They'd slept on the floor that trip almost three decades ago—my word, had it been that long?—their warm skin coiled together inside nylon sleeping bags.

His stomach grumbled. After waking up before sunrise, he'd spent the morning at the gym, and he'd been counting on inhaling a large lunch to compensate for the calories burned before he'd been routed to Burton's.

"I'm gonna need some food," Wolf said.

"Mm," Burton said, looking like he wanted to say *I don't give a shit and it hurts to talk.*

"How long has Cheryl been gone?"

"I don't want to talk about it. Can't you drive any faster?"

He'd been revving the engine to well over the speed limit between jamming the brakes at sharp turns already. "Sure."

Wolf sat back and dreamed about a drive-through, where he would order two of everything on the menu.

Two hours of silence passed as they followed highway 143 southwest, up and down passes, through dense forest and high mountain meadows. A few slivers of snow clung to the shade of the highest peaks, but otherwise the scree-covered slopes above the trees were free of snow, showing streaks of brown, red, yellow, and black.

As they made their way further southwest, the evergreen-choked landscape gave way to sage and low junipers. Their fragrance blew through the vents, while the wind outside continued to buffet the car.

They dropped down into a low canyon that had been dug out by the Dolores River. Darkness grew on the western horizon as clouds gathered, and the wind seemed to double in strength as the incoming weather mass drew nearer until drops began to spit onto the windshield.

They were pelted with rain for half an hour while lightning snapped all around, and then they were through the storm. Wolf thought of Jesse Burton, outside in the elements. Huddling among thousand-year ruins.

Wolf's phone lit up with MacLean's number. He ignored the call and dropped his phone back in the center console.

Burton saw but said nothing. Instead he pointed his dead gaze out the window and folded his arms.

They stopped to gas the car and relieve themselves in Dolores, then traveled another half-hour south before Wolf found a drive-through. Burton seemed irritated at the prospect of stopping for food, but ended up eating a burger and fries, which perked him up. It was just another few minutes' drive to reach the Canyon of the Ancients National Monument.

The ground was drenched. Puddles gleamed in the lowering sunlight, pooling on the rough, pink-hewn asphalt two-lane highway.

"This is it!" Burton said as they passed a sign that read *Sand Canyon Trailhead.*

Wolf slowed the SUV and pulled into a gravel lot.

"That's his vehicle," Wolf said, parking next to a silver Jeep Rubicon and shutting off the engine.

Burton looked at it. "You sure?"

"That's what the BOLO said."

"Pretty nice ride." Burton got out.

Wolf opened his door and they stepped into surprisingly still air. He zipped his Carhartt jacket to his chin, then eased it back down.

The air was cool, heavy with plant oils and moisture rising from the ground. The soil was stained blood red by the rain. Sun sliced through sporadic clouds, lighting the black veil that passed to the north and east.

Thunder rumbled in the west, suggesting the sunshine might be short lived.

Burton pressed his face to the glass of Jesse's vehicle.

Wolf joined him and saw nothing special. He pulled on the handle and the door squeaked open. The air inside was cool, smelling of stale cigarette smoke and old fast food. "No keys."

"Weather's not done. We'd better get going," Burton said.

Wolf sat down in the driver's seat, turned around, and checked the back. At least a dozen wadded plastic grocery bags littered the floorboards, and just as many greasy paper sacks smelling of French fries.

He climbed back out, shut the door and stood, surveying the area. A brown sign with white lettering announced the Sand Canyon Trailhead. Rain clinging to the junipers sparkled in the low-angle sun. The trail cut through pastel-colored cactus, grasses, and bushes and disappeared in a canyon doused in long shadow.

Wolf eyed his cell phone and saw it was just before five pm. There were perhaps three hours of daylight left. He popped the rear hatch of his SUV and took out his Maglite.

"You got another one of those?" Burton asked.

"Nope."

Burton walked. "I guess we'd better hurry."

Wolf stopped at the rear door and grabbed a bottle of water he'd purchased at the Dolores gas station. He eyed the paper sack of groceries Burton had bought but decided to leave it. They'd be back soon.

As he shut the door there was another clap of thunder, again from the west, and he wondered how bad he'd screwed them by thinking that last thought.

"Yeah," he said. "We'd better hurry."

CHAPTER 5

THE WIND FRESHENED, carrying the scents of the desert released by the earlier deluge. Mirror ponds shimmered on the trail, reflecting the darkened skies to the north.

The sun still shone through a crack in the clouds, and long shadows cut across blazing red and white stripes of sedimentary rocks on either side of a low canyon. Like Mesa Verde to the south, the sandstone on either side of them had eroded pockets at ground level that burrowed into the cliff walls, leaving natural overhangs where ancient native people built their shelters.

In the first mile of the hike they'd already seen a few orange-red adobe walls built inside these pockets. But Burton seemed unimpressed by the spectacle and kept moving at a decent clip, that athletic bounce to his step revealing itself again.

But a few minutes later, Burton had slowed considerably.

"You doing all right?" Wolf asked, after a particularly long stretch of silence.

Burton stopped and wiped sweat off his brow. The low

angle of the sun tinted his face red. He pointed to a bluff. "There's a kiva on top of that ridge. Anasazi."

"Is that where Jesse is?"

"No. Just saying. It's coming back to me." Burton marched ahead of him, slapping his right shoe straight in the middle of a puddle on the second step. "Shit!"

Wolf hurdled the water, noting the unsteadiness of Burton's steps as the man shook his now-drenched leg. Every few hundred feet, a palsy-like quiver took further hold of Burton's body.

Wolf could only guess how long Burton's bender had lasted. Days? Months? The man's body was leaking sweat, yearning for water, preferably in ice cube form and submerged in whiskey. Wolf knew the drill: Pins and needles in the extremities from all the exertion, possibly bowels demanding a toilet seat.

"You look like shit," Wolf said.

Burton grumbled something under his breath.

"Didn't catch that."

"Jesse!" Again, the shakes as Burton raised his hands and cupped around his mouth. "Jess-" A coughing fit cut off his words.

Wolf stepped close and hooked both his hands under his armpits.

"Get off me."

"Sit down. Here. On this rock."

"Screw you." Burton sat. The red had fallen out of his face now, replaced by a white that rivaled the stripes threading through the rock cliffs.

"Here." Wolf unscrewed the bottled water and thrust it in Burton's face.

Burton guzzled it, letting a stream run down his chin and into his still-zipped Carhartt.

"Unzip this." Wolf helped him, revealing a tee shirt darkened with sweat and sticking to his chest.

It could have been his imagination, but Wolf thought he saw competing cycles of heaving breath and heart jackhammers shaking the man's fleshy breasts. Sweat glistened everywhere, drenching his body.

"That's it," Wolf said. "We're headed back. Can you walk?"

"Shit."

"Can you stand?"

Burton was somewhere else.

Wolf stood and surveyed his surroundings. They'd gone a little over a mile so far. He stretched his back straight, rolled his shoulders. A twinge of pain bloomed, a remnant from the morning workout.

He'd been pushing himself hard in the gym lately and felt strong. Or, at least he did while lifting barbells. Carrying an overgrown man was another matter.

He pulled his phone from his pocket, saw there was no reception.

"All right, old man. We're going back to the car."

Burton looked up from under drooping eyelids. "Jesse."

"Jesse can wait. We'll send the Ouray SD to come get him."

"No."

Wolf turned and looked up the canyon. He put his hands to his mouth and sucked in a deep breath. "Jesse!"

The sound of his yell was smothered by a passing gust of

wind. The sun was covered by the clouds now, and the temperature had dropped.

"Jesse!" Wolf tried again, and then a few more times. "It's not gonna happen, and you're getting worse."

"I have medicine in the car."

"What kind of medicine? For what?"

"Heart. Blood pressure."

"Are you feeling faint?"

Burton's non-reaction said yes.

"Let's go." Wolf bent and put a shoulder into his chest. "Raise your arms."

Burton pushed him away. "No. You go back. Go get the medication. You can bring it back to me."

The wind freshened again, and the scent of rain came on hard.

Wolf bent low and heaved Burton forward over his shoulder. Wolf had spent a lifetime watching the other man's weight grow unchecked. Now he was startlingly light.

Wolf reluctantly recalled looking at the man's bare ass earlier and remembered more bones than fat beneath that skin. The oversized clothing he still wore had acted like an optical illusion.

"You son of a bitch. Put me down!"

Wolf marched back the way they'd came, one hand wrapped around Burton, a half-empty two-liter bottle in the other.

Burton clawed at his holster. "I'll shoot you."

Wolf winged his elbow, easily blocking the half-hearted grabs.

He stepped straight through a puddle and the water burrowed into his shoes.

"I can't leave him. I can't."

Wolf felt the man's chest heaving against his shoulder. More coughing. "Just relax."

Burton squirmed once, giving real effort to his escape, but it was dismally weak under Wolf's arm.

"Relax."

The totality in which Burton followed his order made Wolf's heart jump. "You still with me?"

No answer.

He reached back and grabbed Burton's wrist. Underneath the clammy skin a pulse bumped strong. Concentrating on keeping his footing and ignoring the pain now shooting through his shoulder, Wolf moved quickly and steadily down the smooth packed-dirt path.

He rounded a bluff and saw the winding canyon yawning ahead of him. There were still two or three hillsides they needed to pass, and then they would reach the mouth that led to the wide-open space that signified the trailhead and the parking lot.

He ignored the breeze, the rain drops, and upped his pace some more.

The next bluff leaned into the canyon from the right, the west, providing some shelter as the brunt of the storm hit with sideways driving rain.

Wolf stopped and slapped Burton's behind. "You with me?"

Still no answer.

The rain soaked his right side like a shotgun blast as he continued onward.

His feet moved faster now, almost too fast, he thought. The last thing he needed was to trip and fall forward, dropping Burton and injuring both of them in the process. A bolt of lightning zapped straight in front of him. Thunder followed almost instantly, a hard pop like a gunshot.

Then he slowed to a stop, because as if delivered by the thunderbolt, a man now stood directly in his path.

CHAPTER 6

"What's going on?" the man asked. He was young, early twenties. He had the same pudge nose as Hal, the same facial structure. "Who are you?"

Wolf lowered Burton to the ground, keeping his eyes locked on Jesse Burton's hands. "Your uncle's in trouble!"

Jesse Burton wore desert camo pants, which were pasted to his legs by the rain, and a black sweatshirt with the hood drawn up and tied tight around his face. He had one black eye and a split lip, suggesting he'd recently seen a few punches.

"Your uncle's having a heart attack or something! Help me!"

Jesse moved closer.

Wolf pulled his gun and aimed at his center mass. "Put your hands up and get on the ground."

Jesse raised his hands, but hesitated, as if thinking about not complying.

"I said get on the ground. On your stomach. Now."

Wolf shot a round into the side of the dirt hill next to him.

Jesse flinched as the pop exploded from Wolf's Glock and he laid on his stomach.

Wolf searched Jesse's waist and immediately found a Kimber 1911 nine-millimeter tucked into a paddle holster under his jacket. He took it off and threw it behind him for the moment.

Jesse put a cheek on the ground, exposing half of his face. His blue eye, surrounded by bruised flesh, was relaxed, resigned to the moment. Long strands of electric-orange hair wormed out of his hood. A dye job. Nobody on earth had hair that color naturally.

Wolf remained tense, ready to spring back if Jesse twisted after him. The kid, the man, was big, the soaked fabric of his hoodie revealing the back muscles of somebody who spent a lot of time and effort in the gym.

Wolf had gone much of his career without carrying a backup piece, but now it was hard rule that he and his team carry a small pistol strapped to an ankle holster underneath their pant leg. Jesse had only the one gun on his hip.

"Stand up. Turn out your pockets." Wolf backed away and aimed.

Jesse did as he was told, producing a pair of keys, a wallet, a couple of pieces of gum wrapped in foil, a flip phone, and the battery that had been removed from it.

"Okay, hand them over."

Jesse complied, and Wolf shoved the paraphernalia into the zippered pocket of his jacket.

"Where'd you get those marks on your face?" Wolf went to the Kimber and tucked the holster into the waist of his pants on the free side. With his own holster on the right, along with the Smith and Wesson M and P 380 on his ankle, he felt like somewhat of a walking arsenal.

"Got in a fight the other night."

The ice-cold rain fell more heavily. Jesse seemed weighed down by the water streaming off of him, but unfazed. His eyes stared ahead without blinking.

"All right, you walk in front of me."

Jesse walked down the trail as instructed.

"Wait. Grab that water bottle. We'll need it."

Jesse came back and picked up the bottle, eyeing Hal.

"Now let's move! Your uncle's in trouble."

Jesse flicked his eyes back to Burton's inert body still lying on the ground, put his hands up and walked. "I can help!"

"Just keep walking."

Another bolt of lightning lit the sky and thunder followed.

Wolf had to holster his gun and pick Burton up from an awkward position and get him back over his shoulder, but with a long grunt and by flexing every muscle in his body, he managed.

"Jesse!" Burton shifted on Wolf's shoulder. "Jesse!"

Jesse stopped and turned around, that same unblinking gaze.

Wolf pulled and pointed the Glock again. "Move."

Soon they reached the left turn in the canyon, marked by the brow of rock jutting in from the east side. A sandstone overhang dug into the rock beckoned as perfectly good shelter, but Wolf pressed on. Tall oaks lining the middle of the canyon whooshed sideways.

Wolf's right ear caught the rain like a thimble. Repeatedly he shook his head to dump it out, and now a cramp in his neck was tightening like a vise.

Hal went quiet, but Wolf could feel he was moving his limbs periodically, lifting his head, flexing his torso.

Whatever was wrong with the old man, Wolf got the sense the rain was slapping him out of his funk. Perhaps the medication in the car would finish the job.

When had the cell phone reception gone out? On the hike? Or on the drive before they had arrived?

Wolf's phone was in his left pocket, sheltered by his own body and the one draped over his shoulder, but he could still feel his jeans stuck to his bare leg underneath. He could only hope the phone was undamaged.

"There's the parking lot," Wolf said. "We're almost there, Hal."

The canyon opened up, revealing the two vehicles parked just over a football field away. Beyond it was a sight worthy of a professional photographer. The terrain beyond the vehicles rolled out and down for hundreds of miles. Red hewn mesas crusted with green shone in the fading sunlight. The rain still fell, but the clouds to the west had run out and the sun poked through for one last blast of light, illuminating a rainbow framing it all.

Wolf felt like someone had a taser to his lower back, and his shoulder screamed in pain with each movement, as if sand had been sprinkled into the ball and socket. Burton was milliseconds from sliding off when Jesse came up and took the weight, handling his uncle like a sack of flour.

Wolf reached for his gun, but Jesse seemed preoccupied with his uncle.

Catching his breath, Wolf rolled his neck and shoulder, stretched his back, and watched as Jesse maneuvered his uncle to the ground and up against the wheel of the car.

Burton reclined against the tire and put his arms on his bent knees. He reached up a hand to his nephew. Jesse looked at it for a moment and clasped it. The two of them stared at one another without saying a word.

Wolf dug the keys out of his pocket and unlocked the doors. "Let's get him up and into the passenger seat."

Burton shook his head and waved them away. "I'm okay now. Just get me my duffle. And that water."

"I'll get it." Jesse uncinched his hood and unveiled his shock of hair, the color of orange Play-doh fresh out of the can. He ducked into the back seat with athletic grace.

Wolf holstered his gun and let the action play out.

"This it?" Jesse asked, producing the duffle bag Burton had packed before they left.

"Yeah."

"You have any weapons in that bag?" Wolf asked.

Burton frowned at him. "No."

Jesse set the antique Sluice County SD bag on Burton's lap. "You need help?"

"No. I got it. I got it. There. There they are."

"Jesse," Wolf said. "I need you to back away from him."

Jesse ignored him for a beat, but then followed orders.

"Let's go."

"You're not armed, are you, Jesse?" Burton asked. "You're not gonna hurt us, right?"

"He was." Wolf pulled out the holster with the Kimber still inside. "And no offense, son, but I don't know you from a rock."

"Jesse," Burton said, more than a little disappointment in his voice.

Jesse stood with his arms folded, watching Burton take a handful of pills big enough to choke a rhino.

"That's a lot of pills," Wolf said.

"No shit."

"How long's it been since the last time?"

"Couple days."

"And how often are you supposed to be taking them?"

"You sound like Cheryl." Burton put another handful in his mouth and sipped the water.

"Hands behind your back, please," Wolf said.

Jesse unfolded his arms and did as he was told.

"He's not gonna do anything." Burton tried to push himself up.

"Just stay there." He cinched the cuffs tight.

"You can turn around now."

Jesse turned. His head was tilted back, defiant.

Wolf pulled out his cell phone and eyed the screen. Still no reception. He pulled out Jesse's flip phone, and the removed battery.

"Battery's dead," Jesse said.

"And that's why you took it out? Looks to me like you're trying to stay off the radar. You have reception?" Wolf asked Burton.

Burton patted his pockets and shrugged. "I think it's in the car."

"Where's the nearest hospital?" Wolf asked. "Dolores?"

Jesse stared with a lazy expression.

"Hospital?" Burton scoffed. "I'm not going to a freakin' hospital."

"Like hell you're not."

Color had returned to the old man's face, but he was still pasted to the ground like a thousand-pound boulder.

"You'll go in the back." Wolf zipped Jesse's phone back in his jacket and led Jesse around the car to the rear passenger seat. He put the kid in, and when he returned, he found Burton still sitting on the ground. "Ready?"

"For what?"

"For some medical attention, that's what."

"Dammit."

Wolf pulled him to his feet. Burton teetered for a second, then shook his head and sucked in a breath. "No problem. Feeling better."

Wolf darted behind him and caught him before he fell over sideways, then gripped him around the waist and dragged him backwards as Burton's heels gouged into the wet earth of the parking lot.

"Shit, man. Listen, you know what I really need. I got it in the back seat. In the gas station bag."

"What are you talking about?" Wolf popped open the front passenger door and helped Burton climb in. "Seatbelt. On."

He pushed the door closed but Burton stiff-armed it back open.

"What are you—"

"It's in the back seat. In the grocery bag. Come on."

Wolf opened the back door and saw the grocery bag between Jesse's feet. He opened up the wadded top of the bag and saw another paper bag inside, this one holding a bottle. "Excuse me."

He reached down and gripped the neck of a fifth of Jack Daniels, pulled it from the bag and shut the door.

The last thing he saw before the door shut was a confused look on Jesse's face.

Wolf set the bottle on Burton's lap. To his credit, the old man gripped it slowly, almost reluctantly.

He shut the door and took his time rounding the rear of the vehicle, taking in the blood red sky and silhouetted sculptures of the landscape to the south, knowing there was a good chance this was the last bit of peace he would feel for a while.

CHAPTER 7

HEATHER PATTERSON STARED at the sunset through the squad room windows, thinking of her two little boys and Scott, and her aunt not returning her calls.

"You've reached David Wolf. Leave a message."

She hung up. She'd already harassed him enough with a previous voicemail and text message.

MacLean's office was closed up, the lights off. The sheriff had left a few hours ago, looking angry and asking about Wolf, which had driven the spike of concern deeper into her thoughts.

Shutting her laptop, she shoved it in her work pack.

"You outta here?" Deputy Nelson looked up from his keyboard.

"Yep."

"You've been in here all day?"

"Yep."

"Had a lot of activity. You think they'll kill each other tonight?" Nelson smiled and shook his head, referring to the earlier Carl and Minnie Yorberg incident.

"I hope not." And she meant it. She'd once seen Minnie Yorberg honest to God kick a pigeon into Main Street traffic. The bird had gotten up and flown away, but the memory of that angry woman's face had not. "See you later. Have a good night."

"Just getting started."

"Yay."

She walked out of the squad room, calculating how much time it would take her to drive up the other side of the valley to visit Margaret. It would tack on another thirty minutes, but at least she could try to wring a few answers out of her aunt.

With that settled, she thought again about the Yorbergs. Rachette and Yates had been handling the ordeal all day, and she hadn't had a chance to talk to them about it yet.

She dialed Rachette's number as she walked down the hallway to the elevators.

"Yeah," Rachette answered after a single ring. A kid screamed in the background, and it sounded like somebody was banging pots.

"I never got to ask, did you get Carl and Minnie figured out?"

"We'll see."

"Meaning?"

"Meaning, we'll see if he wakes up tomorrow with a gaping baseball bat wound to the head."

She ignored the arrival of the elevator, knowing if she got in, she would lose the call. "So what was the problem?"

"I don't know, just a second." Rachette put a hand over his phone, and in a moment the background noise disappeared. "There. Good lord. One of these days I'm gonna have to buy TJ a drum set, along with a rope to hang myself."

Patterson smiled, thinking of Thomas Rachette Junior smacking pots and pans as hard as he could, Charlotte and Rachette taking every second of it without batting an eye. Their parenting style was the opposite of hers. She wasn't afraid to use the phrase "shut up" when it came to her kids.

"So, we brought them both in, and Minnie was talking about how Carl was getting scammed online, and she was smashing the computers so he wouldn't spend their life savings. Apparently, he was getting ready to do just that. Carl was spouting off that he knew exactly what he was doing, and that the woman should shut up."

"What was he going to do?" she asked. "You get the specifics?"

"He kind of blew us off. 'Too complicated for non-financial-types like you two,' he said. Anyway, he backed out of pressing charges."

"I wonder what he's up to."

"Like I said, I don't know, and now that he's not pressing charges I don't care."

"But they might be right back at it in the morning. Hell, one of them's probably laying in a pool of blood right now."

"I hope." Rachette spat, which told her he'd gone outside and put in some Copenhagen.

"That's not nice."

"Neither is Carl Yorberg. I'd rather spend the day at the dentist than with that guy again."

She stared out a sliver third-floor window. The resort mountain stood tall in front of an orange sky. "Okay. I'm headed home."

"Geez, you still at work?"

"Not anymore."

. . .

Only a faint blue glow remained behind the western peaks of the Chautauqua Valley when Patterson rang her aunt's doorbell.

The windows were lit but she leaned close anyway to see if anyone was home.

Margaret appeared, wiping her hands on an apron. She slowed when she saw Heather filling the glass pane, then opened the door.

"You scared the crap out of me."

"Why aren't you answering my calls or texts?"

Margaret sighed. "Come inside."

"Nope."

Margaret gave Heather a look that made her cringe—the one that looked exactly like her mother scolding her for coming home after school with mud all over her clothing.

But the mayor blinked first. "Listen, Heather. I can't talk about this."

"About what? About putting Wolf on the chopping block, and not telling me about it?"

"Chopping block?" Her aunt looked genuinely surprised.

"That's the word going around the station. Your confidential interviews are causing a lot of problems."

"What kind of—"

"Rumors."

Margaret shook her head, staring at the ground. "I told John we should have—"

"I don't care. I care about what you're not telling us. Why those interviews? What's going to happen?"

Margaret lifted her chin. "I can't tell you anything, Heather."

"Why not?"

"Other than to not worry about it. You trust me, don't you?"

She didn't answer.

"Heather. You trust me, right?"

"I just don't want to see anything..." she swallowed, feeling an unexpected rush of emotion, "challenging happen to Wolf. He's gone through so much in the last year."

"I can't guarantee that the changes ahead are not going to be challenging." Margaret's expression was unreadable.

"What does that even mean? What changes? Why is MacLean saying I would be good at Wolf's job?"

Margaret's eyes narrowed. "It means the next County Council meeting is on Tuesday morning, and we'll go forward from there."

"He said I'd be better at doing Wolf's job than he is at doing his job. That's what he said right to my face today."

Margaret said nothing.

"I don't want Wolf's job if it means he's demoted to my job."

Margaret closed her eyes. "Heather. You have to go now. We can't talk about this."

"Is that what's going to happen?"

Margaret's eyelids only rose to half-mast. "Trust the process, Heather. Go home to your kids."

"That's it, isn't it." Patterson's voice sharpened to a dagger. "Tell the council I do not want Wolf's job. You got that?"

"Heather."

"Good night." She stepped off the porch and walked to her car.

Without looking out the windshield, she fired up the engine, backed out, and pointed the SUV back down toward town. Only when she took her foot off the gas did she glance toward the house. Expecting to see her aunt on the porch or standing in the front windows to watch her leave, she was more than a little concerned to see that Margaret was gone, the front of the house bathed in darkness.

She rolled down to the center of the valley, her thoughts on her aunt's slack-eyed stare.

Heather knew that look, too. That particular crease of her aunt's forehead had appeared on her mother's the day she'd told Heather about her grandfather dying.

There was nothing more she could do about any of this except talk to Wolf. And she wasn't about to do it over the phone. She would get to work tomorrow morning and corner him at the first opportunity.

She hung a right on Main and steeled herself for that conversation, and another sleepless night.

CHAPTER 8

THE CELL PHONE in Wolf's hand glowed, washing out his view of the road outside the windshield. He pinched on the display to zoom the map, but the name of the street never came up. He zoomed back out, knowing he hadn't looked at the road, the real road, in too long. The wheels hit the rumble strip and he jerked the wheel.

"Having trouble?" Burton put the bottle to his lips, took a slug, and finished with a satisfied exhale.

"It'd help if you could navigate."

"Not a chance in hell."

Wolf zoomed back out and hovered his finger over the button that would start spouting off directions in a feminine digital voice, thought better of it, and dropped the phone in the console.

"Hee hee." Burton sipped again. "Damn things are the devil. Back in my day we used to drive around for hours gettin' lost. We earned our way to places. Then you got that shit burned into your brain. No way you'd ever get lost on the way there again. You know, I still have all my friends' phone numbers memorized from childhood?"

Wolf had the same superhuman ability, too, but opted to not encourage him and said nothing.

They passed a sign that read "Cortez – 11 miles." A blue hospital sign signaled they were nearing Wolf's destination. When they'd finally found cell reception, a quick search online told Wolf what he had feared—the nearest hospital that was in the direction of home was over two hours away. Cortez was only a few miles, but straight south.

Burton pulled down the sun visor and flipped open the mirror, angling it just so to eye Jesse in back. "All right, Jesse. It's time to 'fess up, son. What's going on?"

Jesse looked like he was trying to sleep.

"You gonna talk or what?" Burton asked.

Jesse kept his eyes shut.

"Come on. I'm down here, aren't I? You just gonna sit there now like a rock after we drove four hours to come get you?"

No answer.

Burton twisted in his seat, then fluttered his lips and pulled on the bottle again. "Your girlfriend said you were with her the night all of this business with this Alexander Guild went down. Maybe you're hiding something about her. Maybe she's a killer. Is that it? That's why you're being so quiet. You don't want to give up that she's lying, and that she was out blasting that guy with a fifty-caliber rifle."

Jesse's eyes flicked open. "She had nothing to do with that."

Burton leaned into the mirror. "He's awake!"

Jesse locked eyes with Wolf in the rearview for a moment, then averted his gaze.

"Why are you running?" Burton asked.

Jesse took his time answering. Wolf watched him as much as he could without running off the road.

"Everything's lining up to make it look like I killed that guy, that Alexander Guild guy."

"Did you?" Wolf asked.

"No."

Burton gave Wolf a sideways glance. "How's that? You were with your girlfriend all night, weren't you?"

Jesse leaned back. "Yeah."

"Then why did you run? And how about that gun you were just carrying?"

"And how about taking the battery out of your cell phone?" Wolf asked.

"I told you, some guys are after me."

"Who?" Wolf asked.

"Kyle's dad and his brothers."

"Who's Kyle?" Burton beat Wolf to the obvious question. The old man was loud and alert- looking, moving a lot in his seat. The alcohol was back behind the wheel.

"He's my friend. My best friend."

Jesse's face was now hidden in the darkness of the back seat. They waited for him to continue talking.

"His dad called me this morning. He said they got a call from the sheriff's department, telling them Kyle was missing and they had found blood at his house, and that they were very concerned for his well-being. They wanted to know where he was, and they seemed to think I was the one responsible for him being gone. And they were coming to talk to me about it."

"The cops thought you were responsible?" Wolf asked.

"No, I mean, the Farmers, Kyle's dad, thought I was responsible."

"Why did they think you were responsible?" Wolf asked.

Jesse shook his head. "Because the cops were looking for me, I guess."

"So, you ran?" Burton asked.

"You don't know that family. Them saying they're going to come see me means they're coming to start ripping my skin off until I tell them what they want to hear."

"Where do the Farmers live? Ridgway?" Wolf asked.

"No. Up in Gunnison."

"That's hours away from Ridgway," Burton said.

Jesse said nothing.

"So why did you run? Why not go to the cops? They would protect you from Kyle's dad, or his brothers, or whoever the hell you're talking about."

Jesse made a noise. A passing car illuminated his face. His eyes were closed, his head back.

"Why did you run, Jesse?" Wolf asked. "Because you knew the cops were after you, too?"

"No. I...I can't explain it. I was confused."

"Try." Burton's voice was loud.

"Why did Kyle's family think you had something to do with Kyle gone missing?" Wolf asked again.

Jesse took his time. "I got in a fight with Kyle Friday night. That's why my face is all messed up. Everyone in town knew about it."

"So the cops were after you," Wolf said. "And you knew it?"

"I...called Kyle Saturday morning. You know, to apologize, but he wasn't answering. I figured he was just ignoring me. But then..."

"But then what?" Burton asked.

"But then I heard from Kyle's father that they were looking for him, and there was blood. So, yeah, I started thinking that, you know, I didn't have an alibi for last night. For Saturday night. And the cops would be coming after me, too."

"Where were you Saturday night?" Wolf asked. "Last night."

"Just ... home."

"Alone?"

"Yeah."

Wolf watched in the rearview. The kid was picking answers out of the sky.

Burton looked at Wolf, maybe sensing the same thing. "Who's this girlfriend of yours?"

"Hettie. And she's...she's not my girlfriend. Hettie's Kyle's girlfriend. She's the reason me and Kyle got in a fight Friday night."

Wolf and Burton eyed each other.

"I've been seeing Hettie behind Kyle's back," Jesse said.

"Whoa," Burton threw his hands up. "Wait a minute. Say that again?"

Jesse said nothing.

"You're shacking up with this guy Kyle's lady behind his back?"

"I know what it sounds like."

"What does it sound like?" Wolf asked.

"You know, that I'm...I don't know what it sounds like. But I can see how somebody would think I might have something to do with it if Kyle went missing."

The silence took over for a bit.

"Go on," Burton said.

Jesse shook his head.

"Come on, Jesse. Spit it out."

"Spit out what? It's like I said. I got a call from Jed Farmer this morning, Kyle's dad. He was going all ape shit, talking about how the cops found blood at Kyle's house and that Kyle was missing. He was demanding to know what was going on and where Kyle was. He said he heard me and Kyle got in a fight. And he said he was coming down from Gunnison to talk with me. And, like I said, that means he's coming down to pull my fingernails out.

"That's when I started freaking out. I drove into town to go talk to Hettie. And on the way there, I saw them driving at my house. Lights flashing."

"Who?" Burton asked. "The cops?"

"Yeah."

"So you ran."

Jesse shut his eyes and shook his head. "I was freaking out, Hal. I figured out what they were thinking from the Jed Farmer phone call. And from talking to Hettie. They found blood. They were coming after me for it."

"Why not just stay and talk to them?" Wolf asked. "And tell them you had nothing to do with it?"

Jesse shut his eyes and put his head back.

The wheels howled on the asphalt as the dotted lines flickered past.

"This isn't looking very good for you, Jesse." Burton used a fatherly tone Wolf recalled from back in the days of sitting in his office after a particularly bad day on the job.

"I know. I know. I screwed up. I was just freaked out, Hal. Just freaked out. I'm sorry. I shouldn't have texted you. I shouldn't have brought you into this. But...something weird is going on. I'm not involved in this. I swear to you, Hal. I'm not."

Burton tipped the bottle back again.

"I shouldn't have texted you. I made a mistake."

Burton said nothing.

"I should have called someone who cares."

"Oh, you're pulling that card, huh, son?"

"I'm not your son." A passing car lit a resigned look on Jesse's face.

"No, you are not."

"Drink up," Jesse said. "Even while you're on your way to the hospital because of it. Drink up, old man. Just like dad. Stupid—"

"All right." Wolf put up a hand. "Listen up, both of you. Let's keep it quiet until we get to the hospital. Jesse, you and I will talk when we get there. And you."

Wolf reached over and grabbed for the bottle. But Burton was lightning quick with his countermove snatching it back, as if he'd been anticipating it since slipping it out of the bag.

"Don't make me regret giving you that," Wolf said.

Burton tucked it away next to his right leg.

Jesse closed his eyes and leaned his head back again.

Burton sat in silence and Wolf let his line of questioning drop. The lights of Cortez were glowing on the horizon, brightening by the second.

Now it looked like Jesse really might have gone to sleep. Wolf thought about how sometimes guilty men looked innocent, and innocent guilty. That was still up in the air with this kid, but one thing was for certain, it looked like he was hiding something. Sheriff Roll and his investigators had a big job ahead of them.

Fifteen minutes later Wolf drove into the glowing lights of Cortez, following the hospital signs toward a well-lit modern building. He pulled into a puddle underneath a drive-up awning in front of the ER and shut off the engine.

"Stay here," Wolf said as he climbed out.

The air was damp and clean, the surroundings lit brightly by the glow from the windows of the hospital.

"Need some help?" A security guard stood outside sucking on a cigarette.

Wolf looked back at the car and saw Burton tipping the bottle, and in the back seat, the young orange-haired man staring out at nothing.

"Yeah. I do."

CHAPTER 9

WOLF STOOD outside under the hospital ER overhang, watching the lightning flicker to the north and listening to the digital trill of the cell phone pressed to his ear. He wondered how hard it was raining up in Rocky Points. In front of him, drizzle streaked through the cones of light out in the parking lot.

"Yeah." MacLean cleared his throat. "Wolf?"

"Hey."

"Where the hell have you been? I've been calling you all day."

"Sorry. I'm down south with Burton."

"Where? What? Why?"

Wolf explained the situation and received dead silence as a response on the other side.

"You there?"

"So you were lying to me earlier," MacLean said. "Which means I was lying to Roll."

Wolf exhaled, considered a long explanation, but instead said, "Sorry about that."

"Sorry about that." MacLean scoffed. "So, I hope you've told Roll what's going on."

"I have. He's on his way."

MacLean let out a long breath. "What's wrong with Burton?"

"Not sure."

The static clicked and scratched in Wolf's ear.

"When are you coming back?"

"I haven't talked to the doctors yet. They're running some tests. I'll have to see what they say."

"Fine. Listen, the reason I wanted to talk to you today was to inform you we have a meeting set up on Tuesday morning."

"Okay."

"At the Town Hall. It's going to be with you, your squad, me, Wilson, and the County Council."

Wolf pulled his eyebrows together. "What about?"

"We'll discuss everything at the meeting."

"Why can't we talk about it now?"

"Because this isn't something we discuss over the phone."

Wolf said nothing.

"Tuesday morning. Eleven a.m. You do what you have to do with Burton to get him back home, or leave him there in that hospital if you have to. But you get home. Tuesday. Eleven a.m. Got that?"

There was a click.

"You there?"

He lowered his cell and stared at the storm clouds roiling to the north. Through the rain-streaked windows behind him, Wolf could see the security guard, who had introduced himself as Scotty, sitting in the waiting room with his arms crossed. Three seats away, Jesse sat with his hands cuffed behind his back, his chin resting on his chest, neon hair draped across his face. Scotty was a talker, and Jesse was fake sleeping to avoid chatting it up. Or maybe Jesse was exhausted from spending the day out in the wilderness and the psychological tension of running from the cops.

Wolf raised the phone and dialed another number.

"Hello, you've reached Cheryl Burton. I can't come to the phone right now, but if you leave me a message, I'll get right back to you."

Wolf eyed his watch—10:17 pm—as the digital beep chimed in his ear.

"Hey, Cheryl. This is Dave Wolf. Listen...I'm in Cortez... Hal's fine, he's fine, but I'm at the hospital, where he's been admitted. We were out hiking around the wilderness and he got light-headed. I just...listen, give me a call. I'm not good with these messages. Just give me a ring." He disconnected and pocketed the phone.

He'd dumped the job of watching Jesse on Scotty, and there was still time before the Ouray law enforcement could feasibly show up. With the rain, he estimated they were still an hour out.

The picture of little Ryan's toothless, seven-month-old grin illuminated the lock screen of his cell phone, and Wolf couldn't help but feel joy swirl in his chest.

When no return call from Cheryl came, he went back inside. The automatic doors slid open and a warm blast of hospital-scented air hit him.

"Any luck?" Scotty unfolded his arms and stood at attention.

"No. Not yet."

"Huh. Wonder what she's doing? Must be sleeping," Scotty said.

Wolf nodded.

Jesse's lips smacked but his hair held still.

"Sleeping," Scotty said.

"Thanks for watching him."

"Sure. No problem. Just let me know if you need me again. I'm going to make the rounds, you can—"

Wolf held up a finger, because his cell phone was vibrating in his pocket. He pulled it out and read the name—Cheryl Burton.

"It's her," he said. "Do you mind watching him a little longer?"

A hint of disappointment flashed across Scotty's eyes, but he smiled and nodded. "Yeah, sure. No problem."

Wolf put the phone to his ear and headed back outside. Strange that relief flooded him, given the conversation he was about to have, but he didn't have a good history with hospitals.

"Hey, Cheryl."

"Hey." She cleared her throat, sounding like she'd just woken up. "What's going on? Hal's in the hospital?"

"Yes."

She spoke to somebody in the room with her. "He's in the hospital...I don't know...okay...sorry, you there?"

"Yeah."

"What's wrong with him?"

"Doctor says he was dangerously anemic—not enough oxygen in his blood. Said he had high blood pressure...and some other things. They're doing tests right now. I haven't gotten the latest update."

"They'll just say the same things they always say. And he has pills for all that. Let me guess, he wasn't taking them and he was drunk as a skunk."

"Something like that."

"Why were you guys out hiking around?"

Wolf let silence take over for a bit. "Where are you, Cheryl?"

"At my sister's."

"Ohio?"

"Yes."

"Visiting?"

"Living. Been here for three months."

"How did I not know about that? You go to the bathroom in Rocky Points, people know about it."

She didn't answer. Burton could be a good hermit, and he was the best poker player Wolf had ever known. That probably had a lot to do with it.

"What's happening between you two?" Wolf asked, aware he was no therapist and had probably just overstepped his bounds.

"His drinking. His lifestyle. Everything. I told him I wasn't going to sit there and watch him kill himself, and I meant it. So I left. Period."

Wolf watched the steady rain and the webs of lightning crawling across the sky. He remembered his open hand connecting with Jack's face over a year ago. He still felt the sting in his palm, and the shame that followed.

"I understand."

"I know you do, Dave. I told him to talk to you. Everyone saw how you turned yourself around, and I wanted him to do the same. You know? He needed to cut it out. One drink became half the bottle. Then he started never even coming to bed at night. I'd wake up and find him passed out on the couch, the TV still on. I told him to talk to you."

Wolf closed his eyes and rubbed a hand over the closely shorn hair under his ball cap. He'd become the Rocky Points poster boy for sobriety, although he had no desire to fulfill the role. Something about the public collapse on the mountain coupled with the decision to quit drinking made a good story, if not in the newspapers, then in coffee shop lines around town.

"—told him never again. So, here I am."

Wolf snapped back to the conversation. "I understand."

She sobbed and sniffed. Blew her nose. "I guess I'll head back. What are they going to do with him?"

He thought of the state of the house they'd left. For his friend passed out in the hospital bed, and for her sanity, he wanted to get back to Rocky Points and clean the place before she saw it. But what was the point? The truth was the truth. To mask it would only do more damage.

"I'll bring him up to Rocky Points tomorrow," he said. "Whenever they get him out."

"What were you guys doing out hiking?"

He considered his answer. "I'll let him explain that later."

"Sounds cryptic."

"We were helping out your nephew, Jesse."

"Jesse?" She all but grunted the word. "Helping? What happened to him?"

"I'll have to let Hal explain."

"Was it something terrible? What did he do?"

Wolf narrowed his eyes. "What makes you think he did something terrible?"

"I don't know. The kid's one of those survivalist-militia-types. Has a YouTube channel that will make your blood curdle. I made the mistake of watching one of the videos he posted on Facebook once. And then there's the incident back in middle school."

"What incident back in middle school?"

"He tried to stab a teacher for giving him detention."

Wolf turned to the glass and looked at Jesse again. The kid was staring up at Scotty's moving lips with glazed-over eyes.

"Hal said he was troubled growing up. That definitely sounds a bit more than troubled."

She snorted. "He was messed up."

"Did he use a knife?" Wolf asked.

"I'm not sure. I think it was something from the classroom."

Wolf contemplated the difference between bringing a knife to school and using it on a teacher versus picking up a sharp pencil in a fit of rage. "Hal said he used to go camping or something with him."

"Yeah," she said. "He did."

"But then he stopped?"

"That's right."

"I'm getting the sense Hal is beating himself up for not being there."

"Jesse was too much for him to take on." She sighed. "For us to take on. Hal's always beaten himself up about that kid. My goodness. No wonder he's in the hospital. What did Jesse do?"

"He's in some trouble in Ridgway."

"Did he hurt somebody?"

"Maybe. We don't know."

The cellular connection hissed. Her phone made a scratching sound.

"I'll pack up now and drive back. Dave, thank you. Thank you so much. I'm glad he's with you right now."

"Yeah. No problem. I'll stick with him until we see you back in Rocky Points. And relax, please. He's in good hands now. Don't drive tonight. Get some rest and leave in the morning."

"Rest. Yeah, right."

"I'll keep you posted."

They said their goodbyes and he pocketed the phone. When he turned back to the window both Jesse and Scotty were looking at him.

He went back inside, and Scotty met him halfway. "Everything okay?"

Wolf nodded. "Thanks, Scotty. I appreciate the help."

"No sweat. You let me know if you need anything more." He left without giving any contact info should the need arise, but Wolf figured the man had done enough.

Wolf sat down, feeling relief in his lower back as the plastic chair squeaked under his weight.

"Thought that guy would never leave," Jesse said under his breath.

Wolf watched Scotty get a cup of coffee from a vending machine and disappear through a set of double doors.

He stood, went to the machine himself and filled a cup with the weak-looking brew. When he came back, he sat across the aisle from Jesse and studied the kid.

"How old are you?"

Jesse said nothing and looked like he was ready to keep his mouth shut for the rest of the night.

Wolf reached in his pocket and pulled out the piece of gum he'd confiscated from Jesse. "Want this?"

Jesse shook his head.

Wolf put it back in his pocket.

"Twenty-two," Jesse said. "I'm twenty-two."

Wolf sipped. "So why are you running from the cops?"

Jesse locked his tired, blue eyes on Wolf's. "I didn't kill that guy."

"Right. And you didn't hurt your buddy Carl."

"Kyle."

"Right. Even though you got in a fight with him over you having an affair with his girlfriend. And now he just happens to be missing and there's blood at his house."

Wolf sipped his coffee, feeling the immediate kick of caffeine, but it was a drop in the gas tank compared to what he needed.

"I had nothing to do with whatever's going on with Kyle."

"Okay, fine. You didn't. But you hear how it all sounds, right?"

Jesse stared at the floor.

"What about this other guy?" Wolf asked. "Alexander Guild."

Jesse said nothing.

"Some rich guy up there in Ridgway?" Wolf asked. "That's how the papers are painting it."

Jesse shrugged, and when a tear rolled down his cheek, he squirmed in his seat, trying with all his might to wipe it away with his shoulder. Due to the handcuffs, it wasn't working.

Wolf studied him, wondering why showing that weakness was such a punishable offense.

"It's all right," he said.

Jesse stood and walked to the end of the row, sat down, and pressed his head against the glass. Now that his face was hidden, Jesse let the waterworks loose. Sounds of uncontrollable sobbing echoed in the empty waiting room, wracking his shoulders.

The nurse behind the desk looked up at Wolf. He frowned slightly and walked to the nurse's station.

"How's it going?" the nurse asked.

"Not too bad. Could be better." He plucked a wad of tissues from the box and walked over to Jesse.

"Don't make me regret this. Or you will." Wolf reached down and uncuffed Jesse, then handed him some tissues.

He sat opposite Jesse, ignoring the now-alarmed look on the nurse's face in the corner of his eye.

Jesse sat up straight. He wiped his nose, then looked at Wolf through red-rimmed eyes. His one bad eye was brick-red.

"Thanks."

Wolf tossed him the open handcuffs. "Put them on in front."

Jesse obeyed, and Wolf cinched them tight when he was done.

"Did you know Alexander Guild?"

Jesse looked past him.

Just then, red and blue strobes reflected off the windows and Jesse's blanched face, and Wolf didn't have to turn around to know the Ouray County cavalry had arrived.

CHAPTER 10

"You're Detective Wolf, I take it?" A deputy flicked his eyes between Wolf and Jesse. He wore a black jacket with a name strip that read Sobeck.

"Hi." Wolf shook the man's sturdy grip.

"I'm Deputy Sobeck, this is Deputy Triplett."

Sobeck was average height and muscular. His hair, eyebrows and eyclashes were a powdery blond.

Triplett extended a large hand that gripped like a wounded squid. He was taller by a couple of inches than Wolf's six-foot three, but looked like he still had his awkward teenage physique and hadn't quite filled out yet.

"Jesse." Deputy Triplett shook his head and winged out his long arms, hands on hips. "The hell you doing running, man?"

Triplett took off Wolf's cuffs and returned them, then pulled Jesse's hands behind his back with ample force and cuffed him using his own.

A man strode in through the front door wearing jeans and a tucked-in button-up shirt. He had gray hair cut tidily at the edges. He was short and thin, with a thick gray mustache beneath a chiseled nose and hard blue eyes.

Wolf recognized him from years ago, though Wolf had trouble placing exactly where they'd last seen each other. "Sheriff Roll."

Sheriff Lance Roll nodded and took Wolf's hand in an iron grip. "Detective Wolf. Been a while."

Wolf nodded, matching the shake with equal force.

Roll kept his grip on Wolf. "Crested Butte. Rocky Mountain LEO conference."

"Good memory." When Wolf pulled his hand away their hands all but snapped apart.

Roll jutted a thumb over his shoulder. "Get him out of here."

With a nod, the two deputies led Jesse out to an Ouray County Sheriff's Department SUV parked under the awning.

"Oh, yeah," Wolf said. "I have this." He unzipped his inside pocket and handed over Jesse's phone, the battery, two pieces of gum, and a wallet. "Here's what I found on him."

"Battery's out of the phone," Roll said.

"He seems concerned about tracking," Wolf said.

"That's Jesse Burton for you. Bastard's untrackable. And it doesn't help when we have other agencies hiding his whereabouts."

Wolf ignored the comment. "I have a Kimber 1911 nine-millimeter I took off him in the back of my cruiser."

"Lead the way. Sobeck! Bag this stuff, please."

Wolf walked through the doors and to Deputy Sobeck's vehicle, where Roll dropped the evidence into a plastic bag.

"Let's go," the sheriff said.

Wolf led Roll through the steady drizzle to the parking lot. He opened the rear door of his SUV and handed over the gun.

Roll opened another evidence bag and Wolf dropped it inside. After sealing the top and studying the weapon, Roll's eyes slid up. "So. You care to tell me what the hell is going on here, detective?"

Wolf looked back at the hospital. Deputy Sobeck and Triplett stood near their vehicles, watching them. Jesse was already inside the car.

"I'm not following, sir," Wolf said.

"Don't bullshit me. I spoke with Sheriff MacLean this afternoon, he even mentioned you by name, telling me you had checked with your former sheriff Hal Burton and had learned Jesse was not there, and that Burton hadn't heard anything."

"That's right."

Roll's eyes popped open. "So, you were lying. You knew exactly where Jesse Burton was while I had my entire department, and then some, looking for that kid."

"Correct."

Roll stared at him. He cupped a hand over his mouth and turned around. When he turned around, he looked at him hard. "Okay, tell me what's going on. Tell me straight."

"Sheriff Burton got a message from Jesse. Jesse seemed to think some people were after him—specifically, Kyle Farmer's family. He says Jeb, or Jed, Farmer called him and threatened him."

"Jed," Roll said. "Did he tell you what happened to Kyle?"

Wolf shook his head. "He doesn't seem to know. Or, at

least that's what he told us. He said he knew from Jed Farmer that something had happened to Kyle, and he knew you guys were coming after him for it."

Roll narrowed his eyes. "All right, he texts Burton and says he's in trouble. You guys come down to get him rather than call us."

"We thought it best to come get him ourselves and deliver him."

"You mean Burton thought it was best for you guys to come get him," Roll said.

"We meant no foul play, sir. If it weren't for Sheriff Burton's health emergency, we would have been hand-delivering the kid to you hours ago. It wasn't our intention to string you guys along."

Roll lifted his chin, managing to look down his nose at Wolf despite his height. "What exactly did this message say?"

"It's on Burton's phone. But it was something along the lines of 'Uncle Hal, please come help me. I'm in trouble. They think I killed that guy Alexander Guild, but I didn't. Now this guy Kyle's family is after me and I'm scared. Come help.'"

Roll nodded. "We'll need that text. Just in case Jesse disabled his phone."

"I'll forward it to you at the earliest."

Roll read off his phone number and Wolf put it in his phone. "And I need a full, official report from you two."

Wolf nodded. "We'll stop by on the way home. You're still in downtown Ouray, right?"

"Yeah. But we've set up a headquarters in Ridgway, in the Marshal's Office. You know it?"

"I have my cell phone. I'll figure it out."

"We'll be there at eight a.m. for a status meeting, but then I have no idea where I'll be pulled to with this case. If you're later, there's a receptionist who knows how to get hold of me." Roll stared at him. "I've read about your exploits over the last year, Wolf."

Wolf said nothing.

"This stunt you've pulled today is mighty ballsy. I could make it my business to make it bad for your career."

"Understood, sir."

"But I know you were most likely acting out of loyalty for Burton. And I respect that." Roll leaned sideways and looked past him. "I'm not gonna press the issue. I have too much bullshit to wade through as it is right now."

"I appreciate it."

"You're welcome." Roll stared hard at him. "How's he doing, anyway?"

"He seems to be stable."

"What was it? Heart attack?"

"No, but it could have been, had we gotten here any later."

Roll put a hand on his own chest. "I've had a bypass myself. Not fun."

"Sorry to hear that."

Roll sucked in a breath and looked into the countryside next to them. The lights of Cortez were few and far between, and a half moon had poked out from behind the breaking clouds.

The sheriff's head turned toward him, his eyes landing on him heavily. "You stop by on the way back to Rocky Points and give me Burton's phone, along with two official reports, or you're in for another long year, Detective Wolf."

The man could have walked away right there, but he stood, waiting for an answer, which Wolf put as a tick in the plus column for the man.

"You have my word," he said.

Roll nodded, then slapped Wolf on the shoulder on the way past. "Let's go!"

The sheriff walked fast back to the building. They climbed into their vehicles and drove away at speed, their wheels hissing behind revving engines.

Still standing in the parking lot, Wolf's eyes rose to the upper floors of the hospital and caught the sight of Burton staring back at him from a lit window.

CHAPTER 11

WOLF RAPPED TWICE BEFORE PUSHING open the heavy hospital room door.

"Oh, it's you."

Wolf shut the door behind him. "How are you feeling?"

"Pretty good." Burton had a tethered remote control in his hand, his eyes on the ceiling-mounted television. "Isn't shit on TV."

Wolf walked to the window and looked outside.

"Saw our man Roll was here to take Jesse."

Wolf nodded. "They want us to stop into Ridgway on the way back home to give official reports."

Burton shut off the television and set the remote down. "Good."

There was a knock at the door and a woman entered, dressed in a lab coat. She wore thick glasses over tired-looking eyes, and her disheveled curly hair suggested she may have been called in to work to tend to their man in the bed.

"Hello," she said with an easy smile. "I take it you're the

Detective Wolf who was just speaking to our nurse down the hall?"

Wolf nodded and shook her well-lotioned hand.

"And you must be Mr. Burton."

Burton twirled a finger in the air.

"I'm Dr. McCarthy. I was called in by the ER doctor to check on your condition. How are you feeling?"

"Like a thousand dollars. A million God damned dollars."

Her smile faded, and she raised the tablet tucked under her arm and swiped the screen. "Well, that's good you feel okay, but the test results tell me you may be just saying that."

"Oh, really."

"The initial blood tests show your red blood cell count is extremely low, which could account for the lightheadedness you reported to the ER doctor upon your arrival."

Burton had the remote control back in his hand and he was engrossed in an infomercial about flipping distressed real estate for profit.

Dr. McCarthy continued reading a paragraph-worth of what was wrong with Burton, and then turned to Wolf. "His BAC was .21."

Wolf nodded. "He had some whiskey on the way here."

She looked at the tablet. "Mr. Burton, you should be good to go tomorrow morning, if you—"

"Yeah, screw that. Television's not good enough for me to stay here."

Her finger froze on the tablet and she looked up. "It's my recommendation you stay overnight."

"I'll take my pills, doc. Thanks. Now why don't you take a hike, hon."

Wolf's face went hot.

Hers looked like it cooled a few degrees. "Hon?"

"I'll be okay. I know the drill. Take the meds, some with food, some without. Don't drink. Got it."

"The serum myoglobin tests showed you were close to having a heart attack. Your EKG shows abnormal palpitations. Looking at the structure of the arterial walls, you're lucky you didn't have a massive cardiac event leading to complete failure."

Burton kept his eyes on the infomercial.

"You're lucky to be alive."

"Doc," Wolf said gently, "could I please speak to you outside for a moment?"

"I'll get dressed while you guys are out there." Burton slid off the side of his bed.

"We're not going anywhere," Wolf said. "You stay there and get comfortable. You're staying the night."

"I can't sleep in a hospital."

"You have something that would help him sleep, don't you?" Wolf asked.

"With his current blood alcohol level? I don't think so."

"Oh, yeah. I'll take a sleeping pill. You get me one of those, I'll be set."

Dr. McCarthy blinked rapidly.

"Doc," Wolf motioned for the door. "We'll be back in a second, Hal."

"That man is not well," she said when they had stepped outside.

"I know. Believe me, I know. So, what does he need to do?"

"Well, aside from being extremely drunk he's technically fine now. But he really dodged a bullet today. I would say absolutely no strenuous activity whatsoever, and for the sake of his heart he needs to refrain from drinking whiskey. I saw from his record he's been seeing Dr. Floyd up at Sluice-Byron County. I've talked to him tonight, and we're scheduled to have a call tomorrow morning. As for Mr. Burton, he needs get home soon, back to Dr. Floyd, for further treatment. And he needs to stay here tonight. If you want to give him the best chance of living, I'd recommend talking him into that."

Wolf nodded. "What about the bag of medication I gave the ER doctor? Is he set with all those pills there?"

She exhaled heavily. "All set there? No. He needs to drastically change his diet, his intake of alcohol needs to drop. He needs to stop drinking completely. He needs to begin to exercise... but not before the first two change and he can get off such high doses of pills. Until then, the man is a ticking time bomb."

"I can't guarantee I can keep him in that bed," Wolf said.

She nodded. "He's properly dosed with medication at the moment. We'll give him another round in the morning, and then it's up to him to keep up with his normal medication regimen. If he decides you two have to get out of here, then have him take those pills first thing in the morning. And get him to Dr. Floyd as soon as possible. And pray that if Dr. Floyd is gone that cardiologist on call is not a woman, or he has no chance."

"Thanks."

She turned and walked away, lifting her hand in salute as she passed through a set of double doors.

Wolf pushed his way back into Burton's room. Hal still stared at the TV.

"So?"

"You have to keep up with your pills and stop drinking so much," Wolf said. "And eat better."

"The sleeping pills. You get any?"

"No."

"Shit."

Wolf walked to the bed, pressed the power button on the remote control and walked to the window again. The sky outside had stopped spitting. The heavy low clouds over Cortez glowed, reflecting the artificial light. "All right, let's talk straight here."

"Yes, sir."

"You've turned into an out-of-control drunk. You know that, right?"

"Oh, right, I forgot I'm with the great saint of sobriety, David Wolf. Hey, I seem to remember you fell flat on your ass, too. Had to have a bunch of your peons pick you up off the ground and fly you to a hospital. For a panic attack. You see me have any panic attacks when I was with the department? And I had a hell of a lot more responsibility than you ever had."

Burton's eyes flicked around the room, then settled on Wolf's.

Wolf let the muscles around his jaw relax. "I talked to Cheryl."

"Good for you."

"She's headed back to Rocky Points to see you."

"Where's the bottle?"

Wolf shook his head.

"You heard me. Where's the bottle?"

"It's back in the car."

"Please get it."

Wolf looked back out the window, considering his options. He could leave. He could update that ride-sharing app on his phone, call someone to come pick up Burton and take him back to Rocky Points.

"What did she say?" Burton asked.

"She told me she didn't want to watch you kill yourself. I don't blame her." He checked the reflection in the window and saw Burton was wiping his face.

"This is so messed up," Burton said.

Wolf let the sound of Burton's sobbing fill the silence.

"What did the doc really say?"

"She told me you had to stop drinking. That your blood oxygen levels were low and living up in the altitude like you do isn't helping any. That your heart had to work overtime, which was tiring it out. Your shit diet and drinking make your heart a ticking time bomb. That it's about to fail if you don't pull your head out of your ass."

"She said that?"

"Verbatim."

Burton chuckled. "How about Roll? They treat my nephew okay?"

Wolf shrugged.

"I saw Roll talking to you. Looked pretty pissed."

"We're expected to stop in Ridgway to give our official reports and hand over your phone for inspection."

"You said that already."

"After we stop in Ridgway, you're getting back in the car and we're driving up to County Hospital, where you're going to check yourself in with Dr. Floyd. And if you had any sense, after that you'd check yourself into some rehab therapy sessions with Dr. Hawkwood down at the Old Church Building."

Burton laughed, a big hearty chuckle that turned into a coughing fit. "No way in hell."

"Whatever. I don't care what you do."

Burton dug a finger into his mustache and scratched with the vigor of a man who was being attacked subcutaneously by insects. Sweat beaded on the old man's forehead. "Wolf. Please."

"What?"

"I need a freaking drink. I really, really need a drink."

"Sorry. The doctor thinks you're a ticking time bomb. Doesn't that bother you?"

"I've been a ticking time bomb for the last decade."

"Yeah? And how many times have you been put in the hospital for it?"

"You're the one who brought me here."

They stared at each other.

"I'm not staying here tonight."

"If I give you a drink, you're staying here."

Burton's eyes widened. "Okay. Deal."

Wolf set down his duffle bag, unzipped it and produced the burbling bottle of Jack Daniels.

"Holy cow, you had it all along."

Wolf pointed at the covered plastic mug of water and ice next to his bed. "Drink all of that water, right now."

Burton wasted no time sucking down the liquid until the straw slurped. The pain and underlying anxiety that had pinched the man's eyes was gone, and they now sparkled like a child's in an amusement park.

Wolf tipped some of the amber liquid into the ice and

screwed the top back on. Then he tucked the bottle away in the duffle bag and zipped it shut.

Burton slowly put aside the straw and lid and reached for the cup, brought it to his lips and took a greedy sip. "Ah. That's the stuff."

Wolf immediately regretted his decision. But if they left, the old man would have hounded him until he could drink. Better here than anywhere else, he rationalized.

Burton's eyes glazed over in thought. "Wolfie, my nephew is caught in the crossfire of something up there in Ridgway. I have a feeling."

Wolf shrugged again. "They have competent individuals on the job. From what I read in the newspaper this morning, CBI's helping."

"I'd like to still know what they're looking at. Make sure they're going at it the right way. You know, peace of mind."

"No offense, Sheriff, but I'd just as well leave it to them. I have plenty of my own issues to get back to at home."

Burton's eyes narrowed. "What kind of issues?"

Wolf sat down in a chair by the window, feeling the weight of his thoughts press him into the leather. "County Council meeting Tuesday morning."

"Ha! Screw those jackals. Just tell them 'yes, sir' and 'yes, ma'am,' and walk out. That's how you deal with them."

Wolf said nothing.

"You think it's serious?"

"I'm not sure, but the writing is on the wall."

"What's this writing saying?"

"It's wondering if I'm good for the job anymore."

"Why?"

"I assume it has to do with peons picking my ass up off the mountain last summer."

"Then why wait almost a year to oust you?" Burton asked. "If they wanted you gone, you'd be gone by now. Right?"

Wolf shrugged. He'd considered the question, too. The only answer he could come up with was things took time. Especially when the mayor was Wolf's close friend. Maybe Margaret's protection had finally been perforated.

They sat in silence.

"You're the best cop Colorado's ever seen. And the routine remains the same. You give them a 'yes, sir, yes ma'am' and if they don't want you anymore, then screw them."

Burton flipped a hand, like he always had when he was done speaking on a topic. He held the plastic cup up to the light, looking slightly disappointed by the level of the contents within.

"Good tasting stuff. Thanks, Wolfie. I could always count on you."

Wolf knew he could have said the same thing to the old man.

Burton and Wolf's father, Daniel, had been longtime partners, and when Daniel Wolf had become sheriff, Burton had been his right-hand man. When Wolf's father had been killed in the line of duty, Burton had been appointed sheriff. Wolf was just a freshman at Colorado State University, still a teenager, and had gone dark after his father's death. He'd quit the football team. Without his father in the stands, what was the point? He went out for revenge half a world away, enlisting in the Army, and instead had found more pain and destruction.

And when Wolf had come back from Afghanistan, broken and suffering flashbacks, with a wife hooked on drugs and a son in diapers, Burton had hired him into the department.

Burton had been there with open arms, always loyal to Wolf, no matter how bad he screwed up.

"Tell me about Jesse," Wolf said. "No more deflecting."

Burton's eyes glazed. "Yeah. Jesse." The cup came back to his lips, then back to the table. "Jesse's my little brother's kid."

"Mike's kid?"

"Yeah."

"He died of a heart condition?" Wolf took a stab in the dark. He'd never known how the man had passed. He'd never known anything about him.

"Aneurysm. Died in his sleep. But he was pretty much dead to the world a decade before that. Ever since Jesse's birth, to be exact."

Wolf put up his feet on the window sill. His feet felt like two blood-filled balloons, and when he leaned into the seat his lower back ached from the day's exertions.

"Let's see...where do I begin with this shit show?" Burton sipped again. "I guess I gotta start with my story. I was an only child until I was seventeen years old, when my mother informed me she was pregnant. It was a shock to everyone in the family, but mostly to me." Burton's gaze was far away.

"I was off to Colorado Springs that next year, where I was going to study criminal justice at Colorado College. And here were my parents, having another kid. Starting over from scratch.

"They were supposed to be crying over me leaving the nest, but instead they were all preoccupied with a new baby."

Burton looked embarrassed and sought the cup to hide his face. The remainder of the liquid disappeared, filtered through the ice cubes.

The first slurp snapped him back to the present. His eyes darkened, went to the duffle bag on the floor.

Wolf unzipped it, pulled out the bottle, and poured him another couple of fingers. "That's it. Make it last."

Burton left the drink and slipped back into his story. "Anyway. I went to college, and a few months into my first semester I got the news my little brother had been born. I went back and visited."

Burton waved a hand in the air.

"I stayed out on the front range, got a job with Denver PD. Became detective. Saw my kid brother Mike every once in a while, you know, every year for Christmas and stuff."

The drink went back to his lips.

"You know about my parents dying, right?"

"No." Wolf knew they were deceased, but he'd never heard how, nor had he pressed the issue.

"They died in a car crash." Burton put a fist into his open palm. "Head on collision with a truck up on I-80 in Wyoming."

Wolf didn't know what to say as he watched Burton wade through tangled thoughts.

"I was down in Denver." Burton lifted an eyebrow. "You know how dangerous it was to work the Denver beat back in the sixties?"

Wolf nodded.

"Pretty dangerous. The criminals had all the new

weapons of choice, and the cops had billy clubs and whistles. No way I was signing up for that. But I'd heard from a guy named Charlie Davidson about a small up-and-coming ski resort town called Rocky Points, and a hard-ass sheriff named Daniel Wolf. The rest is history."

Burton raised his cup and took a sip.

Wolf had heard that part of his life story plenty of times. He waited for Burton to pick up the thread about his kid brother, about his nephew, but the story had evaporated.

"And Mike?" Wolf asked. "Jesse?"

Burton's eyes clouded. "Right. We buried my parents. Mike was twenty, or twenty-one at the time. When he came to the funeral, he introduced me to his wife, some high school sweetheart kind of thing. She was pregnant with Mike's kid. We said next to nothing to each other at the funeral. It was weird. Neither of us could find the words. And we parted ways again."

Burton drank.

"The next time I saw Mike was when he was walking around with Jesse in his arms. He was alone with the kid. His wife died in childbirth."

Wolf stared out at the window.

"Mike didn't take his wife's loss too well. By that point, me and Cheryl had already decided we weren't having kids. We were up in Rocky Points, living our lives, when here comes my brother with his little baby in a stroller, this time without his wife, all depressed looking."

Imagine that, Wolf thought.

"Me and him went out drinking once on that visit, and he broke down crying, telling me how he was scared for the future. That he didn't know what was going to happen and he didn't know if he could handle it.

"I told him he could handle it. And to not give up. But he'd already given up, and I knew it right then and there. I wasn't going to take his kid. I wasn't going to help him out of what he'd got himself into. I had my own burdens, what with the job and Cheryl, and...."

Burton shut his eyes.

"Anyway, he left and went about his life, and I went about mine. About ten years later, I got word that Mike had drunk himself to death. Aneurysm, they were calling it, but from what I could figure out, he'd been drinking heavily every day since his wife died."

The irony bounced off Burton's slack face. He was starting to slur.

"And then I learned that after that trip to Rocky Points, Mike had given up on raising Jesse. I guess there was this woman named Bertha who used to babysit Mike growing up. She took over.

"It was not official, you know, with the state or anything. But Jesse had lived with her for nine of the first ten years of his life, never seeing his father for more than a few minutes at a time, maybe once or twice a month, if at all, until his death."

Burton wiped tears from his cheeks.

"That's when something finally clicked inside of me. I started going camping with Jesse. I realized the boy needed a man in his life. That living with old Bertha wasn't going to cut it. I took Jesse two or three times that first summer. Then I took him fishing that next year, and then we started going to Canyon of the Ancients, and he loved it. It was kind of our thing for a while."

Burton looked at his hands. "But I couldn't keep it up."

"Why's that?" Wolf asked.

Burton snorted. "There's no reason why." He put the cup back to his lips and sucked the liquid out of the ice. "He wasn't my kid. He wasn't my responsibility. That's why."

"Was it something to do with the teacher stabbing incident?"

Burton looked at Wolf with narrowed eyes. "Who told you about that?"

"Cheryl."

"Oh."

Wolf put his feet back on the ground. They throbbed with pain as the blood rushed back in. "What did he try and stab his teacher with?" he asked.

"A compass."

Wolf raised his eyebrows. The pointy metal tip of the math tool was definitely a step above a sharpened pencil as far as harmful intent goes.

"Shit," Burton said. "I mean, I wanted to help. I was considering bringing Jesse up to Rocky Points and taking him into our house, but Cheryl was freaked out. Like I said, we'd already decided we weren't going to have kids. And here's Jesse. The wild animal nobody wanted."

Burton shook his head.

"I could have fought her. I could have put my foot down. I could have fought for him." A tear streamed down Burton's cheek. "I remember that last time I saw him. Before that incident when we were done with one of our camping trips. I told him to keep me on his speed dial. That we were going to spend more time together. Especially after he got his driver's license. That he could come visit whenever he wanted."

Burton pulled the flimsy sheet up to his shoulders and his arms went limp underneath. His head lolled to the side.

"That was the last time we went camping," Burton said, eyes still closed. "I let him down from that moment on. He was getting too close. I was getting too close."

The old man took a deep, shuddering breath.

Wolf stood and tucked the sheet around his arms, then pulled a thin comforter to cover his torso.

The sheet moved, and Wolf saw Burton's eyes were open.

"I lied to his face. He called after that, and I ignored him. I ignored him."

"It's okay."

"It's sure as shit not okay. I ignored him before that incident. Before he tried to stab his teacher. I know if I would have just answered the phone, that would have never happened."

Burton closed his eyes again. His voice was sleepy. "He knew what he was doing, texting me like that today. He knows what I said after that trip and how I wriggled out of my promise like a slimy rainbow trout." He opened his eyes. "I have to help him out of this, Dave."

Wolf stood straight. "We'll talk about it in the morning. You need to get some sleep."

"I have to help him. He's acting like he didn't do whatever they think he did, so I have to believe him. I have to be there for him, and I have to help him."

Wolf thought of the gun Jesse was carrying. He wondered what the kid's past did to his psyche. In Wolf's experience people's pain could cause them to do rash, terrible things. A lifetime of harsh words or circumstances could mean certain actions were on the table that weren't for law abiding citizens.

He thought of Jesse's shock of flaming red hair. His camouflage pants. His past. His present as a militant YouTuber that disgusted Cheryl. He thought of Cheryl all those years ago, appalled and fearful of the child who had tried to stab his teacher.

"I think you might not know this kid," Wolf said.

"He's telling me he didn't do it. Don't you get it? I have to believe him, even if he's not telling the truth. I owe this kid. Because even if he's a murderer, it's my fault." His teeth were clenched.

Wolf said nothing.

"I want to thank you for being here for me now." Burton's words ran together. "You've always been the best of the bunch, you know that? You've always been my best go-to guy. My right-hand man, when I was young and spry enough to be out there in the field." Burton smiled. "You remember that?"

Wolf pressed his lips together.

"And I am sorry. I'm sorry for what I said earlier about you breaking down last year."

"It's all right," Wolf said.

"No, it's not."

"Okay. Go to sleep. We'll talk in the morning."

"I'm not dumb, Wolf. He looks like the type of hoodlum who just might shoot and kill somebody. He's got the history. But if he didn't, if he's telling the truth, I want to make sure they're giving him a fair shake up there. We need to be part of that investigation."

Wolf nodded. "Sleep."

Burton's arm shot out from under the bedsheet. He poked

a finger into his own chest. "I was the Sheriff of Sluice County, damn it. You're the chief detective of the department now. They'd be happy to have two people like us lending a hand."

Wolf waited for the redness to subside in Burton's face, and said, "I'm not sure if I would welcome an outsider into an investigation involving a murdered resident of Rocky Points, and I wouldn't blame Sheriff Roll for thinking the same way."

Burton tucked his hand back under the sheet and a sly smile stretched his lips. "I have a history with Sheriff Roll. He'll let us in."

"What does that mean?"

"You let me worry about that. I just need to know about you. What do you say, Wolf? You in? For old time's sake?"

"We'll go up there tomorrow. Sleep."

Burton's lips curled in a sly smile and he closed his eyes.

Wolf picked up the duffel bag and left.

"Where are you going?"

Wolf twisted the knob. "To sleep."

"You can sleep right here."

He had heard the impaled rhinoceros sounds the man could make during a deep snooze. "No thanks."

"Wolf!"

He stopped, poked his head inside. "What?"

Burton nodded seriously. "Thank you."

"You're welcome." Wolf nodded and shut the door.

CHAPTER 12

"Go see them now, then," Scott said.

Heather Patterson considered her husband's words. "I don't know."

"You got no sleep last night because of it. Go see them."

"It's not just them that kept me up. It's Wolf." Patterson opened the front door and stepped onto the porch.

Hummingbirds swarmed the feeder. Down the hill from their townhouse, the valley north of Rocky Points spread out in peaceful silence. Steam rose off the Chautauqua River. A trio of deer nibbled grass near the bushes lining the water.

She loved these early hours, when Tommy and Lucas were still asleep. But she loved when they were up, too, breaking the peacefulness of the Rocky Mountain nature with demands of cartoons, breakfast, and attention.

She deemed the air too frigid to leave for work in only her flannel, so she stepped back inside to get her fleece.

Scott stood inside, sipping his coffee.

She sighed and stopped in front of him. "You're right. I'll go to their house this morning on the way to work. I can't take the suspense. When I did sleep last night, I had a dream that Minnie buried her husband alive in the back yard."

Scott nodded. "Not a bad dream."

She leaned into him, her head reaching his chest.

He wrapped a long arm around her and rubbed her back. "You know where they live?"

"I was there once, years ago. Do you know how to get there?"

"Take Wildflower and hang a right just before the hill heads down. Dirt road. County 187, I think it is?"

"Oh, yeah." She wrapped her arms around him, and they squeezed each other.

"Tell Carl he's a crazy bastard for me."

She snorted a laugh. "Will do, if he's not dead already."

"Don't worry. She's just psychotic, not a murderer. At least, I think."

She tilted her chin up and he kissed her on the lips.

"Sorry to leave you with the kids again." She grabbed her fleece off the hook and put it on.

"Tina will be here at nine. The kids don't wake up for another hour. I'll survive."

She looked up the stairs. "Another two days straight of not seeing the kids. Asleep when I come home, asleep when I leave."

"Just be grateful they're sleeping and let's leave it at that," he said.

"Okay, yeah." They had gone through a year of Lucas not sleeping well, waking up at all hours of the night. How quickly she had forgotten such a hellish twelve months. She opened the door and turned around. Then she stepped back inside and closed the door. "What if I have to take Wolf's job and be his boss?"

Scott shrugged. "I think he'd agree there are worse people to have as a boss."

"Such a ringing endorsement."

He smiled. "You know what I mean. I truly think he wouldn't mind. Rachette? Now, that's another story."

She opened the door and stepped outside. "Bye. Love you. See you tonight."

Fifteen minutes later, she slowed to a stop in front of Carl and Minnie Yorberg's house and shut off the engine to her department-issued Ford Explorer.

It was early, the sun still not risen above the eastern peaks, but the lights in the Yorberg's windows were on.

She shut off the engine and got out into cold, damp air. She zipped up her fleece all the way and walked, her feet swishing through grass matted down by dew, and then crunching on the gravel driveway.

The single-story structure stood in a meadow, surrounded by the occasional pine tree. Movement caught her eye, and she saw a deer wandering at the side of the house.

She noticed a cloud of smoke rising from the front porch and saw Carl was outside.

"Mr. Yorberg?"

"Who is that?"

She walked along the dirt path toward him, passing garden gnomes half-buried in weeds and wildflowers on the way. "It's Heather Patterson."

Carl squinted, sitting in a cross-legged stupor on the concrete step. "Oh."

"I just came to check on you two." She walked up, eyeing the windows. "How's Minnie doing?"

Carl held a pack of cigarettes in one hand, a lighter in the other. A steaming mug of coffee sat next to him.

"She's fine. Why?"

"Just wondering if she was, you know, still upset."

"Why would she be upset? She was the one bashing the computers. Anyone should be upset, it's me. Gotta buy us new computers now."

Minnie Yorberg came to the front door. "Oh, hi, Heather, how are you today?"

"Hi Minnie."

Minnie Yorberg wore a floral nightgown that looked decades old.

"How are you doing?" Patterson asked.

Minnie opened the screen door. "What are you doing here?"

"Just came to check on you two. See how you were." And to make sure you didn't bludgeon your husband to death, she thought.

Minnie looked at Carl and scoffed. "Ask him. I'm doing just fine."

"Shut up, woman!"

"You shut up!"

Their shouts echoed in the still air.

Patterson stepped onto the porch and put up her hands. "Please. Okay, thanks, Minnie. I just wanted to check on you. Listen, do you think you could give me a minute so I can have a private word with Carl?"

Minnie eyed Patterson, like a batter eyes a lob in the strike zone.

"I'm just making sure everything went okay with our detectives yesterday."

The screen door slapped shut and she closed the interior door, too.

O-kay. Patterson stepped off the porch, clearing out of the cloud of smoke.

"So, Carl."

"What?"

"Detective Rachette says he's still not sure what happened between you two yesterday morning."

"Yeah?"

"He says you never explained it to him."

"Nope." Carl sucked on his cigarette.

Maybe it was the lack of sleep mixed with the fresh coffee buzz, but Patterson decided to improvise. "You know I double-majored at the University of Colorado?"

"That right."

"Yeah. Law enforcement and finance." She felt her face go red at the lie, but Carl was studying his cigarette and failed to notice.

"Good for you."

"Thanks." She nodded. "So, Detective Rachette said that you said there was a disagreement between you two about finances. That Minnie thought you were getting scammed online or something, and she was trying to stop you."

"It's too complicated for an outsider to hear. That's what I told Rachette and Yates."

"Yeah. That was it. But I majored in finance. I can handle it. Come on."

They sat in silence for a beat while Carl finished one cigarette and started another. "Okay. Fine." He sounded like he was taking an impossible challenge.

"Ever since I closed the pawn shop, I've been dabbling in online trading. Making a little cash here, a little there. You know, penny stocks, all that."

"Good," she said.

He eyed her. "You women, you're always nagging for more cash, but when it comes to ponying up to make the money, you get all emotional. Freaked out."

She put up a hand. "Hey. I'm just like you in my household. My husband is the emotional one, I'm the cool-headed one who sees opportunities and acts. That is, if the opportunities are good."

She pictured Scott staring at her with raised eyebrows right now.

"It...sounds weird to a person who's, you know, fresh off the street. Doesn't know the situation."

"Try me."

Minnie's voice appeared in the doorway. "Tell her about how much cash you were going to send to some guy you met in a chatroom."

"Shut up, woman!"

Patterson walked toward the porch. "Please, Mrs. Yorberg."

Minnie disappeared and shut the door.

Damn it. Now she had to get the momentum rolling again. She stepped away from the smoke. "Dang," she said. "I see what you mean."

Carl's eyes twinkled. "You know about cryptocurrencies?"

She nodded. "Sure."

"Well. You can trade these things. You know, buy low, sell high."

"Right."

"Super volatile stuff. But done right, and you can make a fortune because of this volatility."

"Like the stock market," she said.

"Nope. Not like that." Carl sucked another drag. "This is different. This is currency."

She nodded. "Right. Please, continue."

Minnie walked by the window.

"Well, I've been talking to people online," Carl said. "You know, in forums, online communities, etcetera. We help each other get going in the different systems. Anyway, I've met a friend, and he's been giving me tips for a few months now."

She nodded, trying to hide any skepticism.

Carl read her. "But I'm not stupid. I'm not listening to the guy. He could be a fraud for all I know, could be blowing smoke up my ass for his own gain. So I've been, you know, just talking to him. That's it."

"I hear you. Go on."

Carl looked at her, trying to read her. She waited out the silence.

"Anyway. This guy is spot on with picks. Picks that you couldn't be spot on with, unless you're spot on. Do you understand what I'm saying?"

She did not, but she nodded.

"I mean, you have to be able to rig the price of Bitcoin to predict what this guy knows. And I don't know if you know anything about Bitcoin, but that's impossible. Anyway, there's really not much software out for trading cryptocurrencies yet.

It's fresh. It's new. But this guy has it, and he's been selling it. But it's not cheap."

She said nothing.

"Like, really not cheap. But, if you had it, you could make a shitload of money in weeks. It would be a drop in the bucket cost in the long run."

Patterson ignored the gaping hole in logic, namely why the guy was selling the software if he could just sit back and watch money roll in. She nodded instead.

"So, I told Minnie about it. Told her about the predictions this guy has been making for the last three months." He looked sideways at her, his eyes glittering in the rising light. "Months of correct predictions."

"And Minnie didn't like the sound of this?"

"No. She wonders if it works so good, why is this guy selling it to me?"

"Valid concern."

"Yeah. But she doesn't know this guy. He's nice. I have a sense with people, and she's never talked to the guy in her life."

"And you've spoken to him?"

"Online, yeah. I've messaged with him."

Patterson looked up and saw a jet leaving a glowing contrail in the sky. "Okay, so, you met this guy online. Sounds reasonable enough in this day and age. But how exactly did you meet him?"

He looked annoyed by the question. "Personal message in a forum."

"And he was spot-on with some predictions."

Carl nodded. "He introduced himself, said he'd been following my comments, wanted to reach out. And he didn't really come off like Nostradamus and tell me some predictions. He was like, 'Here's what I'm banking on to happen in the next four days.' And then, bam. Four days later it happened exactly like he said he was banking on. Made him a healthy five figures in four days."

She nodded. "And then he…"

"He did it again. He told me about two more moves that would happen with two different currencies, because of markers his software was indicating. And bam. Happened just like he said again. And again. And again."

Carl shrugged. "I was intrigued, and I became friends with the guy. Name's Jon Spillman. Lives in North Carolina. The guy has been infallible for the last two months. I've been bugging him to get his software, and he's finally agreed to send me a version. He's not a professional developer or anything, just really good with databases, all that stuff I've never been good at. He didn't even want to tell me the price. So, like I've been telling Minnie, the guy's not a scammer. He's just a good guy.

"But he doesn't want everyone using his software, you know, stealing it and spreading it on the internet for profit and whatnot. So, he was like, fine, I'll sell it to you. But it's gotta be for a price. One that shows you're playing real ball, not trying to scam me."

She nodded. "Okay. I think I got it. He's worried you're going to scam him."

"Yeah."

"I understand now."

"It's good talking to a sane individual." He chuckled. "Haven't talked to one of those all day."

She tilted her head back, dipping her toe into some things

she wanted to say next. Finally, she settled on, "Let's talk about a hypothetical situation, okay?"

Carl looked perturbed at the change of subject. Another cigarette came out of the pack.

"What if this guy sent out ten thousand personal messages that first day?"

Sounds of frustration struggled to come out of Carl's mouth as he sucked the new cigarette alight. "Ten thousand? What are you talking about?"

"Just bear with me. Let's say there were ten thousand messages he sent. Let's say he had some software that helped him accomplish this task. These messages were segmented into ten versions. Could be more versions—twenty or thirty—doesn't matter. Let's say message version one talked about Bitcoin dropping and...I don't know...what's another cryptocurrency?"

"Hypercoin."

"Hypercoin, thank you. So the first message talks about a Bitcoin drop and a rise in Hypercoin, and how he's going to bank on that gamble with some information he has obtained from his software."

Carl stared into the distance.

"The second version of the message, sent at exactly the same time, goes out to another segment of people. This version talks about Bitcoin going up and Hypercoin dropping. The opposite of the first. A third version goes out talking about the movement of two completely different cryptocurrencies."

Carl's drags per minute increased.

"There's a fourth version sent to other people mentioning

those same currencies with different outcomes. There's a fifth version with those same currencies that—"

"Okay, okay. I get it." Carl shook his head. "There's no way. You couldn't keep up the level of detail with ten thousand messages like this guy's been doing to me. He knows my name. Calls me Carl. Knows about my kids, mentions them..." He stopped talking.

She continued. "At first, your friend is sending out ten thousand messages, then, after that first iteration, there's only a segment of people he sent the correct prediction to. He drops those other nine thousand—or whatever the number is —people that he sent the wrong prediction to, never worries about them again, then concentrates on the remaining one thousand.

"He sends out the second message, also segmenting those now one thousand people into some new predictions. Maybe another ten or twenty of them. After that message, perhaps there are only a few hundred people left that he's sent correct predictions to. After the next message, there are only, heck, I don't know, a few dozen? At some point, he probably has a small pool, one that he can personally communicate with. Get to know their kids' names."

Carl dropped the cigarette into a beer can and it sizzled. He picked up the coffee mug next to him and sipped.

"At that point," she said, "he has a few piping hot people who are amazed by his software's abilities. Let me guess, he probably stopped predicting after a while?"

Carl's face was slack at first, then he started shaking his head.

"With only a dozen or so people on his hot list, he can't risk making a wrong prediction now."

Carl made a sound somewhere between choking and scoffing. "I don't know."

"It's an inverted pyramid." She resisted telling him the scam had been around for a long time, and when she'd learned about it in Criminal Science classes in Boulder the scam had involved mailed letters and stock picks.

Carl stood and walked to his door. "See you later, detective."

The door shut and the lock twisted.

"See you later," she said, walking back to her Explorer.

As she sat behind the wheel, she stared at the Yorberg's house. Carl had been looking out, but now moved away from the window. Minnie came up and took his place. She glared and disappeared.

"See you later," she said under her breath, and fired up the engine.

She picked her phone out of her pocket and took a look at the screen. Still no reply from Wolf. It was seven-thirty a.m., and she wondered if Wolf was in the office yet. It was time to find out.

CHAPTER 13

WOLF'S PHONE RANG AGAIN, and he picked it up from the center console.

Patterson.

He pressed the silence button and put both hands back on the steering wheel.

"More avoiding calls," Burton said.

"Forget me. Back to you." Wolf said. "Blackmail? You want to blackmail the guy so we get included in the investigation? Not a good idea."

"It's not blackmail." Burton sipped his coffee and looked out the passenger window. "It's leverage."

"It's the definition of blackmail."

"I want to know what they have. They might give it to us, they might let us hang around, but they might not. I'm not gonna come out swinging with my guns blazing, I'm just telling you, if he gives us any flak, I'm gonna hit him with it."

Wolf frowned. "Mix metaphors much?"

"Huh?"

Wolf flipped down the sun visor and shifted in his seat. They were coasting the final stretch of road toward Ridgway.

The clock read 7:35 a.m. Burton had been awakened by a nurse checking his vitals at four a.m., and they'd been moving ever since, starting with Burton walking out of the hospital without so much as a goodbye to Scotty the security guard.

"I thought you were in on this with me," Burton said. "I thought you were going to help me help Jesse."

"Do you even remember our conversation last night?"

Burton said nothing.

Wolf eyed him. It was a miracle the man was upright. His eyes had dark bags under them, and his face was pallid, covered in stubble, but there was a spark that danced inside the old man for some reason this morning. Maybe it was the intravenous saline last night, or the hangover just hadn't kicked in yet.

"I told you I have to get back to Rocky Points by tomorrow morning. I have a meeting with the County Council."

"Yeah, I remember that. The BS meeting with the County Council. And I told you screw them. They don't know their asses from their elbows. Look. I just want to see what they have on Jesse. There's no harm in hearing what they have to say."

"And if Roll doesn't want to share what he has?"

"Then I'll use my leverage."

Wolf rolled his head side to side. Carrying Burton over his shoulder and then sleeping across three plastic waiting room chairs overnight, and now speaking with the old man, had his neck screaming in pain.

"What do you have on Roll? Either tell me or we're not even stopping in Ridgway."

Burton smirked. "Okay, fine. I used to have a buddy named Rip Reedy, used to work for Roll down in Ouray. One time I came down to visit, and I was supposed to meet Rip at the station. I was early by about an hour, but I thought nothing of it. I hadn't even looked at the clock, and I just went into their little station they have down there. You seen that little thing? It's like a closet."

"They have a new building now," Wolf said.

"Whatever. Anyway, I went to the door and pulled on the handle, but couldn't get inside. I peeked through the window, and caught more action than I bargained for. Because on the other side of that glass, I saw Sheriff Roll with some woman from town. I stood there frozen, you know, afraid to move but afraid to keep watching."

"But you kept watching," Wolf said.

"Yes, I did. Anyway, they were groping each other, really going after it. The woman had all sorts of hands down his pants, and vice-versa. And then he saw me."

Burton laughed at the memory.

"Oh, he came to that door faster than a bullet, and then he came outside. I was out there on that sidewalk, smiling like I am now."

"And he was married at the time," Wolf said.

"Yes, he was. To none other than the famous Mrs. Lindsay Roll. You've met her. Worked in the San Juan DA's office. Used to come up with Roll to Rocky Points every now and again. Big curly blond hair?"

Wolf sipped the cold remnants of coffee out of his cup and put it back in the center console. "Yeah, I remember her.

Okay, so if I agree to stick around for the day and see what Roll and his team have on Jesse, then we agree that you let me do the talking, and you keep that little story to yourself."

Burton exhaled. "Fine."

The speed limit dropped as they passed a Ridgway City Limit sign.

Like Rocky Points, Ridgway was built on rugged Old West foundations that still shone through. The side roads off the main strip of the town were unpaved dirt, and most of the buildings had been built at least a hundred years ago, with the ragtag local population dressed for function over form.

And just like Rocky Points, the Old West was gilded with the modern. Craft brewers had taken over some of the smaller brick buildings, their hanging carved wood signs adorned with shiny metal. A freshly painted grocery store with plenty of windows touted itself as a healthy market. The vehicles on the roads ran the gamut from mud-slung tractors to luxury European SUVs.

Burton looked up from his phone screen. "Take a left at North Railroad Street."

Burton pointed out his window toward mountains rising in the south. "Whitehouse Mountain. That's Potosi. And ..."

"Sneffels," Wolf said.

"Yeah, Mount Sneffels. I love the skyline here."

"It's pretty beautiful," Wolf said, looking at the jagged mountains to the east.

Wolf rolled down his window, letting in a cold morning chill scented of bacon coming from a diner called Lucille's. Even though they'd already eaten from a drive-thru in Cortez, his mouth watered. But Sheriff Roll had said he'd be at the Ridgway Marshal's Office at eight a.m. for a meeting and there was no sense missing that boat. If they wanted to get all they could on Jesse's case, this was the opportunity Burton was waiting for.

"Left here," Burton said.

Wolf turned and followed a dirt road a couple blocks, where a cluster of vehicles from a variety of Ouray County agencies choked the street, and parked behind a large pickup with a lightbar on top.

They got out, and Wolf took a minute to stretch his body. A breeze rolled down from the southern peaks. Nearby, a trio of uniformed men chatted near a large van adorned with the circular Colorado Bureau of Investigation logo.

Wolf nodded.

"Can I help you?" one of them asked.

"Yeah," Burton said. "We're looking for Sheriff Roll. He inside?"

The guy saw Wolf's badge on his hip. "Who you guys with?"

"Sluice County," Burton said.

"Sluice-Byron," Wolf corrected.

"Yeah, he's inside. Center door."

"Thanks," Burton said, leading the way with the practiced gait of a man who always belonged.

They walked into a dimly lit building that was full of conversation and movement.

Wolf counted six people, all of whom ignored their arrival. Three of them wore Ouray County Sheriff's Department uniforms. Two of them Wolf recognized from last night at the hospital—the tall guy, Triplett, and Sobeck, the powdery haired man. They were at the far end of the room pouring coffee from a drip carafe.

A woman sitting at a front and center desk looked up and nodded. She lifted a pencil by way of greeting, then waved them over and placed the pencil on a sign-in sheet.

Burton leaned a butt-cheek on her desk, ignoring the offering.

"Okay, I'll let him know...I said I'll let him know." The woman hung up. "Can I help you?"

"Need to see Sheriff Roll."

"And you are?"

"Burton."

She leaned sideways and looked at Wolf. "And?"

"Detective Wolf, ma'am."

"And your name?" Burton asked, extending a hand.

The woman eyed it suspiciously and shook. "Cassandra."

"Beautiful name."

She pulled her hand back.

"Hey, it's you." The tall, skinny guy, Deputy Triplett, stood behind her, pointing at Wolf. "This was the detective who wrangled Jesse Burton last night. You must be Jesse's uncle."

"He's back here." Sobeck came up behind Triplett and gestured them to follow.

"Who's that?" Sheriff Roll appeared inside the doorway of a back room. He raised a coffee mug in salutation. "You guys made it. Great. Come on back, please."

Wolf let Burton go first and got a whiff of the alcohol stench coming off the man.

If Sheriff Roll had looked exhausted last night, this morning he looked dead to the world. His eyes were puffy, his face slack. Hair, unkempt and greasy, poked out from a ball cap.

"Sheriff Roll, good to see you again."

"Sheriff Burton." Roll gestured to the coffee machine. "You guys need a cup?"

"Please."

"Pour one, then come on inside. We'll get started."

"No thanks, I just had a cup," Wolf said, stepping into the room past Roll.

Plastic tables and chairs, enough to seat a dozen, stood on a linoleum floor. Florescent lights flickered above, illuminating a board scribbled with notes and a bulletin board covered in photographs.

The room was cool, and the hanging pictures seemed to drop the temperature another few degrees. There was a lot of blood.

"This is Detective Milo. Milo, this is Chief Detective Wolf from Sluice-Byron and the former Sheriff Hal Burton."

A man stood up from a laptop computer. "Pleasure."

They shook hands, and Milo stood with a stiff spine, chin up, hands clasped behind his back. With his short-cropped blond hair and muscular physique, Wolf took him for military.

"I heard about how you guys brought Jesse in last night," Milo said.

"That's right," Wolf said.

"We're glad you found him."

Wolf sensed no animosity behind the man's words.

"You've met Deputies Sobeck and Triplett?" Roll asked.

Wolf nodded and got the same dead fish from Triplett, the strong clasp from Sobeck.

A third man, dressed in a pair of jeans and a CBI logoed polo shirt, rose to greet them.

"This is Special Agent Charlie Rushing with the Colorado Bureau of Investigation."

"Nice to meet you," Special Agent Rushing said. He had a warm, soft grip. The lights overhead reflected off his bald pate and his silver-rimmed eyeglasses.

"Special Agent Rushing's a forensic specialist. You might have seen the van outside. We called in the CBI pretty early on this for assistance," Roll said. "Our department is more like what you guys had a decade ago. We need a lot of outside help when something like this comes up. Not that something like this comes up too often."

"It's just you?" Wolf asked Special Agent Rushing.

"No, I have two other colleagues up at a crime scene right now. I'm just here to help with the morning briefing."

Wolf nodded, noting Special Agent Rushing, along with everyone else in the room, looked almost as tired as Sheriff Roll.

Burton walked in with a steaming cup of coffee. He did the rounds of introductions, and Wolf watched as each man sucked in the aroma of Jack Daniels and eyed Burton suspiciously.

"Right," Roll said. "Why don't we get started. Mr. Burton, if you wouldn't mind letting me see your phone for starters."

Burton pulled up the text message and handed it over.

"Please, you two take a seat. And, Detective Wolf, could you please tell us about what happened yesterday?"

Wolf told the room about Wolf and Burton's adventure into Canyon of the Ancients and their extraction of Jesse Burton.

"Did he look like he was ready to use that gun?" Deputy Triplett asked.

Wolf shrugged. "I never gave him a chance."

"How did you find him?" Roll asked.

"He found us. Like I said, Mr. Burton here was in trouble, and I had to get him out of there."

All eyes went to Burton.

"I'm better now."

His stench told them otherwise.

A few minutes later, and after Wolf fielded another few questions, Roll and the team seemed satisfied with the timeline of events.

"So, what exactly did he say during your car drive to Cortez?" Milo asked.

Wolf shrugged. "I got the feeling that he was piecing together a story as he was speaking with us. I got a chance to watch him in the mirror, and I saw somebody hiding something. I mean, he had a gun, and a flip phone with the battery removed."

Burton shook his head. They ignored him.

Wolf continued. "He mentioned that Kyle...Farmer, is it?"

"Yeah," Milo said.

"He mentioned Kyle Farmer's father called him and told him about the blood you guys had found up at Kyle's house. And that he was coming after him for answers. Jesse freaked out because of this, and he ran."

Wolf eyed the men, gauging their reactions. Nobody seemed concerned with what he'd just said.

"Something bothering you, chief detective?" Roll asked.

"I guess I've just been wondering—is that true?" Wolf

asked. "Did you tell Kyle's dad that there was blood found at the scene, and that you were looking for his son?"

They looked at Roll.

The man seemed to shrink. "I probably shouldn't have told him about the blood," Roll said. "He kept insisting on knowing the reason we were searching for Kyle. Why I was calling him in the first place. I had to tell him."

Wolf nodded. "Anyway, Jesse said he was freaked out about this news, and he saw you guys coming to get him. He said he was confused and decided to run. He also talked about getting in a fight with Kyle over some girl named Hettie, which he thought would make him look suspicious if something had happened to Kyle."

Burton cleared his throat. "He said he had nothing to do with any of this. That it was lining up too perfectly, like somebody might be setting him up."

"Did he mention Alexander Guild?" Milo asked.

"We didn't get much of a chance to talk about that," Wolf said.

"Tell him what you heard from MacLean." Burton slapped Wolf on the shoulder.

"What did you hear from MacLean?" Roll asked.

Burton answered. "That guy Alexander Guild was killed Friday night, right? You told MacLean my nephew Jesse had an alibi for Friday night. That he was with that Hettie girl all night."

Roll nodded. "That's right. I'm aware of what I told Sheriff MacLean. I'm wondering if Jesse said anything to you about the matter."

Burton held up his hands, and Wolf shook his head.

After a few more questions, Roll folded his arms. "Right.

Well, we appreciate you coming in. If you don't mind, we'd like you two to write up an official report before you head back up to Rocky Points. Cassandra can help you with everything."

Wolf and Burton looked at one another.

"Listen, Sheriff Roll," Burton said. "I was hoping Detective Wolf and I could stay for a bit and hear what you have on the case so far."

Roll took his time with a sip of coffee. "I don't know, Hal."

Burton eyed him with that sly lift of his lips Wolf had seen last night.

Wolf cleared his throat. "Sheriff Roll, I have to be back up in Rocky Points tonight. What Sheriff Burton is saying is we'd love to offer our help for the time being. I've been involved in a few murder investigations myself, and I know how overwhelming it can be at the beginning, with all the outside pressure. The onslaught of information. That kind of thing. We're not trying to add to that pressure, just offer our help. A little more experience in the room never hurts."

Roll's eyes went to Burton.

Burton had the good sense to put his mouth to his coffee cup.

Roll nodded slowly, looking like a man carrying a heavy load on his back. "Okay, yeah. That would be fine, I guess. You all okay with that?"

Special Agent Rushing shrugged. "No problem with me."

"Fine by me," Triplett said.

Sobeck and Milo nodded.

"All right, well let's stop screwing around and get started, then." Roll paced at the front of the room. "We'll have to back track a bit for you two."

"We would appreciate it," Wolf said. "Maybe we can add a fresh perspective."

The Sheriff nodded and walked to the bulletin board. "This is Alexander Guild."

He pointed to a full body shot of a man in a suit. He flashed a smile and thick jewelry on his wrist and hands. A thin, attractive brunette stood next to him, flashing her own brilliant smile. They held champagne flutes and looked off camera as if someone had just cracked a joke.

"Guild owned a weapons manufacturing corporation. Multi-billion-dollar company that makes bombs, drones, heavy-long-range artillery for tanks, boats, airplanes. Multiple ongoing contracts with the government. Which means he's very rich, and kind of a big deal around these parts."

Triplett made a noise into his coffee, drawing eyes to him. "Sorry. Go ahead."

"Kind of an asshole," Roll said. "A lot of people didn't like him for what he did."

"What did he do?" Burton asked.

"You hear about the shooting we had down here last October involving Guild?"

"I haven't heard of that," Burton said.

Wolf vaguely remembered reading something about a shooting down in Ridgway, but he'd been too preoccupied with his own life last fall, with the court appearances and all, to pay it much attention.

"Right," Roll said. "Might as well start there. Milo?"

Detective Milo stood, then sat on the edge of a plastic

table in front of Wolf and Burton. "Last October a local man named Ray Winkle, Hettie Winkle's father, began a feud with the now deceased Alexander Guild. Ray was a former enlisted. Served in Afghanistan the same time Sobeck and I did. Ray came back with some issues. PTSD."

Wolf nodded.

"You serve?"

"I did."

Milo nodded, as if confirming what he'd already suspected. "Ray lived here all his life. He was an elk hunter, and he used to take a trail west of town that leads into the Uncompahgre wilderness called the Chimney Mountain Trail to get to his favorite hunting grounds.

"Alexander Guild moved in ten or so years ago onto a plot of land up near the trailhead, built one of his many houses up there. Anyway, that trail passes through a small piece of Guild's land.

"For years, he let people use that section of trail. But, for some reason, this last year Guild decided he was going to make that piece of land off-limits."

Milo picked up a pen and drew a square on the white-board. "Here's the barbed wire fence he put up." Milo drew a line that came up from the bottom of the board, cutting across two points on the square on the lower right corner. "And here's the public trail, which is now cut off in two places by that fence."

"Why not just walk around the bottom corner of his land?" Burton asked.

Milo drew another square butting diagonally with the first square. "Because he owns that piece of land, too. And it's already fenced."

"Everything above those two squares is public land?" Burton asked.

Milo nodded. "Everything north and south of his two parcels is public. And everything to the north is now cut off... unless you want to drive for three hours to access it from the south."

Milo drew an X in the two spots the trail crossed the land. "He installed two gates with combination locks on them—one to get into that piece of trail passing into his land, another gate to get out. The only people who could go through it had to get the combinations from Guild. And those people had to be Guild-sponsored hunting outfitters. He flat-out refused other access to the public. Not even to government agencies."

"Devious bastard," Burton said.

"Devious bastard who was acting completely within his rights," Sheriff Roll said.

"Still a devious bastard."

Roll shrugged. "Not gonna argue with that."

"Ray Winkle thought the same," Milo said. "First, he was hopping the corner of the two parcels of land, and Guild was calling us up there to intervene. We gave Ray a slap on the wrist, but Ray escalated things and showed up with some lock-cutters a week later. Cut his way through the gates and went about hunting as he always did. Mr. Guild came in to our office and complained. We brought Ray in, slapped him harder on the wrist. Gave him a trespassing ticket. From that point it got out of hand quickly, ending with Guild shooting Winkle." Milo splayed his hands. "Apparently Ray showed up again with the lock cutters, and according to Mr. Guild, this time he was brandishing his rifle and slinging threats. Mr. Guild was armed himself, felt his life was in danger, and fired his own weapon, shooting and killing Ray Winkle. The DA wasn't inclined to take any action against him."

Triplett made another noise. "Guy had high-priced lawyers coming out of his ass. Money buys you the right to be a cold-blooded murderer."

"It was a little more complicated than that." Sheriff Roll shot his deputy a glare. "We found Ray Winkle, shot from close range inside Guild's property fences and still clutching his gun. All indications showed Guild was telling the truth. Contrary proof just wasn't there."

The sheriff looked down at his feet.

"And now you know the story," Milo said, breaking the silence.

He tapped the photograph next in line, which looked more like a closeup of highway roadkill than the man in the previous picture. "This is how we found Alexander Guild the other night."

"Which night?" Wolf asked, with the lack of sleep he had to strain his mind to remember it was now Monday morning.

"Saturday night."

"My God. They said he was shot," Burton said. "That looks like he had a stick of dynamite strapped to his head."

"Fifty caliber bullet does interesting things to a skull," Special Agent Rushing said.

Wolf had seen a similar aftermath in person once. He had to rein in his thoughts from straying too far.

Detective Milo gestured to the line of photos showing the body at different angles. "Here's his back deck. You can see those woods in the background. They're a little over a hundred yards away."

A stone's throw for a sniper rifle, Wolf thought.

Detective Milo picked up some papers, found a pair of frameless reading glasses and put them on. The man's already intelligent eyes seemed to go up a few IQ points.

"You said you found Alexander Guild on his back-deck Saturday evening?" Wolf asked. "Who found him?"

"Deputy Triplett had the good fortune to see him first."

Triplett lowered his coffee cup from his mouth. "We got a call from two men who had planned to meet Mr. Guild, a father and son up here visiting from California. They said they'd been driving the day prior, Friday, all the way from San Diego and ended up staying down in Farmington." Triplett looked over at Sobeck.

Sobeck nodded.

Triplett continued. "They said they'd been keeping in touch with Guild and told him they'd be up from Farmington in the morning after a night's rest. When they arrived here Saturday morning, on schedule, they went to the front gate of his property, called on the intercom system, got no answer. Cell phone, no answer.

"They figured he was out on an errand, had his phone off or something, so they hung out in town for a while. Tried again, no answer. After the fourth or fifth try they started getting worried and they came to us.

"Sobeck and I were first responders. Sobeck stayed out with the two guys while I hopped the fence and walked up to the property." A shudder passed through Triplett and he huffed a breath. "I went around the back of the house, where there's a walkout basement. I saw a bunch of blood and brain had dripped between the wood down onto the ground."

"Thank you, Deputy," Roll said.

Triplett snapped a nod. "Yes, sir."

"And the father and son's alibi checks out, I take it?" Wolf asked.

"We checked with the motel down in Farmington," Milo said. "The father used his credit card to pay, and the motel operator confirms they were down there Friday night."

Wolf nodded and looked at Special Agent Rushing. "And do you have an estimated time of death to corroborate their alibi?"

"Nine-thirty-eight p.m., Friday night."

Wolf popped his eyebrows. "That's specific."

"We have security video from Mr. Guild's house." Milo gestured to Special Agent Rushing.

Agent Rushing turned the device's screen toward them, showing a video window. The video was paused, showing the back of a man, presumably Mr. Guild, leaning on a deck's railing. A white time stamp on the bottom of the screen read 9:38:03 p.m.

"Want to see?" Special Agent Rushing's eyebrows were raised, his words heavy with seriousness.

"Sure, why not?" Burton said.

The man swiveled his eyes to Wolf, who considered the question, then nodded.

After tapping the keyboard, Rushing leaned back, allowing room for the men to crowd around the screen.

"Here it comes," Triplett said.

And come it did. One second Alexander Guild was standing, smoking a cigarette on the deck, the next he was hurled back, his head becoming a much wider and amorphous entity. Mist swirled angrily, and when it dissipated, Alexander Guild lay still on his back, arms and legs splayed like he was making a snow angel.

Knowing for certain what was coming when Rushing had pushed the button, Wolf had anchored his eyes on the blackness beyond the man's moment of death, and he'd caught a flash in the distance.

"Did you see it?" Detective Milo asked.

"Yes," Wolf said. "Just about Guild's one o'clock."

"See what?" Burton asked.

Rushing scrubbed the video back.

Wolf took the opportunity to stand and look away, and he almost ran into Deputy Sobeck. The man's skin was slick with sweat.

Sobeck turned and shook his head. "Seen enough death in my days to last me."

Wolf's mind reached back to his time in the Army, and the sound of chattering gunfire filled his ears again.

"I saw it," Burton said. "The gunshot in the trees. So how does that bring us to my nephew?"

"Sir, I'm gonna go use the restroom," Sobeck said.

Roll nodded. "Sure thing." He and the others watched the man leave.

"He's been spooked by this case," Triplett said.

There was the sound of tires squealing outside, and car doors thumping shut. Roll went to the window and spread open the blinds with his fingers. "Shit." He hurried out of the room.

"What is it?" Triplett got up and followed him.

"The Farmers," he said.

Wolf trailed after them, and caught Roll telling Cassandra to stay seated and inside, which only fired Wolf's adrenal glands.

Everyone poured out of the building at a full run.

"Get back! Freeze!" One of the deputies had his gun pulled and was aiming at three men in front of him.

"Freeze right now!" Another pulled his sidearm.

Down on the dirt road, three men dressed in camouflage and flannel stood defiantly. In front of them a man in uniform was on his knees, holding his face. Behind them, a black Chevy pickup with raised suspension, knobby tires, and tinted windows was parked at an angle across the road.

Sheriff Roll waved his hands over his head. "Whoa! Stand down, deputies. What's going on?"

"This asshole just punched me in the face!" The deputy stood up.

The oldest of the three men clenched and unclenched his fist, looking none too sorry for what he'd done.

"Okay, let's put our guns down," Roll said. "You heard me. Please back away."

"What's going on?" Burton asked Wolf, standing next to him on the lawn.

Wolf shook his head, watching with tensed muscles. His first clue the three men were related came when Roll had called them the Farmers, but even without that tidbit of information it was easy enough to see they were a father and two sons. The oldest looked to be in his fifties. He stood over six feet tall and had muscles to spare. His two sons were a touch shorter, but just as sturdy. All three had the same red hair.

"Jed, what are you doing?" Roll asked.

"You know damn well why we're here," the elder Farmer said. "We're here for some answers about my son."

"And you're punching law enforcement? You know I can arrest you for that right now, right?"

"He was in my way. Where's my son?"

"We're trying our best to figure that out, sir." Sheriff Roll held out his hands. "That's why we have all these people out here, working around the clock. We're searching for your boy."

"That him?" Jed Farmer pointed his log of an arm at Burton.

Burton poked his own chest. "That who?"

Mr. Farmer stepped forward and the crowd of men closed in.

Guns were raised, but Jed Farmer was unconcerned. His boys stepped forward to flank their father.

"Are you the one who brought Jesse in last night?" he asked.

"I am."

"He's your nephew?"

"He is."

"Well? What did he say?" There was desperation in his voice.

Burton shook his head. "About what?"

"About what? You piece of shit. I'm talking about where's my son!" Spittle flew from Jed's mouth.

They all stood in silence, watching Jed.

"He told us you three were chasing him," Burton said. "He said you think he did something to your son, but he didn't."

"He's lying."

Burton said nothing.

"He's lying to all of you! He knows where my son is! He knows! He might be hurt!"

"We're working on that piece of the puzzle right now, Jed," Roll said. "That's what we're doing. Right now. Right now, we're working on this. You coming in here like this is not helping."

Farmer's eyes searched the men, skipped over Wolf and then came back. "Who are you?"

"Chief Detective Wolf of Sluice-Byron County."

"Were you the one with him last night, too?"

Wolf nodded.

"Is your friend telling the truth?"

"He is."

Farmer stared at him, then backed up and walked to his truck. The two boys turned and walked to the passenger side.

"Sheriff, it's probably time you figure out what Jesse Burton said to his dear old uncle last night when he was out in that desert hiding from you all. Like, why was he running? Maybe he mentioned something about that. Maybe you should ask him why's he acting that way if he's not guilty? And then ask him where my son is!"

Roll opened his mouth to speak.

"I'm through talking to you, Sheriff." Jed climbed into the truck and the engine roared to life.

"Watch it!" somebody yelled, as exhaust shot from twin oversized pipes and gravel spat from the tires.

The crowd moved over to the lawn and watched the truck speed off, skid into a left turn and rev out of sight.

"Sir," Triplett said. "We can go after them. Put them away until they cool off."

Roll shook his head. "We don't have the time or manpower for that. Let's get back inside."

CHAPTER 14

THE ROOM WAS ELECTRIC, filled with the sounds of heavy breathing and sniffing as they all piled back in and took their seats. Wolf's body vibrated with tension. Burton sat next to him, looking like the action had ignited his hangover. His skin was pasty and covered in a sheen of sweat.

They were all stunned, and Roll looked lost in contemplation as he paced at the front. "Jed Farmer's right. We have to get going. We have to move on this."

But the sheriff stopped pacing and stared at the carpet.

"The Farmers," Burton said. "They seem like a nice bunch."

Milo blew air from his lips. "Jed's the father. Seymour's the older kid, Gabriel's the younger brother."

Wolf raised his hand, which seemed a prudent gesture. "Going back to what we were talking about...I'm wondering: how did you go from finding Alexander Guild on his back-deck Saturday night, with only two men in town from California as persons of interest, to involving Jesse Burton and Kyle Farmer at all?"

Milo nodded. "That goes back to a few months ago. After Alexander Guild shot and killed Ray Winkle out there on the corner of his property, there was some serious local blowback. We're talking pitchforks and torches kind of stuff. People were up in arms. Wondering how he was getting away with murdering Ray Winkle the way he did."

"Serious local blowback is an understatement," Roll said, looking up from the floor. "Rage. That's the word. As we said, Hettie Winkle was Ray Winkle's daughter. She's the same age as Kyle and Jesse and she's been dating Kyle for the last two years. Hettie was close to her father, and when Guild shot him, she was extremely, and understandably, upset."

"And so was Kyle," Burton said.

Roll nodded. "Right. And Jesse, too. And like we said, there was some serious blowback from that incident. Some rage. Whatever you want to call it. But Jesse and Kyle took it to a new level with a video they posted on their YouTube channel."

"What video?" Burton asked. "I never heard of a video."

"They have a YouTube channel called the Sons of Righteous Light," Triplett said.

"Sons of Righteousness and Light," Sobeck said.

"Yeah, whatever," Triplett said. "Anyway, they put out a video of them ranting and raving about how the rich man put the government in place, paying for their campaigns and whatnot. And how now the rich man can lock out even the BLM employees, and the public. Which is all true, mind you."

"Okay, Triplett," Roll said.

Triplett ignored the interjection. "It was the same argument the rest of the town was making. I mean, this frickin' guy up there on that hill, Alexander Guild, had a big party once a couple years ago with thirty or forty politicians, a bunch of bigwigs, and we had to shut down the roads around his house, pulling security duty like a bunch of rent-a-cops."

"Okay, thanks, Triplett," Roll said.

Triplett leaned back in his chair.

Deputy Sobeck cleared his throat. "In their video, Jesse and Kyle put a watermelon on top of a dummy. The dummy had the name Alexander Guild pinned to its chest. They shot the watermelon with a .50 caliber rifle. You don't have to be Hercule Poirot to suspect Jesse and Kyle when we found Alexander Guild's body."

"Can we see this video?" Wolf nodded towards Special Agent Rushing's laptop.

"Their video only made everything worse," Roll said. "I had Sobeck and Triplett go up and talk to them. They agreed to take the video down."

"We sweet talked 'em," Triplett said with a cluck of his tongue.

Wolf nodded. "Okay. Let's go back to Saturday night. After you found Guild on his back porch, you immediately thought of Kyle and Jesse. How long did you wait to talk to them?"

"We went up to Kyle's the next morning, Sunday morning at sunup," Milo said. "What is it, Monday? Geez, yesterday morning we went to Kyle's place. I need some sleep."

"That seems like a long time to wait to me," Wolf said. "Why not go up to Kyle's Saturday night after you found Guild's body?"

Milo looked down, and Roll raised his chin. "Like I said,

chief detective," Roll said, "we don't see much of this kind of thing happening around here. We were up all Saturday night at Guild's. It took us a while just to convene there, then to get up onto the deck itself. Sobeck had to climb up. The alarm went off when he finally got inside and opened the front door, we had a whole thing with the security company about that. That father and son from California were demanding answers, so we had to talk to them. We called in the CBI. We did an initial sweep in the woods, in the house, looking for anything."

Roll shook his head, looking as if he wanted to forget the night altogether. "It was an easy realization about Kyle and Jesse. But it still took time with all that was going on."

Wolf nodded. "I understand. Did you find anything out of the ordinary inside of Guild's house?"

"Nothing. Place was locked tight, except the one open door on the deck Guild had used. As far as we could tell, he was watching ESPN, having a drink, and went outside to have a cigarette. There's no sign of anyone else being there on any of the security footage."

"Okay, and then you realized," Wolf said, "remembered about Kyle and Jesse's video and you guys went up that next morning to Kyle's house. And what did you find?"

Milo exhaled. "A whole lot of dried blood on Kyle Farmer's porch, for one."

"A large area suggesting Kyle was shot on his front porch," Roll said, "where he bled out. And was then moved. And boot prints tracking that blood all over the place when it had been still wet."

Wolf looked at Special Agent Rushing. "But there was no body."

"No," Rushing said.

"What about Kyle's cell phone? Did you track it?"

"We found it," Rushing said. "It was sitting on the kitchen counter. We're taking a look at it."

Wolf nodded. "It rained last night here, didn't it?"

"That's right," Rushing said. "But the porch was covered. It didn't disturb any of the blood evidence."

Jesse Burton's phone sat in a plastic bag on one of the tables.

"What have you learned from Jesse's cell phone?" Wolf asked.

They all looked at Rushing. "Not much. Especially for Friday night. In fact, most of the night is completely missing from a data perspective."

"Missing?" Roll asked.

Rushing nodded. "The only explanation I can come up with is he took out his battery. The last cell tower ping was 7:49 pm, which was initiated by a call he made to Kyle's phone. We triangulated his location to the Soaring Eagle Bar. With the local tower ping cycle, the next ping would have happened an hour later, or when he initiated or received another call. But, an hour later, at 8:49 pm, there is no ping. And there are none until the next morning, Saturday, when it looks like he powers on his phone. At that point, the triangulation shows him at his house."

"And what time is that on Saturday morning?" Roll asked.

Rushing looked at a note scribbled on a sheet of paper. "9:32 am."

"And what about Hettie's cell records?" Roll asked. "Did you get into those last night, too?"

Rushing kept his eyes on the paper. "Yes, sir. We analyzed the tower dump data from the cellular company. She makes a call to Jesse Burton at 9:15 pm, Friday night. She doesn't connect the call, meaning they do not talk. We traced her to her mother's house when she made that call."

"She lives there," Roll said.

Rushing nodded. "And then she makes another call ten minutes later, at 9:25 pm. This time it shows her location as Jesse Burton's home."

"Who does she call?" Roll asked.

"Jesse Burton again. The call does not connect."

Roll scoffed.

"So, they don't talk," Milo said. "And our obvious question here is why? Why go to his house and call him?"

"Because she gets there and sees he's not home," Roll said. "That's why."

"Or he was taking a dump and couldn't get to the door, so she called. Or he was taking a shower. Or they were angry at each other and he was ignoring her calls. There's a million different reasons why she could have called Jesse when she arrived."

Roll glared. "But there was no tower ping. He pulled his battery."

Burton looked at Rushing. "Are you one hundred percent sure about that? That he pulled it and it wasn't a malfunction?"

Rushing shook his head. "We'd have to get an electronics expert to look at it, but to me it seemed in perfect working order."

"He had his battery pulled when you got down to

Canyon of the Ancients and picked him up!" Roll's face was red.

Burton said nothing and the room went silent.

"And can you track Hettie's phone's one-hour ping cycles, too?" Milo asked.

"Yes, and I did," Rushing said. "And it appears she was at Jesse Burton's house all night from that point on."

"Does she make any more calls?" Roll asked.

"No, sir."

"And what is Jesse telling you?" Wolf asked. "Did you interrogate him last night?"

Roll shook his head. "He wanted a lawyer. Said absolutely nothing the whole drive back, kept his mouth shut until we threw him in the cell up in Montrose."

"What about this fight we keep hearing about?" Burton asked. "The black eye and split lip on Jesse?"

Roll gestured to Sobeck.

"I was there," Sobeck said. "On Friday night, Kyle, Jesse, and Hettie were eating at the Soaring Eagle Bar in town here. At approximately eight-thirty, Jesse and Kyle started throwing punches at one another across the table. All hell broke loose, and they went outside. I followed and broke it up, made them get in their cars and drive their separate ways."

"You were there," Burton said. "You saw this."

Sobeck nodded. "Everyone at the bar did. A crowd spilled outside. Kyle was yelling at Jesse about Hettie. It was clear at that moment that Jesse and Hettie had been having an affair behind Kyle's back. Kyle was screaming at Hettie, who also came outside. Calling her a slut, Jesse a back-stabbing son of a bitch, that kind of stuff.

"Like I said, I split them up. Finally got Kyle off of Jesse, who was giving Jesse quite a beating. I told Kyle to get in his pickup and leave, and he did. Peeled off, all pissed. And then, when everything calmed down, I told Jesse and Hettie to leave. They left in Jesse's Jeep."

"Agent Rushing, how about the weapon?" Roll asked. "What did you guys find out last night?"

Agent Rushing gave Wolf and Burton a courtesy nod. "We found a Barrett M107A1 fifty-caliber rifle equipped with a suppressor and thermal imaging scope at Kyle's house. It's definitely the weapon that killed Alexander Guild. And, before you ask, no, we didn't find any prints on it."

"Add that to the other prints we've found anywhere, and that's zero," Roll said. "Okay, anything else?"

"We towed Jesse's Jeep from Canyon of the Ancients up to Montrose last night. The vehicle is waiting to be examined by my team."

"When are you going to get to that?" Roll asked.

Agent Rushing shrugged. "I could have one of my team get up there later today."

"Good."

"What else?"

"We're waiting on the DNA match from the blood outside Kyle Farmer's house to the DNA samples we took from inside the house."

Roll nodded. "What else?"

"I'd like to get into Jesse Burton's house and check his drains for blood," Agent Rushing said.

"I know. We're working on the warrant." Roll's cell phone chimed, and he put it to his ear. "Hello? Okay, we're on our way up...twenty minutes." He pocketed his cell. "That

138

was Pete. He's back from the walk between Kyle's and Guild's."

The room erupted in movement as everyone stood.

"Who's Pete?" Burton asked. "I still have some questions."

"Sorry, Hal, we don't have the time. Oh, and did I mention I received a call from Senator Chadwick this morning asking how the case is progressing? Join the growing line of people looking for answers." Roll looked at his watch, then clapped his hands. "Okay, people. Let's get back up to Guild's place and see what Pete has for us."

Everyone walked out of the room, but Roll hung back. The man looked freshly bullwhipped. "Sorry, Hal. You see what I'm up against here."

"How about we tag along," Burton said. "Just a little observation."

"You're getting a little heated about defending your nephew already, Hal. It's personal with you."

Hal held up his hands. "I'll stay out of it."

Roll looked too tired to fight. "Do what you want. I don't care." He, too, left the room.

Burton and Wolf followed, giving the receptionist Cassandra a nod on their way out.

She ignored him, too engrossed in a hushed conversation with Sheriff Roll to notice.

As they left out the door, Wolf looked back and caught a glimpse of Cassandra massaging the sheriff's arm, speaking what looked like soothing words.

CHAPTER 15

"NEVER DID GET to use that leverage," Burton said.

"And if you want to keep tagging along in this case, I'd recommend you keep that leverage to yourself." Wolf pressed the gas, running a turn light that had gone red. They were the caboose in a train of vehicles now flowing north on 550 at high speed. The highway twisted and turned along the Uncompahgre River, up and down, through groves of tall oaks and pines.

Burton gazed out the window to the east. "What is that blocky-looking mountain?"

"I believe that's called Courthouse Mountain," Wolf said without looking.

"I remember driving with my father up and down this road, so many years ago. He used to say the San Juans made it look like the sky was jagged as broken glass."

Wolf remembered the story about Burton's past from the previous night. Did Burton? He was wrenched back to the present moment as they rounded a blind bend in the highway. Up ahead brake lights blossomed, and the train slowed before hanging a right.

After the turn they passed over the river on a steel bridge, through a flat plain where cattle fed on bright green grass, and up into rolling hills. The view of the San Juan mountains grew before them. Red rock streaks painted the slopes of the highest peaks, as if Burton's father's broken glass sky had made them bleed.

"That it?" Burton asked, leaning into the windshield.

The pavement ended and they entered a cloud of red dust rising from the road. Brake lights glowed again, and they slowed and hung a left and followed a long drive up a gentle rise. An upside-down U-shaped headgate stood a quarter-mile or so ahead. They passed underneath without slowing, and on the way through Wolf saw heavy iron gates that had been propped open with rocks. At the top of the rise stood a dark brown house, measured in the tens of thousands of square feet by the looks of it, covered in gleaming glass.

The rumbling in the cabin ceased as they rolled onto black asphalt and slowed to a halt next to the other vehicles. Wolf got out and stretched his limbs overhead, spotting another Colorado Bureau of Investigation logo on an already parked sedan.

The air was cool and as clean as it got.

Once the cacophony of slamming doors ceased, the utter silence of the place closed in. Ridgway sparkled on the bottom of the valley, at the foot of the towering mountains to the south. A herd of antelope sprang across the verdant slope they'd just driven up, leaping over a barbed wire fence like it was nothing.

"The famous fence."

Wolf turned to see Detective Milo standing behind him.

"See there?" Milo stepped up next to Wolf and pointed, then swung his hand to the left. "The parking lot?"

Wolf saw a dirt clearing in the field up the road from where they'd veered off onto the drive.

"There's the trailhead right there, leads all the way up and around the land." Milo kept swiveling, keeping his finger pointed until he stopped at what looked like a wreath hanging from the fence.

"Hettie comes and puts flowers." Milo walked toward the house. "I personally think she does it to provoke the guy as much as commemorate her father. She is her father's daughter after all."

They continued on, stepping toward the side of the house.

"And he was a fighter, huh?" Wolf asked.

"Oh yeah. A lesser man, or a smarter man, would have taken Guild's threat to stop trespassing and gone home. Not Ray. I don't think Guild knew what he was doing threatening Ray. I grew up with him. He was a bit older than me. But I'd seen him get into some fights over the years, and I tell you that man never came out the loser." Milo stopped at the top of the rise at the side of the house and made a point to look into the distance. "Until now, of course."

Wolf followed his eyes and whistled softly.

The mountains stretched left to right as far as the eyes could see. Before them lay a continuation of the gentle pasture, and the dense wall of pines Wolf recognized as the spot from where the shooter pulled the trigger, ending Alexander Guild's life.

People in uniform and white forensic suits were milling about in the distance near the trees' edge.

Wolf looked to the back of the house and saw a wrap-around deck that overlooked all of the majesty before them.

"Not a bad spread." Burton's breathing was already labored. "Not enough you have all this to look at, you have to cut off people using it, too, eh?"

Milo said nothing.

"What did this guy do for a living again?" Burton asked. "Made military guns?"

"Heavier than that," Milo said. "Stuff dropped from jets. Shot from naval destroyers."

Sheriff Roll, Deputies Sobeck and Triplett, Special Agent Rushing, along with two others had disappeared into an open garage door.

"Let's go." Milo walked toward the bumpers of four cars shining inside the garage.

"Can't wait to see this," Burton said.

Wolf had to admit he was curious to see how a billionaire bomb-maker who shot the locals lived. Judging by the four vehicles lined up in the garage, the man was not one for blending in. The two cars on the left were near-identical Ferraris, one black, the other red. Their paint jobs were polished to a liquid shine. Next to the Ferraris sat a Mercedes SUV and a Land Rover. Beyond the cars was another perpendicular bay that housed a small fleet of ATVs and dirt bikes.

The door leading to the house was propped open and Sheriff Roll stood inside waiting for them. "Booties. Gloves."

Wolf and Burton took the offered slips for their shoes and latex gloves. Burton gripped Wolf as he struggled to bend down to get the sheaths over his feet. After three attempts the man was still without the proper shoe coverings, as well as breathless.

"Give me those." Wolf bent down and put them on for him.

"Sucks getting old, eh Roll?"

Roll pretended not to hear Burton as he stepped up the stairs and into the house with the pep of a much younger man. Wolf and Burton followed. They walked down a long silent hallway and entered a vast kitchen.

Two refrigerators, three ovens, three sinks, a granite island the size of a ping pong table, copper pots hanging off an iron rectangle dangling on chains from a vaulted ceiling, all backdropped by huge windows framing the mountains outside—the place was impressive.

In the next room, a hand-carved table about the same size as the kitchen island was surrounded by eight heavy chairs carved from the same wood.

Another hallway led to the other end of the house. Photos of Alexander Guild smiling and shaking the hands of U.S. presidents hung on the walls. Another photo showed Guild in a line of military men wearing foreign uniforms, one of them adorned with enough gold to sink a ship.

"Out here," Roll said.

The opulence of the house fell away as Wolf looked through the sliding glass door. They stepped through it, back into blazing sun. A breeze ruffled the side of a forensic tent that had been erected on the expansive deck, and the unzipped door yawned open, revealing a reddish-brown stain on the composite deck board.

"Ground zero," Roll said.

Burton leaned inside. "That's appetizing."

Triplett and Sobeck were at the edge of the deck looking toward the trees.

"You get a good look, old man?" Roll said to Burton. "We're headed up to the trees. You still want to tag along?"

"Up there?" Burton wheezed.

"You should stay in the car," Wolf said, thinking about the doctor's warnings the day before.

Burton's eyes flashed. "Nope. I'm okay. Let's go."

Five minutes later, they had walked the stretch of grassland and reached the edge of the trees.

"You gonna make it?" Wolf asked Burton.

Burton's face had that slick white look again, and Wolf was asking the question sincerely.

"Yeah. I'll be fine."

"Any of you have some water?" Wolf asked.

"I said I'll be fine."

A heavyset woman stepped forward and offered Burton a plastic bottle. "Here. Take it, I don't need it."

Burton started waving it away, then grabbed the container and swilled it greedily.

"This is Deborah," Roll said. "She's one of the department volunteers."

"Somebody got after it too hard last night." She laughed and waved a hand in front of her nose. When nobody laughed, she stepped away.

A gruff-looking man dressed in ratty jeans and a red and black flannel appeared next to Roll, Sobeck, Triplett, and Milo.

"This is Pete Hammond," Roll said. "Pete, this is Detective Wolf and former Sheriff Hal Burton down here from Sluice-Byron County."

Pete's hand was a rough chunk of granite. "Nice to meet you."

The man's eyes were hooded, with deep, tanned wrinkles. He was short and squat and the outward sway of his arms suggested he had some muscles under his clothing. He spat on the ground, pushing a wad of chewing tobacco to the other side of his mouth. "You gonna make it?"

"Pete is a local tracker and hunting guide," Roll said. "Pete? How was the walk down?"

"Plenty of sign from Kyle Farmer's house to right here." Pete turned and looked back. "I found two prints with tread in them you'll be able to cast. Otherwise the dirt is loose, and anything detailed is pretty much washed out by the rains yesterday."

Roll nodded. "Good work."

A few paces away, a team of civilian volunteers in yellow traffic vests looked down at a string grid staked into the ground. A man in a white CBI jumpsuit was hunched over inside the grid.

"That's where we traced the line of fire," Special Agent Rushing told Wolf. "We've found a GSR pattern." He pointed at an orange ribbon hanging from a pine-needle laden branch.

"The GSR pattern on the ground indicates the shooter was lying down, using that crook in the branches to steady his aim. Other than that, we're finding very little other forensic evidence."

"You're sure it was a he?" Wolf asked.

"We did find multiple shoe prints of a size and depth suggesting it was definitely male. Shoe size approximately nine to eleven. Weight approximately one hundred seventy to two hundred pounds."

"The two prints I found are pristine," Pete said. "And I'd put the weight at the lighter end of that spectrum. I flagged them, put in the waypoints in the GPS."

"Thanks, Pete," Roll said.

"I gather you walked from Kyle Farmer's house?" Wolf asked.

Pete nodded. "Yes, sir."

"How long did it take you?" Wolf looked up at a valley covered in pines. There was no sign of a trail anywhere.

Pete spat at his own feet and pointed the way Wolf was looking. "Chimney Rock Wilderness trail is over that hill."

"That's the same one that's now cut off by Mr. Guild's new gates and fence down there," Sobeck said.

Pete grunted in agreement. "Once you reach the trail, it's practically a straight shot up the valley to Kyle Farmer's place. He lives a quarter mile or so off the beaten path, so to speak.

As for how long it would take a killer to walk from Kyle's to here, I'm not sure. I was dallying around. Took me a couple hours. I figure it would take no more than twenty minutes at a brisk pace."

"You know Jesse left that bar fight at around 8:30," Wolf said. He looked at Milo, letting the man finish Wolf's thought. He was observing, not trying to step on toes.

"We're gonna need to know the exact time," Milo said. He looked at Roll. "I'll walk it back to Kyle's and time it, sir."

A knot had balled up in the middle of Wolf's back, something that happened every time he sat behind his desk or behind the wheel for too long. "Mind if I join you?"

"I'll come, too," Pete said.

Roll looked at Burton.

"Hell if I'm walking that," Burton said.

"Good," Roll said. "We're in agreement."

"We'll drive it," Burton said.

"That's the idea."

Burton's eyes flicked from Wolf to Roll, then back. He held out a hand, which trembled slightly. "Give me the keys. We'll meet you up there."

Wolf pictured the remaining liquid in the bottle of Jack Daniels underneath his car seat, and a BAC number that started with point two, and shook his head.

"You're in no condition to drive," Roll said, saving Wolf the trouble. "You'll come with me."

"Bah. Whatever." Burton turned and stormed away back toward the house.

"We'll see you three up at Kyle Farmer's house." Roll said and followed Burton down the slope.

Pete checked his watch and walked up the mountain, into the trees. Milo and Wolf pulled out their cell phones, started their timers, and followed after him.

CHAPTER 16

"I GREW UP RIGHT HERE," Detective Milo said over the sound of their marching feet.

"And you said you were army?" Wolf asked.

"Yep."

"Afghanistan?"

"Served three tours. You?"

Wolf nodded. "Six."

"Ranger?"

"That's right. Fort Lewis."

"Gotcha. I was a Green Beret. I was probably over there more recently than you."

Wolf smiled. "I look that old, huh?"

Milo's face went red. "No, shit, well, yeah, I guess. But I meant you were probably closer to 9/11."

"Yeah, we were the first over there after the towers fell."

"I got back just a few years ago."

They walked in silence for a bit, taking long strides to keep up with Pete. The old man kept up a relentlessly quick pace, and Wolf thought of ruck-marches through scorched earth in the middle of summer, carrying a weighted pack and rifle over his shoulder and wearing boots that never fit right with the matching blisters on either heel to prove it. He remembered walking through narrow ravines, and the fear of hot lead punching into his body from above.

"Not quite as beautiful as Afghanistan, though, is it?" Milo asked, one side of his stubbled lip curled up. "Driving up into valleys, listening to them Taliban on the radio, calling out to each other as they were watching us come. IEDs. Frickin' kids and old men the only ones coming out of the woodwork to talk to us. That feeling. Don't miss that shit. Heck, you know."

Wolf nodded. "You said Pete was a hunter outfitter. A local tracker. Was he given the combinations of those locks down there?"

"As a matter of fact, he was."

Wolf raised his eyebrows.

"Pete was in Vietnam," Milo said loudly, eyeing Wolf.

Pete grunted.

"And Pete was down in Durango Friday night," Milo said, this time lowering his voice for Wolf's ears only. "And that's confirmed."

Wolf took his word for it, but didn't like it. Pete was carrying a .45 Ruger on his hip. Was Pete a disgruntled outfitter? Out to get revenge on Guild for a deal gone bad? With tracking skills like his, he would be good with faking tracks and covering his own.

"And I haven't killed anyone since Vietnam," Pete said over his shoulder, apparently reading Wolf's mind.

Wolf checked his phone. The stopwatch ticked onward, showing they'd just passed the eleven-minute mark.

Milo squinted and surveyed the land ahead. "I think the house is over that second mountain on the north side." He pointed to the left side of the valley. "Can't be more than the distance we've already traveled."

"How sure are you about that 8:30 time for the bar fight between Kyle and Jesse?" Wolf asked.

"That's according to Sobeck," Milo said.

"Have you double-checked with the bartender? Other witnesses?"

"Not yet. Ever since we went to Jesse's place yesterday morning, we've been on the move. It's on my to-do list to check with the bartender and servers to lock that time down."

A pair of female deer watched them from the clearing, ears swiveled like radar dishes.

Sweat slid from under Wolf's ball cap and down his temples. It felt good to be getting some exercise. The knot in his back was loosening.

"So, you have them reportedly leaving the bar at 8:30 pm, but from a reliable source," Wolf said. "How long does it take to drive from that bar to up here? To Kyle's house?"

"Let's see." Milo pulled out a small notebook and flipped some pages. "I did a Google Maps search, and mind you this is at the exact speed limits, here...it takes sixteen minutes from Soaring Eagle Bar to Kyle Farmer's place. I'm gonna tell you right now Jesse Burton takes the speed limit and doubles it most of the time."

Wolf eyed him.

"Okay, say sixteen minutes," Milo said. "So, he gets up here to Kyle's at 8:46 p.m."

"And he's pissed off. You guys said that Jesse was getting

beaten up pretty good by Kyle before Sobeck broke up the fight. So, out of anger, he shoots Kyle?" Wolf asked.

Milo shrugged. "There's a blood stain the size of a lake up there at his front door. Looks like it to me."

"And Jesse grabs the .50 caliber from up here at Kyle's house," Wolf said, pointing up the valley.

"The rifle is kept in an external shed. You'll see. Kyle has an arsenal bigger than ours down in Ouray."

"How does he get access to the shed?" Wolf asked.

Milo shrugged. "He shoots Kyle, takes his keys, gets in the shed to retrieve the fifty-cal."

Wolf continued. "So, starting over with the Jesse as the killer scenario: he gets in the fight, comes up here, arriving at 8:46, give or take a few minutes."

"He shoots Kyle," Milo said. "Takes the .50 caliber sniper rifle from the shed. Walks down here to Guild's place." Milo checked his phone.

Wolf did too—eighteen minutes, twelve seconds had elapsed on their hike.

"We're almost there," Milo said. "It's only going to take another few minutes. The timing works perfectly for Jesse."

Wolf put himself in Jesse's shoes. The kid would have had a fresh shiner on his eye, a fat lip. Wounded pride. But he had the girl. He'd lost the battle but won the war. Why the rampage when he had the girl?

"How did Hettie get to the bar?" Wolf asked.

"She told us she got there with Kyle. But she left after the fight with Jesse."

"And Jesse dropped her off at home," Wolf said. "As her phone indicates."

Milo nodded. "And Jesse takes out his phone battery. I mean, come on. It was him. This is all him."

"When did you talk to Hettie?" Wolf asked.

"Yesterday. We were searching for Jesse."

"And what, exactly, did she tell you about Friday night?" Wolf asked.

Milo consulted his notebook. "She told us that Jesse dropped her off at home. She stayed there for a few minutes, and then drove over to Jesse's, where she stayed the night. I asked her if we could check her phone data to corroborate her story, and she willingly handed it over to us. But now this business about Jesse taking out his phone battery?" Milo shook his head. "I don't know what to think about her. This could be an elaborate murder they've been planning for months for all we know."

They walked in silence for a bit.

"We need to talk to Jesse," Milo said. "Get him to trip up on the details."

If they ever talked to Jesse, Wolf thought. A good lawyer would keep his client's mouth shut.

They rounded a turn and saw Pete fifty yards ahead, flickering in shafts of sunlight as he walked through a copse of trees. He came to a stop and turned around. "Cut up here! You'll see two evidence tents marking the clearest boot treads I could find!"

Pete veered left and hiked into the woods without waiting for a response.

"Almost there," Milo said. "Just on top of that rise."

Wolf looked up the slope and saw an A-frame roof poking up among the trees, beyond it blue sky, the sun a beating heart inside clouds that looked like a giant, wispy ribcage.

They veered off the trail and began climbing up the incline through the pines. Wolf's toes gripped on exposed rock in places, other times dug into soft soil covered in pine needles.

The first evidence tent came into view and they veered sideways to meet it.

The print was a stamp in dust next to a tree trunk. If it were a fingerprint, it would have been a partial. Here the sun failed to reach the forest floor, blocked by dense branches covered in needles, acting as an umbrella against the previous night's rains.

Wolf studied the ground, seeing the rain runoff had veered to either side of the small raised portion of land.

They moved on, using the second yellow evidence tent as a bearing. Above them, Pete stood with his hands on his hips, looking down at his own cell phone screen. "Twenty minutes, forty-eight seconds!" he called down.

"Yeah, at a sprint!" Milo said.

"After you shoot someone's head off, I doubt you take the scenic route back," Pete said.

They slowed and studied the next footprint, and Wolf saw it had the same tread pattern as the first. This one was much more pronounced, punched into crusty earth that held the shape of each circle and square on the underside of what looked like an average-sized men's' hiking boot.

They summited the hill. Behind Pete stood the boxy A-frame structure whose many windows shone in the sun.

"Did you find footprints down by Alexander Guild's back field that match these?" Wolf asked.

"Nothing with definitive tread, but the sizing is the same."

"How sure are you?"

"One hundred percent."

That was pretty sure.

"I only saw one set of prints veering off that trail near Guild's house," Pete said. "One set going up the hill, over to the point the shooting took place, one set coming back. I measured over a dozen impressions I found in the loose soil, compared them to all the other prints around here. I'm sure."

Wolf tapped his cellphone screen and stopped the stopwatch, which showed 23 minutes, 31 seconds.

Detective Milo turned down valley and eyed his own phone. "Twenty-three minutes."

"That's what I got."

"Check me if I'm wrong," Milo said, "but that's perfect timing for Jesse to get in that fight, drive up here, and walk down to Alexander Guild's in time to be our shooter at 9:38 p.m."

"There's only one thing I'm not liking about all this," Pete said.

They looked at the wiry old man. He was staring down the mountain with pinched eyes.

"What's that?" Milo asked.

"You know all those boot prints left in the blood around the front of the house?"

"Yeah?"

"Those don't match these prints."

"How sure are you about that?" Milo asked.

He flicked his eyes to the detective. "One hundred percent."

CHAPTER 17

A DISTANT RUMBLE of thunder rolled through the valley below.

The peaks flanking the south side of Ridgway were engulfed in dark clouds. Streams of rain hung down, sweeping over the town. A thin tendril of lightning snapped from cloud to ground.

"Shit, it's ten-thirty," Milo said. "That's early for a thunderstorm."

Wolf silently agreed, but he'd learned to count on surprises when it came to weather in the Rocky Mountains. He'd seen it snow on the fourth of July and watched the sky throw lightning bolts out of a mid-winter blizzard.

"I'd like to see those footprints," Wolf said to Milo.

Milo nodded and turned to walk. "Follow me to the front."

"Have a good walk?" Sheriff Roll rounded the corner of Kyle Farmer's house, Burton, Sobeck, and Triplett behind him. They met at the side of the house, where Milo and Pete relayed the time information they'd gathered with the walk up from Guild's house.

"You have a good ride?" Wolf asked Burton.

"Peachy." Burton wiped his nose with a shaky hand. His face was only slightly less pale than before. "They ain't got shit on Jesse so far as I've seen."

"Yeah, well I'm not sure if you've been listening to us, old man," Roll said, "but from where we're standing, it's looking like Jesse more and more."

"I'd like to see the front of the house," Wolf said. "Pete gave us some interesting news."

The group walked to the front of the house, where Pete stood near the crime scene tape strewn across the front steps, staring at his phone. Nearby, Sheriff Roll's FJ Cruiser sat next to two other Ouray County SUVs still ticking from the drive up.

"What do you have?" Roll asked.

"These prints are different from the ones leading down to Guild's house."

Roll leaned into the crime scene tape and stared at a foot-print on the deck. Wolf and Burton edged up to get a look.

A large stain of dark maroon, almost black, stood out on the wood next to the front door. Evidence markers littered the deck, indicating now dried footprints that had trudged through the blood when it had been wet. More plastic markers sat on the stairs.

"You can see the smear there," Milo said. "Looks like some-body slid the body away from the front door and down the steps. Probably pulling him by his arms or legs. Agent Rushing and his team found traces of blood on the steps, even with the rain."

A sturdy front door, inlaid with a glass sun, stood open.

"Front door was open like that when we got here," Milo said, following Wolf's eyes.

"I'm not seeing any spatter."

"None to see," Milo said.

Wolf pictured Kyle Farmer answering the door and being greeted by a bullet that lodged in his body, then slumping to the ground and bleeding out. A blade would have left a whole different kind of mess.

There were dozens of footprints that led into and out of the stain.

"Did you find any stray lead?" Wolf asked.

"Nothing," Milo said.

"He's right." Sheriff Roll was staring at a picture on Pete's phone. "The prints on the side of that hill are different from these."

Wolf took his eyes off the blood stain and surveyed the house. The trim, the hinges, the doorknobs, the windows, were all decent quality. It was the kind of place that in Rocky Points would have fetched over a million.

He swiveled and saw a single-car A-frame garage matching the house on the other side of the driveway.

"Not a bad place," Wolf said.

Milo sucked in a breath. "You can smell the weed." The skunky scent of growing marijuana was thick in the air.

"They have a few dozen of them in the basement," Triplett said.

"What about Kyle's vehicle?" Wolf asked, surveying the driveway and only seeing law enforcement vehicles. "Where is it?"

"Rushing and his team sent it up to the forensics lab in

Montrose," Milo said. "At first glance, it didn't look like anything was out of the ordinary with it. No blood. Not like this porch."

Wolf nodded and looked at the garage. There was crime scene tape stretched across the door.

"That's where he kept the guns." Triplett said. "And there are more bloody prints in there."

Roll had his phone out and was taking pictures of the footprints. "Let's compare these prints to those inside that shed." The sheriff led them across the asphalt to the single-car garage. Pete, disinterested, wandered into the woods off the driveway.

Roll pulled on some gloves, then opened a wooden door.

"Keep your distance, please."

They lined up to get a view inside the space. The lights overhead zapped on, rows of machined metal shining brightly. Cool air poured out, smelling of gun oil.

Burton whistled. "Damn, makes my gun safe look like a box of Altoids."

Wolf looked inside and saw rifles of varying makes and models lining the left wall. There was an antique Winchester, a modern model 70, and a half dozen hunting rifles in between. Next to them stood an arsenal of combat weapons—an AK-47, M16A2, and a whole selection beyond that hanging on display.

Lining the narrower back wall, running the width of the converted single car garage, were three shelves angled toward the floor, covered in padded green felt like you'd find on a poker table. The chips laid out were handguns.

On the floor against the right wall, two open wooden crates revealed enough ammunition, some of it illegal, to supply an army. On a nearby workbench sat a Hornady ultrasonic cleaner and reloading station with all the newest, shiniest top-of-the-line toys for a gun enthusiast.

There were more footprints, however, which most interested Roll. He stood over one and took a photo. "Yep, these match the ones on the front porch."

"So there are two different people we're dealing with here," Milo said.

Wolf noted a vacant slot where a rifle should have stood against the wall.

"That's where Kyle kept his .50 cal," Milo said, watching his eyes. "We found it lying on the workbench."

"For you to find it," Wolf said.

"Yep."

Wolf stepped away from the crowded doorway and backed onto the driveway.

"Maybe those prints leading down the hill are Kyle Farmer's," Burton said, backing out of the entrance. "Or all these prints in blood could be Kyle's. Hell, we don't have a body. You guys have no DNA match yet. We have to keep options open. Maybe Kyle Farmer is on the run. You guys ever consider that?"

They stared at one another.

Another clap of thunder echoed up the valley. The sun was covered by a fast-moving cloud, dropping the temperature a few degrees.

"Hey! I got something!" Pete's voice came from behind the shed.

They followed the tracker's voice to the rear of the building and saw him in a crouched position, studying the ground in front of him.

Roll pushed his way to the front. "What is it?"

"Got another boot tread. This pattern matches the bloody ones. See how it has that star tread right in the middle?"

"Shit." Roll got close. "How'd we not see this before?" he looked up at his deputies for an answer.

They said nothing.

"Sorry," Roll said, digging his fingers into his temple. "I know, we've all been going full steam since that call to Guild's house. Anyway, that's why we brought you in, Pete. Good work."

Pete got up and looked down a steep slope that fell off the back of the gun shed.

Wolf stepped close and saw a perfect print set in dried mud. "Just to be clear, it rained Friday night up here? And then last night, Sunday night. But didn't Saturday night?"

"That's right," Pete said. He put up a hand toward the sky. "Friday night it must have rained at a perfect eastern angle to muddy up this backside of the shed. Which left us some mud, so our killer left us a print. But last night's rain must have been angling in from the west, so the shed kept our print dry and preserved." He pointed to the storm approaching now from the southwest. "Can't guarantee what's gonna happen with this approaching rain now."

They turned and looked toward the darkening western sky.

Roll nodded at Sobeck. "Photos, please. And get something to cover this so Rushing can cast it when they get back up here."

Sobeck hurried away.

Pete and Wolf must have had the same thought, because

they both looked down the slope and began walking toward a disturbance in the soil underneath an old-growth pine.

The ground was covered in pine needles rutted from the recent rain, punctuated by gouges where it appeared someone had slipped and fallen. But it was more than that. Beyond the riotous indentations preserved under the tree were tracks of a very different sort.

"What is it?" Roll appeared next to them and looked down. His eyes widened in comprehension. "Shit. Look at that."

"Looks like somebody was walking," Pete said, "and then fell on the pine needles. They dropped something really heavy. And then decided to drag it down the slope."

Thunder rumbled up the valley. A quick glance in the direction of the storm indicated there was a lot of rain coming out of the clouds, and they would be getting soaked within the next few minutes.

"We have to move." Roll's voice was breathy. He turned and looked up the slope. "We have to move! Sobeck, Triplett, get anything and everything we can to cover evidence before this storm hits!"

Sobeck was bending over the footprint at the top of the slope with Triplett looking on.

"Let's go!"

The two deputies broke toward the vehicles.

Pete was already moving down the slope, following the groove and tracks. Milo and Wolf followed. The air flickered from a finger of lightning overhead, followed by a rumble of thunder as they skidded down the loose dirt hill.

"Son of a bitch!"

Wolf turned around to see Roll on the ground, grabbing his arm. "You okay?"

"Yeah. Go!"

A minute later they were down the mountainside and onto flat land. Grass bent in waves, and a grove of aspen trees hissed in the freshening wind. There was a stream that cut through the bottom of the valley, surrounded by tall brush whipping on the gusts.

Milo and Pete had their eyes locked on the ground, walking through the grass. Wolf followed and saw it didn't take a professional tracker to see where they were headed. Because in the distance, amid the green foliage near the aspens stood a single earthen mound.

CHAPTER 18

Wolf joined them at the oval pile of dirt shaped suspiciously like a grave. Clumps of grass had been cut by a shovel blade, strewn aside, the dirt smoothed by rain—a rain that had last fallen on Friday night.

Sobeck and Triplett bounded up to them, out of breath. Sobeck had a DSLR camera around his neck, Triplett a handful of tarps under his arm.

"I would get some pictures of that dirt before that storm hits," Wolf said. "It's been smoothed by rain."

Sobeck snapped some photos, and his flash became indistinguishable from the lightning zapping around them.

"Got three tarps," Triplett said. "That's all I could find."

"Let's cover this up!" Roll said. "And we need to get Rushing up here, ASAP." The sheriff pulled out his phone and looked at the screen. "Crap. I don't have reception. You have any?" he asked Milo.

Milo looked at his phone and shook his head. "You?"

Wolf checked. "No!"

"I do, just barely." Sobeck handed his phone to Roll.

Roll made the call to Agent Rushing, a finger in his ear as he yelled into the receiver of the cell phone. He hung up. "They're on their way. They said to cover this as best we could and wait for them."

Triplett and Sobeck unfurled a tarp. It snapped in the wind, threatening to fly away. Wolf and Milo retrieved some stones by the stream. Together they all covered the mound with the tarp and used the rocks to weight it down.

Wolf looked up the slope and saw Burton still standing near Kyle Farmer's gun shed. The old man made no move to climb down and help them, and Wolf was grateful for it. He didn't feel like carrying somebody back up that slope.

"What now?" Sobeck asked, his voice barely audible over the wind.

The wall of rain slid up the valley, almost on top of them. Wolf zipped his Carhartt all the way and eyed the grove of aspens.

They all had the same idea and moved to the relative shelter of the trees just as the rain hit. The drops were frozen, stinging exposed skin as they came sideways. As they huddled with their backs to the onslaught, Wolf caught sight of something yellow in the grass.

"You have an evidence bag?" he asked Triplett, who pulled one from his pocket. Wolf grabbed it and headed into the rain, bending in front of what was a yellow-strapped headlamp. He bagged it and ran back to the trees with his find.

He handed the bag to Triplett, who handed it down the line past Sobeck, Milo, and then finally to Roll. Roll slipped it into his jacket pocket, not bothering to speak over the raging deluge.

They each took a white tree trunk for shelter and waited out the storm.

CHAPTER 19

SPECIAL AGENT RUSHING knelt over the mound and inserted a gloved hand into the dirt. The rest of them watched in silence.

Wolf stood with his hands in his pockets. The rain had passed, leaving the ground drenched and the grass matted. The afternoon sun had broken through the tail of the storm, and steam rose from the field. Low caterpillar clouds clung to the mountains in the distance. Once again Ridgway glinted below, far in the distance.

Rushing's hand stopped and he looked up at the crowd that had gathered around him.

"You feel something?" Roll asked.

Rushing nodded and pulled dirt away, revealing a black tarp.

Burton leaned into Wolf to get a better view. The old man had finally made the trek down the mountain. Although Wolf was still wondering how Burton would get back up the hill, he was now grateful for the alcohol vapors filling his nose, because the faint scent of death swirled in the still, post-storm air.

Triplett pinched his nose, while Sobeck stepped back. Pete seemed unfazed.

"Okay, we'll excavate." Agent Rushing sat back on his heels. "You guys can leave us to it."

"How long is that going to take?" Roll asked, sounding affronted.

"It could take hours."

"Screw that. Cut it open."

Agent Rushing's mouth hung open. "I'm not going to do that, sir."

"We need to know right now if that's Kyle Farmer. Cut it open."

Rushing sucked in a breath, let it out.

"Move." Roll took a Leatherman multi-tool from his belt and knelt.

"Careful," Special Agent Rushing said, standing up to make room for the sheriff.

Roll flipped out a blade, held it with his fingertips and sank the steel into the plastic.

The blade sliced open the tarp without the slightest resistance. After Roll opened a two-foot section, he pushed one side open with the blade.

The suspense ratcheted higher as another layer of black tarp was revealed. Roll dipped the tip of the blade into the plastic again, and this time when he sliced, ghostly white skin covered in brown hair came into view.

"Careful! Don't cut him." Special Agent Rushing knelt next to Roll. "Give me the knife." He held out a latex-gloved hand. "Come on."

The increase in smell pushed them all back, including Pete this time, except for Agent Rushing, who leaned close.

"Ah, shit." Triplett stumbled away and coughed.

"It's him?" Burton asked.

"It's him, alright," Roll said.

Wolf had never seen Kyle Farmer until now, and just like every other dead body, he could have gone without seeing him today. He turned away and shuffled toward Burton, the image of closed eyes, stubbled face smeared in blood, and a mouth hanging open at an odd angle fresh in his brain.

"Looks like he was shot here, below the collar bone. And one straight to the heart," Rushing called out.

"Damn cold out here." Burton's chin bounced with uncontrollable shivers, and even with a borrowed Ouray County SD rain coat zipped up and hood cinched around his head the man looked pre-hypothermic. "Freakin' freezing."

Wolf's chills were gone, warmed by afternoon sun now poking out through the clouds, though he was still soaked to the bone. He suspected even a raging fire would fail to stop those shivers wracking Burton's body.

"Jesse says he was with Hettie all night," Burton said. "And she's corroborating. What I want to know is what's with the second set of boot prints?"

Wolf had no answer.

"Cause, that means two guys, right?" Burton asked. "One guy offing Alexander Guild, another Kyle."

"Hettie could have been in on this, too," Wolf said.

Burton eyed him. "Hey Roll!"

Roll looked at him.

"What's this Hettie chick like?"

Roll blinked. "Not sure how to answer that question."

"I mean, you think she could have drug Kyle's body down here and buried it? Is she big and burly like that?"

"No way," Triplett said. "She's like a hundred pounds soaking wet. Skin and bones."

"Does she have size twelve men's feet like those boot prints up there?" Burton asked.

"Nope," Roll said.

"You think Hettie could have done this?"

Roll eyed him, then reluctantly shook his head.

Burton looked at Wolf. "You think Hettie did this?"

"I didn't say she brought the body down here. Or buried it. I'm just saying she could be lying about being with Jesse Friday night. He took out his battery. Why? To hide his location, that's why."

"This was definitely somebody big and strong," Triplett said. "You move Kyle Farmer's body, you'd better be big and strong."

"And stupid," Burton said. "Leaving that headlamp here like that?"

The excavation continued slowly while Burton talked to Wolf. Wolf observed Sobeck taking photos with the DSLR, Triplett listening to Sheriff Roll, Sheriff Roll pointing into the distance and complaining about something, Pete looking up at the breaking clouds toward the west, Milo rubbing his temple with one hand and listening to his boss without acknowledging, and Special Agent Rushing bending over the body.

They were a beaten crew. Wolf had seen it before, and too many times—when pressure was pushing in on all sides to get something solved and the only thing breaking wide open were the psyches of the personnel involved.

Later, mistakes would be exposed. Fingers would be pointed. And Sheriff Roll knew it. That's why the man's eyes were filled with resignation, his shoulders slumped as if his body was losing the battle against gravity.

"You listening to me?" Burton asked.

"No."

"Screw you."

An hour and a half later, the sun was back out in full force, warming the bottom of the valley to a balmy mid-sixties. Wolf's clothing was dry, his stomach still empty, his mouth parched for water that nobody seemed to have thought to bring.

Rushing and Jackson had the body fully exposed, and every once in a while, the wind lined up to give them all a whiff of death that reminded them why they were all there.

"I've got something interesting over here!" Rushing called.

"What is it?" Roll asked as they gathered near the body, the smell of decay stronger than ever.

"See this?" Rushing pointed to a piece of jewelry on Kyle's finger, glinting in the light. A silver bracelet with a tag on it.

"It's wrapped around his fingers," Rushing said. "There's an inscription on the tag that reads *Brothers Forever.*"

"That's interesting," Roll said. "Anyone recognize that piece of jewelry?"

Burton turned around and walked away from the grave.

"I find the state of the jewelry interesting," Agent Rushing said.

"Why's that?" Roll asked.

"Because look at Kyle's hand."

"It's covered in blood."

"That's right. You can see, the entirety of the front of his torso is covered in blood, which means he was lying on his front when he fell from the gunshots. He bled out, painting everything, including his hand, in blood. If he was holding this bracelet when he was shot, when he fell, the bracelet would have been covered in blood."

"But it's sparkling clean," Roll said. "Which means somebody put it in his hand after he was shot."

"Precisely," Rushing said. "And like I said, it's wrapped around his finger. Somebody placed this in his hand, then wrapped him and dragged him down here."

"Okay," Roll said. "Now that's interesting."

Wolf saw Burton stood a dozen paces away, staring back at the hole. Wolf joined him. "Did you hear that?"

Burton nodded.

"What's wrong?"

"Nothing. I just feel like shit."

A minute later, Sheriff Roll walked over to where Wolf and Burton were standing and looked up at Kyle's house on the hill, the crease on his forehead deeper than ever. "What do you make of that?"

Wolf shrugged. "Looks like the killer was trying to leave a message."

"You recognize that bracelet?" Roll asked Burton.

Burton shook his head.

"This is a cluster." Roll eyed his watch. "I have to get back down into town."

"Because you have Kyle Farmer," Wolf said.

"Yeah. Because we have Kyle Farmer." The sheriff eyed his watch again.

"If you'd like," Wolf said, "Burton and I could go with you to give the news to Jed and his boys."

"Screw that." Detective Milo walked over. "I'll go with you, sir."

Roll stared at his detective, then nodded to Wolf. "Thanks. I appreciate the offer. But Milo's right. We can handle it."

Triplett walked up and cleared his throat. "Sir. By my calculations, Sobeck and I have been going straight for thirty-nine hours now. Not that I'm bitching about it...I mean I am, sorry. I'm just sure as hell hungry and thirsty and could use a shit and a nap."

Roll put up his hand. "You're right. Something's gotta give here."

Special Agent Rushing stepped up and joined the group now gathering around the sheriff.

"Special Agent, my deputies need a rest. You and your colleagues have been going just as long as we have."

"It's no sweat. The other two are done down at Guild's place and headed up here now. We can work in shifts."

"I need to keep somebody up here with you while you finish."

"I'll stay," Sobeck said. The deputy's eyes were wide open, but he looked dead on his feet.

Roll nodded. "Thank you, Jimmy. Triplett, you can come down with us."

"No," Triplett said. "My partner's staying, I'm staying. We'll get our rest then. I can wait."

Roll nodded. "All right. We'll see you tomorrow at 0800 at the Marshal's office. That okay with you?"

He looked to Burton and Wolf. "Milo and I will take you to your car at Guild's place."

"We don't know where the Farmers are going to be," Milo said.

Roll nodded. "I know. We'll have to call and tell them to meet us somewhere."

"After seeing them in action this morning, I'd say the more people the better," Wolf said. "Deputy Sobeck says Jesse and Kyle said that fight at the Soaring Eagle Bar broke up at around 8:30 pm Friday night. I'm not saying Deputy Sobeck's lying, but I think it's in your best interest to lock down the exact time there. If you're thinking Jesse came up here, took the gun out of Kyle's shed, and marched down to shoot Guild, then if you're off by twenty or thirty minutes there's no way Jesse could have made it by 9:38 to shoot him."

Burton straightened. "Wolf's right, we have to lock that time down. We'll come with you down to the bar. Buy you a beer. You look like you need it, old man."

Roll eyed Burton and laughed, too hard. "Yeah, yeah, okay *old man*. We'll go to the Soaring Eagle Bar to buy *me* a beer." His face fell. "Good a place as any I guess to let a man know his son is dead."

"Doesn't matter where you do it," Wolf said. "There's no good place for that."

Roll took a deep breath, looked up the hill, and then at Burton. "You think you can make this?"

Burton waved a hand and walked.

And, surprisingly, Burton climbed back up the mountain with the spryness of someone half his age.

CHAPTER 20

"THIS PLACE IS BEAUTIFUL, I tell you," Burton said, leaning against the windshield.

Wolf eyed him, seeing that Jack Daniels was behind the wheel again.

The drive down to Guild's place had taken them a half an hour, a drive during which everyone in the vehicle had been accompanied by the soundtrack of Burton snoring in the back seat.

Sheriff Roll had remained silent the entire drive, brooding on the task ahead. Milo had also fallen asleep during the short drive, leaving Wolf plenty of time to stare out the window and contemplate the past, present, and future. He kept his mind off dead bodies and job security and focused instead on his grandson's green eyes, ridiculous giggle, and big smile.

Upon arriving at Alexander Guild's house, Wolf and Burton climbed into the warm cab of Wolf's SUV, the comfortably familiar driver's seat for Wolf, the soothing bottle of Jack Daniels for Burton.

Another twenty minutes later, they were driving toward Ridgway on Highway 550.

"I gotta get down here more often." Burton sat back and sighed. "Freakin' beautiful, I tell you."

The man was in a good mood because he was sipping on the Jack Daniels bottle again, but he was not wrong. The late afternoon sun had dipped behind clouds over the big mountains flanking the valley, and shafts of light lanced down, dappling the ground beneath.

Wolf hung a right off the highway and into Ridgway. They passed the dirt road leading to the Marshal's office on the right, Lucille's Diner with its bacon smells, then parked at an old-western looking saloon building. Neon beer signs hung in the windows, glowing behind a simmering reflection of the sky.

"About time." The cork in Burton's hand squeaked as he sealed the bottle and set it at his feet. Wolf noted the remainder of the liquid had again been cut in half, and estimated Burton had consumed a good six or seven shots in the time it had taken them to coast down from Guild's house. Just a spit in the gas tank.

They stepped out into cool air, moistened by the earlier rain and laden with the scent of bar food. Wolf's mouth exploded in anticipation, but he tamped down his spirits when he saw Roll was on the phone with Milo at his side.

"Don't envy that man right now," Burton said.

They strolled nearer the front bumper of Wolf's vehicle, listening as they approached Roll.

"I'm sorry, I'm so sorry, Jed, I know. I'm—" Roll pulled the phone from his ear and poked the screen with his finger. "Dammit!"

Burton, Milo, and Wolf stood with their heads bowed and watched Roll take a walk away from the parking lot. He tilted his head back, took a moment, and returned with a steely look.

"Okay. He knows. I screwed up. But he knew. There was no hiding it. I couldn't lie."

"I know, sir," Milo said.

"Nothing you can do but what you did," Wolf added.

"Well," Burton said. "Let's get you two a beer, how about that?"

Roll narrowed his eyes and stared at Burton. "Best idea I've heard in a long time."

The inside of the place was classier than the exterior led on. The bar lined the back wall, armed with what looked to be a few dozen pour handles offering craft beer. The floor was stained dark, the walls were painted earth tones, adorned with pictures of the majestic surrounding mountains and antique farming equipment.

It was 5:15 pm, and a lot of patrons were out for what was likely happy hour at the Soaring Eagle Bar. Pool tables occupied the right-hand side of the room, sturdy-looking dining furniture filled the left. Milo and Roll chose a table and sat down.

The bartender came out from the bar and met them at the table. "Sheriff, detective. How are you guys doing?" His somber demeanor, and the glances they were getting, said Roll's phone conversation had been observed through the windows.

"A pitcher of beer, please." Burton pronounced it *pisher*.

"You got it. And here are some menus, in case you need them."

"Oh, we'll need them," Burton said.

"Sheriff, detective? You two okay with the beers?"

"Yes, thank you, Joe. And how about some waters all around."

Wolf ordered a tonic with a lime.

"And we wanted to ask you some questions, Joe," Roll said to the bartender. "About that fight between Jesse and Kyle Friday night."

"Yeah? What about it? You know, I had Kyle's father and two brothers in here earlier asking about that."

"Is that right?" Roll asked. "What were they asking?"

"Just about the fight. About what happened."

"And you told them?"

Joe shrugged. "Yeah."

Roll nodded. "Okay. Well, we'd like to know about what time that fight happened. Do you remember exactly?"

Joe put his hands on his hips and looked out the windows. "Must have been eight or eight-thirty. It was right around sunset." He looked at his watch.

"Is there any way to pinpoint that more precisely?" Wolf asked.

"Maybe. Let me check." Joe turned and headed for the bar.

Wolf faced the windows, and the peaks outside. The Colorado Rockies were playing on the ceiling mounted TV, and it felt good to zone out on the action, if only for a few minutes.

"Here you go." The bartender set down the drinks. "And I have this." He pulled out a piece of paper. "I closed out Deputy Sobeck's tab right after they left. I remember that, specifically, because Jimmy helped break up that fight. I was thanking him, and he told me to just close him out. That was at 8:27 pm. And, that was no more than five minutes after Jesse and Kyle were out of here."

Roll took the piece of paper and handed it back. "Thanks, Joe."

"No sweat."

"How did that fight go down, Joe?" Wolf asked.

Burton took charge of the pitcher and started sloshing cups full.

"Well, Kyle gave Jesse a pretty good beating, the way I saw it."

"And you heard what the fight was about?" Wolf asked.

"Yeah. Apparently, Jesse and Hettie were screwing around behind Kyle's back. Kyle was screaming about it for everyone to hear. It was like a Jerry Springer show." Joe chuckled, then stopped when nobody joined him.

"Anyway, we all piled out of here and watched while they wrestled around. Kyle was throwing punch after punch into Jesse's head. Jimmy finally went out there and put Kyle in one of those cop ninja holds and broke them up. He made them split up and leave. Kyle got into his pickup and peeled off, and then Jesse and Hettie drove away in Jesse's Jeep."

"Thanks, Joe," Roll said.

"No sweat. Now can I take your orders?"

When it was Wolf's turn, he ordered a cheeseburger and fries and handed over the menu. Sipping his tasteless carbonated drink, he leaned back into his chair. Roll and Milo both stared blankly at the television, while Burton drank and tended to everyone else's glass like both were his job.

"It's not looking good for Jesse," Roll said. "Just admit it, Hal."

Hal slurped his beer. "Not from where I'm sitting."

"Oh yeah?"

Movement outside caught Wolf's eye. He stood up.

"What is it?" Roll asked, turning around to see the Farmers' pickup truck sliding into the parking lot, kicking up a cloud of dust.

"You told them where we were?" Milo asked.

"Well yeah, I told him I wanted to meet him, then...you guys stay here." Roll walked to the entrance.

Wolf and Milo hurried after him and slipped out the door before it closed. The air was still laden with dust.

"What happened to him?" Jed Farmer said as he walked towards the sheriff.

"Jed, please..."

"What happened to him!" The man's cheeks were streaked with tears.

The older son—Seymour, Wolf remembered—was crying too. The youngest stared straight at Wolf with an unblinking gaze. All three of them looked like violence was on their minds.

"Answer me!"

"We think he was shot," Roll said.

"You think? What do you mean? You said you found him, didn't you? Did you find him?"

People were gathering at the windows inside, but none dared to come out.

"Yes, Jed. We found him. He was shot. I told you, he's dead." Roll's voice failed him when he said the word dead, and it came out as a whisper.

Jed's eyes flicked to Wolf. "Did he do it?"

Wolf said nothing.

"Did your nephew kill my son?"

Burton came up next to Wolf. "We don't know. But it doesn't look like it to me."

"To you? And how about to everyone else?" Jed looked at Roll. "What did he say last night? You guys brought him in, right? What did he say?"

"We haven't talked to him yet," Roll said.

"You haven't talked to him yet?"

"You know that's perfectly within his rights, you know that."

"Which means he's guilty."

Roll looked down at his boots. "Jed. It means it's within his rights to not speak to us."

Jed Farmer looked at Roll like a predator watches prey cowering at its feet. "Where did you find him?"

"I can't tell you that, Jed. It's a crime scene."

"Where!" The man's voice echoed in the still air.

"I'm sorry, Jed. Really. I am. Seymour, Gabriel, I'm sorry about your brother."

"I want to see him," Jed said.

"You can see him when we get him to the morgue."

Jed closed his eyes. "When's that gonna be?"

"Not for a few hours."

Jed's eyes shot open and found Burton. "You guys talked to him. He ran down to the Canyon of the Ancients. Why? What's that got to do with anything? Did you find him in the Canyon of the Ancients?"

"It was just a spot where he and I used to go hiking," Burton said. "That's all."

"But he was shot. He was shot and killed." Thoughts flickered behind the man's eyes. "And what's this I'm hearing about Jesse and Hettie screwing each other behind Kyle's back? What's this about everyone saying they got in a fight here? Hettie and Kyle were dating, and your nephew was screwing her. It's clear as day, sheriff. Look at the facts. Jesse did it."

"We don't know that for sure," Burton said, the drink in him adding a bit too much force in his voice.

"Jesse was screwing that girl," Jed said. "And her father was killed by Alexander Guild a few months ago. Jesse wanted Guild dead, and he wanted my son dead. All for that bitch." Jed's voice was like a panther's growl. "That's all there is to it, sheriff."

"I assure you, we're working on figuring out exactly what happened to your son."

"Is that why you're here now? Sipping some suds and having some burgers? Maybe shoot a bit of pool before you get back to figuring out what happened to my son?"

"No, you know that's—"

"I want to see him."

Roll nodded. "I know you do. I'll let you know the instant you can."

"What are you doing here?" Jed asked. "You said there's a crime scene. You should be out there. Figuring this out."

"They got the CBI up there working the scene," Burton said.

Wolf cringed at Burton's intrusion. The fact that he slurred half the words didn't help. Wolf jabbed him with an elbow before he could say more.

Jed squinted. "Why are you talking right now? I didn't ask you any questions." Without warning, Jed pushed past Roll and lunged at Burton.

"Hey!"

Jed's arm lashed out and the sound of fist hitting flesh spurred Wolf into action, albeit a moment too late. The two younger men sprinted towards them. An elbow buried hard into Wolf's chest, knocking the wind out of him.

Seconds earlier, Wolf had felt only heartache for the man, and even now he understood the erupting rage, but Wolf was acting on instinct, protecting Burton from the onslaught. He punched, connected with one of Jed's kid's faces, and then tossed Jed sideways into a car.

Roll had one of the kids by the back of his sweatshirt and flung him away.

There was a harsh knocking noise behind Wolf, and he looked back and saw Burton had hit the side of the car before crumpling to the ground.

"Freeze, everybody! Now!" Milo had his gun out and pointed at one of the two Farmer boys.

Jed looked behind Wolf and let up.

"He's hurt," Milo said.

"Let's go!" Jed told his sons. They walked toward the truck and the boys climbed inside, disappearing behind the tinted windows.

Jed appeared over the roof. "I'll be keeping on you, sheriff! You either find out who killed my son, or I will!" He climbed in and slammed the door.

Wolf knelt to tend to Burton, ignoring the rocks pelting his back as the Farmers sped away.

"He's not looking good," Milo said. "I'll call an ambulance."

If it weren't for his moving lips, Burton would have looked stone dead.

CHAPTER 21

"Mr. Wolf?"

The plastic chair under Wolf groaned as he stood up.

"I'm Dr. Wilkinson." A tall gray-haired man with a tablet computer extended his free hand.

"Hi." Wolf shook his hand. "How's he doing?"

"He's stable right now."

"What happened?"

"Blood tests are showing he had a heart attack."

Wolf raised his eyebrows. "How serious?"

"Let's just say if the paramedics were a few seconds later, he wouldn't be with us anymore. As it was, they resuscitated him twice on the way here. I've scheduled an emergency surgery tomorrow morning."

"He's okay until then?"

"No, but his blood alcohol level is point-two-one and that's too high for our surgeon's liking. We've scheduled the surgery for ten a.m. tomorrow morning."

"Can I see him?"

"He's resting. He'll be out for at least twelve hours." He

looked up from under his glasses. "I understand from Mr. Burton his wife is unaware of what's going on?"

"I've told her," Wolf said. "Well, I haven't told her it's a heart attack. But...I'll tell her."

The doctor turned to go, and Wolf returned to his chair. With a sigh he pulled out his phone and checked the screen. Seeing three missed calls from MacLean, he dialed the number.

"You still alive?" MacLean asked by way of greeting.

"Yeah, but Burton's another story. He had a heart attack."

"And he's dead?"

"No, sorry. He's alive. But after talking to the doctor, it looks like it's just by a thread."

"Shit." MacLean drew out a long breath. "Well, I guess that's that for his nephew's case then, huh?"

Wolf said nothing.

"Wolf?"

"Yeah, sorry. I don't know."

Silence. "We're going to see you tomorrow morning at that meeting, aren't we?"

"I'm gonna stick around and make sure Burton's all right. They'll take him up to County Hospital for the surgery tomorrow morning."

"What time tomorrow morning?"

"Not sure," he hedged.

"Because by my calculations you have to leave by nine. It'll take you at least an hour and a half."

"Yeah."

MacLean sat silent for a beat. "They'll get him up to County with or without you, Wolf. What's going on?"

Wolf considered the question carefully. He'd borne

witness to an investigation over the last twenty-four hours. That's what was going on. Other than protecting Burton from beatings, what had Wolf achieved?

"What's this meeting about?" he asked.

"It's about me, and you, and your detectives. And the future of this department."

"Sounds ominously vague."

"I told you, it's not something I'm going to discuss with you over the phone. The time and place are tomorrow morning at eleven a.m. in Town Hall."

"Is it bad?" The question was supposed to stay inside, but it slipped out.

"Yes. I'm afraid it is, Dave."

The speaker in Wolf's ear crackled with static.

"I'll see you tomorrow," MacLean said, and hung up.

He had two text messages from Patterson and one from Rachette, both asking for an update.

He shot off quick replies and pocketed his phone. With the chunk of technology tucked back away he sucked in a slow breath through his nose, closed his eyes, and fell asleep.

"So I said suck it...exactly what I said...doesn't matter, that's not protocol and he knows it. The real problem is he's a little bitch and he needs to learn how *not* to be one..."

Wolf cracked his eyes and squinted at the light lancing through the hospital waiting room window. Outside, the nondescript Montrose parking lot gleamed in the sun.

"Hey, I gotta go. No, he's waking up. I'll talk to you later."

Wolf sat up and rubbed his eyes, revealing the familiar face next to him.

"Hey." Detective Tom Rachette plucked a cup of coffee off the floor and handed it to him. "Good morning."

"What are you doing here?"

Rachette sipped his coffee. "I heard what happened."

"Doesn't answer my question."

Wolf checked his watch and saw it was 6:35 am. His detective would have had to leave Rocky Points before five to be here now. "How long have you been here?"

"A few minutes."

They sat quietly and drank their coffee. The combination of the cool indoor air and the rays streaming in the window felt good on Wolf's weary body—he was like Superman gaining power from the sun and Arabica beans, though he was pretty sure Superman didn't have shooting back pains like he had now.

"Here. Here's why I came." Rachette unfolded a sheet of computer paper and put it on Wolf's thigh. "Here's some of the questions they asked me last week." He stood and walked to the window.

Wolf picked up the paper. There was a numbered list scrawled in Rachette's chicken-scratch writing.

1. Please assess Chief Detective David Wolf's ability to do his job since his June hospitalization for a panic attack.
2. On a scale of one to ten, please rate David Wolf's current ability to do his job, and explain your answer.

Wolf lowered the paper, revealing Rachette staring at him. "Who asked you these questions?"

"The Council. They asked all of us. Yates, Patterson, me. We each had confidential interviews with them. Margaret and the whole council. I couldn't keep it secret from you anymore."

Wolf sipped his coffee, feeling the acid bubbling in his gut.

"Me, Patterson, and Yates all had the same interview. And Patterson wanted to tell you, too. Just so you know. You've just been gone. We never got a chance to tell you. I'm not sure if anyone else had the interview besides us. I asked Wilson, and he told me to shut up about it."

Wolf thought of last night's conversation with MacLean, and last week when Wilson and MacLean had been speaking to one another in hushed tones, stopping when Wolf came into the room. He'd been with Patterson at the time and assumed their hesitation was because of her.

Is it bad?

Yeah. I'm afraid it is, Dave.

"And I answered the questions favorably," Rachette said. "In case you're wondering."

"That's none of my business, Tom."

"It sure is. I answered them favorably."

Wolf nodded.

More signs from the end of last week now clicked together: The looks from Rachette and Yates as they stood talking at the coffee maker, and the way they'd split when he entered the room. MacLean staring out at him from his office window as he talked on the phone.

"You all right?" Rachette asked.

"Huh? Yeah."

"Did you already know about this?"

"No." He eyed his detective. "Thanks for letting me know."

"Yeah. I'm just sorry I didn't tell you earlier."

"Don't worry about it."

They sat some more.

"How's the old man doing?"

"Not good. Needs a triple bypass."

"Jeez. MacLean said he went down hard, too? Something about a fight?"

He eyed Rachette. "You spoke to MacLean about Burton?"

"Well, yeah. Spoke to him late last night." Rachette paused.

"MacLean sent you down here."

"Yeah."

"To bring me back."

"Yeah. I'm supposed to escort you." Rachette looked at his watch. "Got a couple hours before we absolutely have to be on the road. You want to get some breakfast?"

Was the County Council pushing for termination? If so, why was MacLean so keen to have Wolf up there for the meeting? To watch him as the dagger struck home? At one time the man had very nearly been Wolf's foe. Since then they'd become, if not friends, at least civil to one another.

"I think Patterson is taking your job," Rachette said.

The words jangled inside Wolf's brain. He rose and walked to the window.

"I overheard Wilson talking about it."

Wolf saw Rachette's sagging posture in the window's reflection. He focused on his own face staring back. Stubble had grown unchecked for three days, creating a dark carpet fringed with more than a little silver. His dark eyes were puffy from lack of sleep and surrounded by wrinkles that seemed deeper than before.

"Come on. I'll buy you breakfast." There was a hint of desperation in Rachette's voice.

"I have to talk to Burton." Wolf turned and walked away.

Rachette let him pass.

"Excuse me," Wolf said to the woman behind the reception desk. "I was told I could see my friend once he woke up. We have to leave, and I really want to let him know what's going on. Last night, the doctor said he'd be out for twelve hours, I was—"

"His name?"

"Harold Burton. He's in room 313."

"I'll put in a call to the nurse's station." She picked up the phone and dialed. "Hi, I have—"

"David Wolf. Detective David Wolf."

"A Detective David Wolf to see Harold Burton...I know..." she looked at her watch. "Okay... okay." She removed the handset from her ear. "She's checking."

Wolf nodded and gave her space.

"I heard Cheryl wasn't even in town," Rachette said.

"You knew she left?"

"Left? Like, as in left him?"

Wolf shook his head. "Never mind."

"I didn't know she left him. Really? You know, I was at Beer Goggles like two months ago, and he was just sloshed the bar. I asked him about Cheryl, you know, 'How's Cheryl doing?' I asked, and he basically spat in disgust on the counter. I just assumed he misunderstood me. Got Blackman to call him an Uber. Took me and Blackman all our strength to escort him outside when the ride showed up. That was during the playoffs. I remember, cause the Donkos got their asses handed to them."

They stared at each other.

"Good story."

"Thanks."

"Excuse me," the receptionist said. "You can head on up there. He's talking with the doctors now, but once they're done you can visit with your friend." She smiled sympathetically.

"Thank you so much." Rachette leaned an elbow on the counter.

"Uh huh." She busied herself with her computer.

CHAPTER 22

"YOU LOOK LIKE SHIT." Wolf meant every syllable.

Burton's mustache wriggled as if his mouth had stretched into a brief smile, but his upper face held the lifeless gaze of a lobotomy patient.

"How are you feeling?"

"Not particularly bad," Burton said. "Hung over as shit, need a drink, the doc is telling me they're going to cut open my chest and put some leg veins on my heart, which means they'll have to cut open my leg. But they gave me a painkiller that's starting to work on the pounding headache that starts at the five stitches they put in my scalp. So, yeah. Good."

Burton leaned back on the pillow and clamped his eyes shut.

"You okay? You need a nurse?"

"No. I'm just sore. And I don't like thinking about what they're about to do." Burton's eyeballs moved behind his lids.

"I heard you saw the light last night."

"Oh yeah, the dead thing?"

"Yeah."

"I don't remember seeing a white light, if that's what you're getting at. No opening into the next world."

Wolf smiled. "You were probably looking the wrong direction. I'm pretty sure you're gonna want to look down next time."

Burton opened his eyes and smiled back, then he closed them again. "I knew I was headed somewhere like this. Just never thought I'd get there." When his eyes opened, they shimmered. "Cheryl was right. I'm killing myself. And not by a thousand cuts, but with a sledgehammer."

Wolf watched a flock of birds pass by the window. Low clouds skated across the sky, leaving inky shadows on the heaving landscape to the south.

"I can't keep drinking a bottle of whiskey or scotch every two days. I don't know what I've been thinking."

That you would die if you stopped? Wolf thought. *That the liquid hitting your lips sent calming shudders through your body?*

"I'm done. I'm freakin' done. Right now, you're looking at a new person. This...this is the end of Hal Burton the drunk old man. He died last night. Twice."

Wolf nodded. "Good."

"Yeah. Good." He closed his eyes again.

Wolf watched out the window some more. "Listen, you know they're taking you up in the ambulance. I'm not sure what time they're leaving, but..."

"But you have to be up for that thing. The meeting with the County Council."

Wolf said nothing.

"You'd better get up there. But you remember one thing about whatever they've decided they're gonna do to you."

"What's that?"

"You remember that you don't do the work for titles, or money. Or recognition."

Wolf thought there were worse things in life. The titles led to money, which led to a sense of security, which led to him being able to do his job without any fear, which led to recognition for a job well done.

"You do the work because you're a dumbass."

Wolf nodded. "Hmmm."

"You're an idiot. What I mean is, you have no freakin' choice. You wake up, and you skulk around this life looking for people who need help, and you help them. You go to the store, you see some old nitwit who can't reach a box of cereal and you help him." Burton made a fist. "You ain't got no choice."

"What exactly was in that pain pill they gave you?"

"You don't give a shit if people are writing about you in the papers, making you look like a nutty piece of fruitcake." Burton laughed. "You know I'm speakin' the truth, brother."

"Yes. Thank you."

Burton's face relaxed. "You do the job because that's what you're wired to do. Don't you forget it."

"Thank you, sir."

Burton nodded, as if he'd said his final piece about that. Wolf hoped so.

"And don't worry about me. I'll be fine. I spoke to Cheryl a few minutes ago. She's back in Rocky Points. She's going to meet me at the hospital." He smiled, and this time it reached his eyes. A tear fell down past his nose and disappeared into his mustache.

Wolf stared out the window and gave Burton a moment to gather himself.

"Any news on Jesse?"

"I haven't been in touch with anyone," Wolf said.

"That bracelet in Kyle Farmer's hand."

"Yeah?"

Burton looked at Wolf. "It was Jesse's."

Wolf stepped toward the bed, wondering if it was the drugs talking. "You're sure?"

"One hundred percent."

Wolf remembered the way Burton had walked away from Kyle's body. "How are you so sure? You've seen him twice in two decades."

"I gave the bracelet to his dad when he came to Rocky Points all those years ago. Bought it at that trinket place on Main that used to be there. Remember the place that used to have the penny-flattening machine?"

Wolf's eyes glazed over as he remembered going into the shop with his father. They'd left that day and gone to the railroad track to flatten coins the old-fashioned way.

"The Blonde Creek Miner," Wolf said.

"Yeah. Holy cow, that was the name. Place went out of business when I was sheriff, and I can't believe it lasted that long. Sold nothing but useless junk."

Useless junk. That was the going product line of most businesses on Main Street.

"I recognized it when I saw it, with the rounded silver rectangle tag—it's got a particular border. And when he read the inscription...I have the same one at home. We both got one that same day."

"So Jesse got the bracelet from his father," Wolf said,

"and wrapped it around Kyle's finger before he buried him? And then he texted you for help? How does that make sense? He would know you would have recognized it when they dug up Kyle. Why would he bring attention to himself, when he's working so hard to cover his tracks otherwise? Like, by taking out his cell phone battery?"

Burton nodded. "And why the second pair of boots stomping through the blood? And what about that head lamp? That spooked me when I saw that bracelet. What do you want to bet they'll find out that was Jesse's headlamp? Why would he just leave that sitting right there in the grass?"

"Maybe he dropped it," Wolf said, but the answer sounded weak coming out of his own mouth.

"Well, if he did, it was mighty careless," Burton said. "Almost to the point of reckless. And if he left that bracelet in Kyle's hand, then that means he's itching to get caught. Which...shit, that just might be it, I suppose. Maybe he is desperate to get caught."

Burton stared hard at Wolf. "Will you promise me something?"

"What's that?" Wolf asked.

"I'm going under the knife. He's out there, all alone in jail. Scared shitless." He shook his head. "This doesn't look right, damn it."

Wolf went to the window and looked out. The sun cast long shadows, deepening the wrinkles on the pale dirt hills. When he turned back, Burton's head had lolled to the side, his eyes closed.

"Promise you what?" Wolf asked.

Burton lay motionless.

Wolf's eyes darted to the heart monitors and saw nothing

out of the ordinary. He walked up and checked his wrist for a pulse for good measure.

"You awake?"

No answer.

Wolf cycled a breath. "Yeah, old man," he said. "I will." He slipped out of the room and into the hallway, where he was met by a heavyset nurse.

"Did he fall asleep?" she asked.

"Yes, he did. What did you give him for pain this morning?"

"It was a mild sedative. We need him resting up." She slipped inside the door. "And shutting up."

"He okay?" Rachette asked as they walked towards the elevator.

"He's fine."

"You ready to do this or what?"

Wolf looked at his detective.

"What?"

"I'm not going back with you."

Rachette didn't blink. "Why not? What's the problem?"

"I need to see this through for Burton."

They walked down the hallway. "I heard it looks like Jesse did it," Rachette said.

"And that's another thing," Wolf said. "There's something I don't like about those murders down in Ridgway."

"What's that?"

"That's exactly what I don't like. That it looks so much like Jesse Burton did it."

Rachette sucked in a long breath, then nodded. "Then I'm not going back either. I've already told those jackals on the council what I think anyway."

Wolf pressed the down button and the elevator doors opened.

Rachette folded his arms and leaned against the interior wall of the elevator. "You need food."

"I do. But first things first," Wolf said.

"What's that?"

Wolf could hardly stand the smell of himself, the itch on his skin. "I need a shower."

CHAPTER 23

WOLF STEPPED out of the motel room, feeling as fresh as he could get using cheap motel soap and shampoo.

"Looking like a couple dozen cents," Rachette said. "Which is a few cents better than how you looked a couple hours ago."

A housekeeper pushed a cart toward them, clacking over the weathered wooden boards that ran in front of the row of rooms that made up the Ridgway Motel.

"Howdy," Rachette said.

"Thanks a lot," Wolf said, handing over the key to the woman along with a ten-dollar bill. He'd already bribed the guy at the front, having to part with a twenty for the privilege.

She smiled gratefully and disappeared into the room.

Rachette passed Wolf a cup of coffee. "Here you go. Got it in the lobby. Was talking to the guy at the desk. He heard about Kyle Farmer's body being pulled out of the ground last night. And I thought news traveled fast in Rocky Points."

Wolf sipped his coffee, checking out the view of the San Juan mountain sky line.

"I'm gonna eat this cup if I don't get some food soon," Rachette said. "What about that diner?"

The Ridgeway Motel was two blocks up the hill from Lucille's Diner. Wolf figured it was about time to ingest some of that bacon he'd been smelling for the last day. He eyed his watch. It was 7:25. If they could eat fast, they'd have enough time to catch Roll and his crew at the station at eight.

They walked the two blocks, leaving their matching dark grey unmarked cruisers in the motel parking lot. Dust hung in the still morning air, kicked up off the side streets as cars rolled up to Main. An Ouray County SD SUV rolled past them, turned into the diner, and pulled into the alley behind the restaurant.

"You know that guy?" Rachette asked.

The SUV stopped and a woman got out of the passenger seat. She held a waitress apron in one hand and a purse over her shoulder.

Deputy Triplett got out of the driver's side and met the woman in a hug, burrowing in the way a person dives into bed after a long day. She stood still, apron in one hand, the other patting his back, while Triplett wrapped his arms around her. His chin on her head, they could see his lips move, looking like he was trying to comfort her.

Wolf let his gaze drop to the sidewalk, feeling like he was intruding. "That's a deputy named Triplett."

"Dad, I think he's gonna pork her," Rachette said under his breath.

Wolf allowed himself another glance. The woman

squirmed in Triplett's arms and dropped her hand from his back, but Triplett held on, eyes closed.

They embraced another few seconds before parting. Triplett watched her leave, then looked right at Wolf and Rachette. The deputy's eyes flashed with recognition.

Wolf raised his hand to wave, but before he'd completed the full gesture Triplett had his back turned and was rounding the back of his car. The vehicle bounced as he got in and disappeared behind the diner, the tires spitting gravel.

"O-kay," Rachette said.

Triplett's SUV came into view and rolled onto Main without stopping, turned downhill, and sped away.

"Pretty weird guy, you ask me." Rachette pulled open the glass door and bells tinkled, announcing their arrival to Lucille's Diner.

A waitress came to the hostess stand. "Two?"

"You got it," Rachette said.

"Follow me."

The woman they'd seen in the alley walked past, and Wolf noticed her name tag.

Jill Sobeck.

Wolf stopped and watched her walk to consult a sheet on the wall.

"Could we be seated in her section?" he asked.

Jill Sobeck saw them pointing at her and turned away, busying herself with writing something on the sheet.

"Yeah, sure." The hostess looked confused by the request, and at a loss as to where to put them.

Jill Sobeck came over. "What's going on?"

"These gentlemen would like to sit with you."

She frowned. "Okay. Do I know you?"

"Sorry," Wolf said with an amiable smile. "No. I just saw your nametag. We're working with Deputy Sobeck, Jimmy, on the case." He pointed at her nametag.

"Oh. Yeah. He's my husband."

"Oh," Wolf said. "Well, nice to meet you."

"You can seat them here."

"Thanks."

"Get you something to drink?"

They ordered coffee and orange juice and Rachette watched her leave. "Okay, what's going on? Is she cheating on her husband with some other dude in the department? Is that what I just saw?"

Wolf said nothing. There were a thousand different explanations for what they just saw. Although Rachette's version seemed pretty feasible.

"Pretty good-looking woman, if I must say," Rachette said.

"How's Charlotte doing?"

"Yeah, yeah."

They sat in silence, and Wolf replayed Triplett's look out in the alley. Like a guy who'd been caught in the act.

"Charlotte's good," Rachette said. "Sleep deprived. Kids, you know?"

"Here you go." Jill Sobeck placed two waters in front of them, then coffee cups, and filled them with the steaming liquid.

"Thanks, Jill," Rachette said.

She nodded with an eat-shit-and-die look.

"I'll be back with your OJ. You guys get a chance to look at the menu?"

Rachette ordered eggs and bacon. Wolf ordered two meals: eggs with bacon and eggs with sausage.

Wolf decided to bring Rachette up to speed on the case, pausing while Jill Sobeck delivered their orange juice. Rachette openly stared at her rear end as she waited on the table next to them.

"And now," Wolf said under his breath, "I've just been told by Burton that the bracelet we found yesterday, placed in Kyle's hand for all to see, was Jesse's. It said 'Brothers Forever' on it. Burton gave it to his brother years ago, and his brother gave it to his son, Jesse."

"Okay," Rachette said, "but why would Jesse do that? Does he want to get caught?"

Wolf shook his head. "And that headlamp. Why leave it just sitting out? Odds are they're going to find out that was Jesse's headlamp."

"So someone's trying to frame him."

"Right now it seems too clean." Wolf sipped his water.

"Yeah, it does, I suppose," Rachette said. "But, then again, sometimes things are exactly like they seem."

Wolf sat back as Jill Sobeck came to the table with their orders.

"Anything else for you two?"

"No thanks, Jill," Rachette said. "Hey, listen, Jill, was that guy you were with out there—"

Wolf kicked him under the table.

Jill looked like she noticed, and her face darkened. "What was that?" She stared at them in turn. "Why are you two sitting at my table, again?"

"Like we said, we're just working with your husband." Wolf took a bite of bacon.

"Who did you two say you were?"

"We're just two detectives working with your husband," Rachette said. "And his partner."

For an instant her lips curled into an involuntary snarl. "What are you getting at?"

Rachette froze with a forkful of hash browns near his mouth. "Uhhh, nothing."

She slid her gaze to Wolf, then back to Rachette. "Fuck you guys. I'll get somebody else to finish up with you."

"Excuse me." A woman with gray curls and a slouched back appeared out of nowhere, an appalled look on her face. "Jill, what did you just say to that man?"

The way Jill's face dropped told Wolf she was the owner.

"Excuse me, sir. I'm am so sorry—"

"No." Wolf held up a hand. "We're so sorry." He looked at Rachette.

Rachette's eyebrows were arched now, utensils down.

"That was...the rudest thing I've ever said to a woman," Wolf said. "I'm so sorry, ma'am. What she just said to me is mild in comparison, and in fact, I deserve a punch in the nose after that. It's just been a long, long day already. I have no right to take it out on you. I'm sorry."

He stood and thumbed Rachette toward the door.

Rachette got up, eyeing his plate like he was leaving behind one of his children.

"Oh, well..." The elderly woman shook her head. "That's...unfortunate."

"How much was the check?"

Jill stared at him with a blank look, then pulled out the ticket from her bib. "It's like, thirty, probably thirty-three after tax or something."

"Here." Wolf pulled his wallet. "Here's fifty. Keep the change."

"Oh, no. That's too much."

"No, it's not. Please. Have a great rest of your day. You too, ma'am."

They walked out the door and started back up the road.

"Crap, what just went down?" Rachette asked.

"Besides you antagonizing her? The thickness of my wallet?" There went the eighty bucks Wolf had taken out of the hospital ATM before they'd left.

"Yeah, sorry about that. I'm hungry. I can't think straight when I'm hungry."

Wolf eyed the grocery store across the street. His stomach ingested another portion of itself with a long creaking noise he could hear in his skull. "Let's get some—"

"Hey!"

They stopped and turned around, and saw Jill Sobeck running up the sidewalk after them.

"What the hell was that all about?" She asked as she reached them.

"Hey, I'm sorry for being rude," Rachette said.

She glared at Rachette, then looked up at Wolf. "If you want to talk to me about something, then spit it out."

"I'm detective Dave Wolf, and this is Detective Rachette. We're from up north, Rocky Points. We're working the case with your husband. And Deputy Triplett."

"And you saw me with him a few minutes ago."

Wolf looked at Rachette. "Yeah. We did. And that's none of our business."

"He gave me a ride to work. My husband usually does, but he's not staying with me right now, so he was doing me a favor. It's not anything more than that, if that's what you're thinking."

"Like I said. None of our business."

"Well, it's my business what people in this town think, and you're about to go around spreading rumors. Especially if you're working with my husband. So, just so you know, me and Deputy Triplett are not doing anything together. Got that?"

"Okay." Wolf nodded sincerely. "I understand. We're sorry, isn't that right, Tom."

"Yes, sorry."

She put her hands on her hips and huffed a breath, looking back toward the diner. The owner was looking out the door, then ducked inside.

"Shit. Bye." She turned to leave.

"If your husband's not at home, where's he staying?" Wolf asked.

She stopped and turned around. "Like you said. None of your business." She walked away, then stopped again. "And thanks for not getting me fired. I guess."

"I'm in love with that woman," Rachette said.

"And your wife?"

"Her too. But there's just something about that one. I can see why Triplett was groping her like that, then staring at her like that, then clearly fantasizing about her like that."

Wolf raised an eyebrow and started crossing the street to the grocery store. "You're a sucker for women who seethe with hatred toward you."

"I love all women."

"You said it, not me."

CHAPTER 24

Wolf parked next to Rachette in the community lot by the Ridgway Marshal's office building, still chewing the second microwaveable breakfast sandwich he'd purchased at the grocery store across from Lucille's Diner.

He eyed the vehicles out front of the Marshal's office, noting the absence of the CBI van.

Stepping outside, the air was cool with a slight breeze out of the west carrying the sound of children playing in the park.

Two kids were kicking a soccer ball near the back of the building with their mothers sipping coffee and looking on, oblivious to the row of disturbing photos hanging on the interior wall just a few feet away from their backs.

"What kind of reception you think we're going to get?" Rachette asked.

"It might be a good idea if you let me do the talking."

"Understood."

They walked to the front door of the building, passing a man with a Ridgway police uniform talking to Deputy Sobeck.

"Can I help you?" the uniform asked as they veered up the sidewalk toward the entrance.

Both Rachette and Wolf were dressed in button up shirts and jeans, badges on belts next to their service pieces.

"That's Detective Wolf from Rocky Points," Sobeck said, stepping toward them.

They shook hands, and Wolf introduced Rachette.

"Could I speak to Sheriff Roll, please?" Wolf asked.

"I thought you were on your way up to Rocky Points," Sobeck said. "What happened to the old man?"

"Heart attack."

"Whoa. Is he okay?"

"He's stable."

"Glad to hear it. I heard he bit the dust pretty hard last night."

Wolf nodded. "Sheriff Roll inside?"

"Yeah. Go ahead."

They went inside and approached Cassandra Windell.

"Hello Detective," she said with a tired smile. "Back again."

"Hi."

"What are you doing here?" Sheriff Roll stood next to the coffee machine at the back of the room. "I thought you were on your way up to Rocky Points with the old bastard."

Wolf smiled. "I wanted to talk to you, first."

"How's he doing?"

"Stable. He'll be going under the knife tomorrow morning."

"They use a saw for that kind of work." Roll patted his own chest. "Who's this?"

"I'm Detective Rachette, sir." Rachette stepped forward but Roll made no move away from the coffee maker.

"Okay." Roll stirred some sugar into his cup and walked toward the murder room. "Come on in."

They followed after him.

Deputy Triplett sat at one table sipping coffee and staring at his phone. He looked up and frowned at the sight of Wolf and Rachette. "What the hell's this?"

Roll stopped and looked at his deputy. "What the hell's what?"

"Oh. Nothing."

"This is Detective ... what was it?"

"Rachette."

"Oh. Hey." Triplett nodded and went back to his phone.

Roll looked between them suspiciously.

New pictures had been added to the perimeter of the pen board. Photos of Kyle Farmer's exhumed body, covered in dried blood and soil, were on display.

"CBI guys are up in Montrose overseeing the autopsy." Roll sat at one of the tables and crossed his legs. His eyes were almost swollen shut.

"You get some sleep last night?" Wolf asked.

"After the hospital I went back up to the scene. So, not really. You?"

"A few hours."

"What's up?" Roll asked.

"I have some new information."

"Yeah?"

Wolf told Roll about the bracelet wrapped on Kyle's fingers being Jesse's.

"Is that right."

Triplett looked up from his phone. "He's trying to get caught."

"I was kind of thinking along the lines that maybe somebody was trying to make it look like he did it," Wolf said. "He asked his uncle for help, but left the bracelet his uncle would certainly recognize in Kyle's hand?"

Roll sipped his coffee. "Jesse's agreed to talk to us this morning. We'll make sure and ask him about that. I appreciate the intel, thank you."

"You're going to talk to him?"

"That's right. We're leaving in a few minutes."

"And how about the autopsy?" Wolf asked. "Is it done yet?"

"Yes, sir. We'll be seeing Kyle at the morgue this morning, too."

"Prints on the headlamp?" Wolf asked.

Roll sipped his coffee. "They had partials, but no match."

"No match to Jesse Burton?"

"No."

Wolf frowned. "Are they sure?"

"They're sure. They have Jesse's prints, checked them against the partial. No match."

Wolf and Rachette exchanged glances.

"Where'd they take the body?" Wolf asked.

"Up to Montrose. Everything's up in Montrose. One of these days we'll join the twenty-first century down here."

"I hope not," Triplett said under his breath.

Wolf stared at Roll for a beat. "You mind if Detective Rachette and I tag along this morning?"

Roll narrowed his eyes. "I appreciate the help about the bracelet, but I think we have this covered, Detective. No offense. I've just got enough on my plate to juggle anyway. Adding another couple detectives to the mix is more of a hindrance."

"I promised Burton I'd see this through," Wolf said.

Roll clucked his tongue. "Not really my problem." He got up and forked open the blinds.

Triplett swiped and tapped his phone. Rachette sniffed and crossed his arms.

"Just like that? I'm supposed to go back home empty handed?"

Roll shrugged. "This was never your case, Wolf."

Wolf looked out the doorway and saw Cassandra Windell stirring a cup of coffee. She glanced inside the room and walked away. "Sheriff, could I speak to you privately for a moment?"

Roll snapped the blinds shut and, after some deliberation, nodded to Triplett.

Slowly, Triplett rose to his feet and walked out.

"You too," Wolf told Rachette.

Wolf waited for the room to clear and then spoke softly. "When Burton and I first came into town, he told me a story."

"Did he? And what was that story about?" Roll crossed his arms.

"About something he once saw down in Ouray."

Roll chuckled. "You really gonna try this right now, son?"

"Try what?"

"You've been hanging out with that old bastard too much."

"It's true, though. Right?" Wolf looked to the still-open doorway and lowered his voice some more. "You were cheating on your wife with another woman, and he saw it happen."

"You don't need to lower your voice, Detective. I have nothing to hide." He stepped toward Wolf. "Are you really about to try and threaten your way into this case?"

Wolf blinked. "It's true."

"You want to know something interesting about that woman Burton saw me with down in Ouray all those years ago?"

"Sure."

"It is true. I was cheating on my wife with her. Her name was Helen. And you want to know something interesting about Helen? Just like me at the time, she too was in a troubled relationship. In fact, she left her husband right after that. And I left my wife a few days later. And now? Guess what?"

Wolf shook his head.

"Helen's my wife!" Roll's voice all but echoed through the building. He looked Wolf up and down. "When this case is said and done, I might just have to reconsider my stance on David Wolf and the way he kept that information on Jesse Burton's whereabouts from this investigation. I'm sorry, son, but I'm going to have to make this year just as bad for you as your last year. No choice."

Wolf lowered his eyes and nodded.

"Now get the hell out of here. Before I have you thrown out."

Wolf stayed where he was. "I Googled your current wife. She's your second."

Roll stared at him.

"I've met Helen before. She works with Montrose

County. Narcotics task force. Does a lot of planning and admin work for the team."

"Good job, Detective. You want a merit badge?"

"I've met your receptionist before, too. Cassandra Windell."

Roll sucked in a tense breath and his eyes showed his real rage had morphed to the artificial kind.

"It took me some time, but when I saw you two together yesterday, it clicked. The first time I met Cassandra was a few years back at the LEO conference in Crested Butte. She was your companion at that event at the bottom of the ski resort convention center. That's where I met her, and then we saw you two later that weekend together back in town. Sheriff MacLean and I were staying in a bed and breakfast, and you were staying there too. In fact, you were at the other end of the hallway from us, but you were oblivious to that fact. Probably because you were preoccupied with her."

Roll walked to the door, looked out, then shut it.

"I remember MacLean telling me something to the effect that you 'got around more than a carousel,' or something not-clever like that. I thought nothing of it, until Burton told me his story about Helen and your first wife, and I saw you and Cassandra. You know how the saying goes: Once a cheater, always a cheater."

"All right, listen here, asshole." Roll pointed his finger.

"I don't give two shits about you and whatever carousel you're on," Wolf said. "I care about seeing this case through for Burton. He's concerned about his nephew. He's let the kid down in the past and doesn't want to let him down now. I'm here to help, not hinder your investigation. If he's the killer, then he's the killer. I have no stake in the outcome. I just need to see it through."

Roll put his hands on his hips. He scratched his head. "I didn't think anyone else from the conference was in that bed and breakfast."

"Only another sheriff from a neighboring county and his chief detective."

"Shit."

"Three doors down. We spoke a few times."

"Really?"

"You were caught up in the moment."

Roll stared at the floor.

Wolf slapped him on the shoulder and opened the door. "I'm going to grab some coffee. Let me know when we're leaving for Montrose."

CHAPTER 25

"THEY'RE NOT COMING BACK?" Patterson sat down at her desk and wiggled her mouse, waking up her computer screen for something to do. Then she stood back up. "What do you mean they're not coming back? Why?"

"Rachette says he's staying to help Wolf," Yates said. "I guess Wolf wants to stay and help with the case down there. Have you heard about Burton?"

"Yeah." She had heard the news last night, actually. Of course, she hadn't heard the news from Wolf himself but from MacLean.

"We're all supposed to be at the meeting," Patterson said. "All of us. Not just me and you."

Yates shrugged. "They're not coming."

Wolf had been ignoring her calls for two days now, only shooting her a robot-sounding text last night that he was okay and would be home soon. No mention of the harrowing experience of bringing Burton into the hospital after a heart attack. And now this, deciding to skip out on the meeting, and still no word.

She kept her face blank, trying to hide the hurt. "All right. Whatever."

She turned back to face her computer. An update box popped up on screen and she ticked the button to start a minutes-long process to make her computer usable again.

Yates sat at his desk. "You want to carpool to the meeting together?"

"Oh yeah. Sure." She stood up and went for another cup of coffee. She was still running on fumes. Once again, she'd gotten no more than a few hours rest the night before. At least she'd gotten home in time for dinner with the kids.

Wolf and Rachette were staying down in Ridgway.

She knew it must be important, but she just couldn't shake the feeling something more was going on. Was Wolf ignoring her? Surely he'd heard about the interviews now that he was with Rachette. Was he feeling animosity toward her for not saying anything? Or was there just too much going on down there for him to deal with.

For heaven's sake, Burton had had a heart attack the night before. He was in the hospital right now, hanging on by a thread. She poured a cup of coffee, mentally slapping herself in the face. Get it together, woman.

She needed sleep.

And she needed this Council meeting to be over, for better or worse. After that, whatever was to be decreed by the powers that be would be decreed. And she could get on with her life. They all could.

She froze on her way back to her desk, because at the head of the squad room she saw Carl Yorberg walking to MacLean's office.

She watched with interest as the man knocked on MacLean's door.

Through the glass, MacLean looked up from his desk and waved the man in, offering him a seat.

Carl refused the seat and launched into a speech that had them both looking out the windows, and straight at her.

She looked over her shoulder, but that was dumb, they were clearly looking and talking about her. With her face growing hotter, she narrowed her eyes and tried to lip read, but it was impossible through the cracked blinds.

"What's happening?" Yates stood next to her. "Oh, look, our favorite person. What the hell does he want now?"

"I don't know."

Carl gestured, and again the two men looked straight at Patterson.

"What are they talking about?" Yates straightened. "That asshole better not be making a complaint."

Carl seemed to be done with whatever he had to say, and MacLean gave him a hearty handshake.

They walked out of the office and MacLean led Carl straight for them.

"Detectives," MacLean said. "You know Mr. Yorberg?"

"Mr. Yorberg," she said.

"Mr. Yorberg." Yates nodded. "How are you and the missus doing?"

"We're doing great," Carl said. "And, in fact, that's why I came in to talk to the sheriff here."

Carl stared at her, looking like he might pass out or something, and then he broke into a strained smile. "I wanted to thank you for what you said yesterday morning. I went into the library after you left and got on a computer and did some research, you know, some looking into the communications I've had with the man I told you about."

Carl studied one of his yellowed fingernails.

"Well, the more I looked at the messages, the more I realized you might have been right. And I started digging through the forums, and I found some people actually warning about this guy. Heck, I feel like an imbecile, but I'm not too proud to say thank you. You saved our family a lot of money by talking with me."

She felt herself blushing under the attention. "Well, I'm glad I could help."

"Thank you." Carl held out a hand.

She grabbed it and shook, feeling something sticky on her palm. "You're welcome."

"Bye, Sheriff." Carl walked out.

Wiping her hand on her jeans, she eyed MacLean and Yates.

"What was that about?" Yates asked.

"That was a citizen thanking his public servant for a job well done," MacLean said. "Good piece of work, Patterson."

Yates looked uncomfortable, confused, and now she realized she had failed to tell Rachette or Yates about her visit to the Yorbergs yesterday morning.

"Weren't you and Rachette with Carl and Minnie Yorberg for most of a day Sunday?" MacLean asked.

Yates pulled his eyebrows together. "Yeah."

"And yet Patterson here figured out the inverted pyramid scheme Carl had himself wrapped up in. Or was that you guys? Did you help with that?"

Yates looked at Patterson and shook his head. "No, sir. That's the first I'm hearing about it."

"Yeah, I can see by the look on your face." MacLean slid his eyes to Patterson. "Good work, Heather. I told you're good at this job."

MacLean stared at her for an awkward few seconds, and then left back to his office.

Yates stared at her. "You didn't tell us about going to talk to Carl and Minnie yesterday morning?"

Patterson shook her head, her face flushing hotter. "It completely slipped my mind with all the news about Wolf and Burton."

Yates nodded. "Ah."

"I'm sorry. I forgot."

After a long silence, he squinted. "Is it all true? Is Wolf getting axed, and you're stepping in?"

The blood drained from her face. "No. What? Yates, I don't know what's going on. I'm just as in the dark as you are."

Yates looked toward MacLean's office.

MacLean stood on the other side of his office windows. He had a cell phone to his ear, smiling while he spoke. Staring right at her.

Yates left the squad room.

"Yates. Damn it."

MacLean shut his blinds, an act he rarely did. "I like to be as transparent as I can," was the man's catch phrase that he beat into his deputies like a sales slogan.

Fists clenched by her sides, she sucked in a deep breath through her nose and walked toward the sheriff's office.

But DA White strode into the squad room and cut her off.

She stopped and watched the two men converse for a few seconds outside his office and then leave.

"You okay?"

She turned and saw Charlotte Munford-Rachette staring at her with a concerned expression.

"You look like you're about to punch somebody's lights out." Charlotte looked down at Patterson's hands.

Patterson unclenched her fists.

"What's going on?" Charlotte asked. "What did Tom do?"

"What?" Patterson shook her head. "Tom didn't do anything."

Charlotte joined her watching MacLean and White leave down the hall. "Is this about Wolf? Tom told me about his interview with the council."

There was no sense lying to her friend. And she knew that anything Tom Rachette knew, his wife was fully briefed on. "Yeah, it is."

"You think you're going to take Wolf's job?"

She flicked her eyes to Charlotte. "That's what Tom said?"

Charlotte's face flushed. "No. He—"

"I'm not going to take Wolf's job, Charlotte."

Charlotte shook her head, then stood with her hands on her hips. "Well, isn't that what's going on?"

"No. It's not. And I can't believe one of my friends would accuse me of doing something like that."

"It's not something you're doing, Heather. It's something that's happening. It's out of your control."

"Whatever, you don't know what you're talking about, so

why don't you just stop. We all have to stop spreading rumors. It's childish."

Charlotte held up her hands and walked to her desk.

Patterson suddenly felt trapped. Her heart raced inside her chest and there was no stopping it. She grabbed her car keys off the desk and left. Exactly where she was going, she had no idea.

CHAPTER 26

THE DRIVE north from Ridgway to Montrose wound into increasingly open land. The bleached looking hills on either side of Highway 550 were covered in low shrubs and winding motorcycle trails.

Wolf gazed out the window, inhaling the scent of Rachette's chewing tobacco floating through the cab.

"I don't know," Rachette said. "I've been thinking. Maybe Jesse's psychotic. Maybe he came back to the scene of the murder with a different set of boots on. Maybe he decided he wanted to be caught and tucked that bracelet in Kyle's hand."

Wolf looked at him. "And the headlamp?"

Rachette spat in a can. "He borrowed it from a friend. He dropped it in the commotion of burying a dead body. It was dark, he couldn't find it. You know, like when Thelma drops her glasses on Scooby Doo?"

Wolf turned and stared out the passenger window some more. He was dead tired and glad Rachette was here, if not to poke holes in his theories, then to drive.

The monotony of the haul back and forth between

Ridgway and Montrose seemed to add weight to his eyelids, and when he closed them once, he woke up to the jarring of Rachette parking and shutting off the engine.

"My ass hurts," Rachette said, opening the door and standing. "Haven't driven this much in one day in...well, a couple days. But still."

Wolf got out onto tired legs and stretched.

The parking lot outside the Montrose County Morgue baked twenty degrees hotter than the temperature they'd left down in Ridgway. The surrounding land was table flat, albeit backdropped with the mountains to the east and low hills to the west, checkered with crops that filled the air with a spicy scent.

Wolf and Rachette parked between the Ouray County FJ and an Explorer cruiser. They walked to the front entrance of the Montrose County morgue, joining Roll, Milo, Triplett, and Sobeck before walking inside.

The air smelled of chemicals, and if the contents of the building didn't induce gooseflesh, the temperature did.

They were met at the front by the county coroner, a bald, round man wearing frameless glasses named Dr. Fingston.

Wolf followed in the rear as they were led through a series of corridors, each colder and more sterile than the last.

"Here we are," Dr. Fingston said as they entered the formaldehyde stench of the autopsy room.

Special Agent Rushing and Jackson of the CBI were also inside, standing next to a metal table with Kyle Farmer's flayed open body lying atop it.

"Special Agent Rushing, Jackson," Roll said, looking like he was keeping his eyes well away from the brightly lit spectacle in front of them.

Nobody seemed comfortable with the sight. Sobeck hung back, keeping a few feet behind Rachette, who was always at the fringes when a corpse was involved.

"What did we find out?" Roll asked.

"You can see his insides are pretty torn up," Dr. Fingston said. "We found two hollow point .45 caliber slugs, one in his upper chest, one destroyed his heart. That's the one that did him in.

I believe you'll find it interesting that rigor mortis had already set in for a number of hours before the body was buried."

Special Agent Rushing nodded and pointed at the side of Kyle's body. "You can see the bruising on his side. That's where the blood pooled when he fell after being shot. Or, at least the blood that didn't end up on his porch."

"So he was killed, left for a few hours on his porch, and then moved to where he was buried," Detective Milo said.

"That's correct."

"Let's talk about the bracelet," Special Agent Rushing said. He looked at Agent Jackson, who

picked up an evidence bag containing the bracelet and brought it back to the group.

"Agent Rushing tells me he thinks the bracelet was wrapped around Kyle's finger before he was wrapped in the tarps and buried, and I concur. There is minimal blood on this bracelet, and there's just no other explanation."

"Mr. Burton told Detective Wolf this morning that the bracelet was Jesse's," Milo said.

The two CBI men and Dr. Fingston looked at Wolf. Sobeck stepped away, looking at his phone.

"That's right," Wolf said, and he told the backstory of Burton giving the bracelet to Jesse's father.

Sobeck came back with his phone and turned it toward the sheriff. "Sir, take a look at this."

He tapped the screen and a video started playing with sound.

"... Sons of Righteousness and Light—"

Sobeck tapped the screen and the video paused. "Look."

Jesse and Kyle were sitting on the side of a hill, staring into a camera. Jesse had his hand up to his face, and the bracelet was clearly fastened on his wrist.

"I remember that bracelet now," Sobeck said. "He's always worn that thing."

Triplett leaned down over the screen. "Yeah. I remember him wearing that, too. Now that I think about it."

Roll nodded. "All right, what else? If you don't mind, I'd rather get this over with as quickly as possible. Not exactly my favorite place to hang out. Time of death?"

"Impossible to be certain. But, judging by the larvae found in his wounds, it's looking like Friday night."

"And Kyle's phone?" Milo asked. "Is that providing any other clues?"

"He received a call from Hettie Winkle a couple hours before the fight happened," Rushing said. "A call from Jesse earlier that morning. Other than that, Kyle's phone's GPS coordinates place him at the bar, then home. And that's that."

"What about the tarps wrapped around Kyle?" Roll asked. "Any prints on those? Anything there?"

Rushing looked at Jackson.

Jackson shrugged. "There's a lot of blood on the interior of those tarps, as you can imagine. But no prints."

"And on the exterior?" Roll asked. "Any trace fibers, say, a glowing orange hair or two?"

Jackson shook his head. "No, sir."

"How is it the killer wrapped him in the tarp and doesn't leave a single print?" Roll asked.

"It's not the best fabric to begin with to retain fingerprint oil." Jackson shrugged. "He could have been using rubber gloves if he was smart."

"And on the bracelet?" Roll asked. "How about prints on that?"

"Just a lot of Jesse Burton's," Rushing said.

"Prints in blood?" Wolf asked.

"No, sir."

They stood in silence for a beat.

"You know who wears rubber gloves?" Triplett asked the room. Nobody answered. "Weed growers, when they're picking their product."

Roll nodded. "We'll keep that in mind, deputy. We'll keep that in mind."

"You guys want to head out to the garage and check out the vehicles now?" Dr. Fingston asked.

"Yeah, sounds great," Rachette walked out the door and up the hallway.

"The other way!" Rushing called after him.

"Whatever." Rachette about-faced and marched back to them as they poured out of the room.

Rushing led them down the hallway and outside of the building, into warmth that felt like a nurturing blanket on Wolf's skin. The scent of onions growing in the fields smelled like the most succulent dessert Wolf ever compared to the building they'd just left.

"I don't care what anybody thinks," Rachette said, although he kept his voice low, "I'll never get used to that shit."

They walked along the edge of the building toward an open roll door, where Jesse's Jeep Rubicon stood inside, doors open. Next to that, a black Chevy pickup that looked like a relative of Jed Farmer's vehicle stood parked, its doors also ajar.

At Rushing's request, they stopped at a rectangle of light spilling into the smooth floor of the open garage. He walked to Jesse's Jeep and pointed at the driver's side door. "We found a number of fingerprints, in blood, on the exterior handle."

"Whose prints?" Roll asked.

"Jesse's."

"Whose blood?"

"Jesse's."

Roll looked disappointed. "So, probably blood from the fight."

"That's what we're thinking."

"What else?" Roll asked.

"Some more on the steering wheel, seatbelt, stick shift. Again, all Jesse's own blood, which we assume is from the fight. Trace amounts of GSR on all of it, too."

"That's not good for Jesse," Roll said, perking up.

Rushing gestured to the back of the vehicle.

"There're also trace amounts of gunshot residue in the rear cargo area, which we would expect to find in anyone's car who frequented a gun range. And as you probably know, GSR can stick on skin and clothing for many days, weeks. So, the steering wheel GSR could have been from some point earlier. At least, that's what any good defense attorney would say."

"There must have been GSR found on Kyle from getting shot," Roll said. "And we have the GSR from the trees out back of Alexander Guild's place. Can't you match the GSR signature to this here on the steering wheel?"

Rushing nodded. "If the GSR found on Kyle or at Alexander Guild's was somehow tagged with special elements."

"And was it?"

Rushing shrugged. "No. And, keep in mind, there was significant environmental degradation to the GSR samples everywhere. On the steering wheel, it was smeared in blood. Behind Mr. Guild's house, it was doused in rain for hours. To definitively put a match on the GSR on the steering wheel with either the gun that shot Kyle, or Mr. Guild, is beyond our capabilities. We'll have to send the samples to Denver and get a specialist to look at everything."

Roll shook his head. "Okay. What else?"

"We've found Jesse's orange-dyed hairs on his driver's side, and we've found long strands of blonde hair on the passenger side, along with another set of fingerprints, which we're assuming are Hettie Winkle's, but we're going to need a copy of her prints from you guys to confirm that."

"We'll get you that," Roll said. "What about microscopic fibers?"

"I've found nothing that stands out with my initial look at the fibers. We'll have to wait for the Denver lab for a thorough analysis. And that's about everything we have on Jesse's vehicle."

"What about Kyle's?" Milo asked.

"We found a bit of blood, Jesse's blood, on the steering wheel. And Kyle's prints. Suggesting he had Jesse's blood on him when he left the scene of the fight Friday night. Other than that, nothing out of the ordinary as far as we can tell."

Rushing rounded the pickup. "We found Jesse's fingerprints, and what we're assuming are Hettie's, all over the passenger side. But there's no trace of Kyle's blood with either of them." Rushing shrugged. "Kyle and Jesse were friends. Hettie was Kyle's girlfriend. It would stand to reason that they rode in his truck from time to time."

"So, waiting for Denver lab results aside, what are we reading from this?" Roll asked.

Milo cleared his throat. "When we look at Jesse's Jeep, at least from the point of view of a defense attorney, it looks like Jesse got bloodied up in a fight, then drove himself home. There's no evidence here tying him to dumping Kyle's body. But as Agent Rushing said, they scraped the seats. There could be trace fibers from the tarps, found inside his car. That could put him at the scene."

Rushing nodded. "That's something I looked for. But I didn't find anything. That's not to say the labs in Denver won't."

"The killer stomped around in that blood," Wolf said, "how about on the foot pedals? Any blood there?"

Rushing shook his head. "None."

"No mud that matches that soil near the mound?"

"No, sir."

Milo cleared his throat. "Pete told us those boot prints found behind Mr. Guild's house, and the ones going up the hill from the trail below to Kyle's house, were completely different than those found stomping around in that blood on his porch. You agree with that?"

Rushing nodded and pulled out a smartphone with an oversized screen. He tapped it and brought up some images. "I agree with your tracker's analysis of those footprints. He's right, as you can see here."

Rushing showed the screen, which had digital drawings over photographs of the two footprints side-by-side. Next to each print was a measuring stick.

"You can see the two prints are different treads, and slightly different sizes. The ones we found in the blood on the porch, and inside and behind the gun shed, are bigger."

A car passed outside, its tires crunching on tiny pebbles as it disappeared around the corner.

"So, there's two different guys," Roll said.

"Or one guy, two pairs of boots," Milo said.

Roll looked at him. "Why change boots?"

"Maybe the killer did all the killing the first night, Friday night," Milo said. "And then he came back and did the stomping, and the burying of Kyle's body the next day."

"With different sized boots," Roll said.

Jackson lifted his index finger. "Those boots stepped in that blood when it was still wet, which suggests everything we're seeing, the two murders, and Kyle Farmer's burial, all happened Friday night."

"How long does it take for a puddle of blood like that to dry?" Triplett asked.

Jackson shrugged. "It's very difficult to say. One would have to account for environmental factors and the depth of the pool of blood. A droplet of blood left to dry on a surface would probably take around an hour to completely dry. But it was raining Friday night, so it was humid, and there was a lot more than a drop of blood on that deck. I still only give it three, four hours tops, for it to still be wet enough to make those footprints."

"What about fingerprints on that headlamp?" Wolf asked. "You said you found a partial, but it didn't match anybody?"

Agent Rushing smiled with exasperation. "That partial wasn't complete enough to match in IAFIS. But, in my opinion, under the microscope, I'm not seeing the print matching Kyle, Jesse, or the third set we're calling Hettie's prints. I don't want to seem too confident on this, and I've included the prints in what I'll send to the lab in Denver, but," he shook his head. "It's not matching any of the prints we've found. It's a completely different pattern."

Roll sighed. "We're looking for somebody else."

"Somebody with Jesse's bracelet?" Milo asked.

The silence dropped down on them again.

"This is making a frick-all of sense to me." Roll said as he eyed his watch. "Okay, thanks everyone. Right now we're just blowing smoke up each other's asses. We have an appointment with Jesse Burton. He wants to talk? Maybe he's the magic key we've been waiting for." The sheriff walked out of the garage.

"What do you think?" Rachette asked, walking next to Wolf as they followed the group through the parking lot.

"I think the sheriff's right. Maybe Jesse's ready to talk for a reason. And maybe something will start making sense."

CHAPTER 27

THE MONTROSE DETENTION CENTER was a parking lot away. Too far to walk, too close to take more than thirty seconds driving.

Wolf and Rachette finished the drive, parked near Roll's FJ and Triplett's cruiser again, and climbed out of their vehicle.

Outside, Sheriff Roll and Detective Milo stood close to one another, with Triplett and Sobeck keeping their distance.

"What's going on?" Rachette asked Triplett.

"I think they're discussing their interrogation strategy," Triplett said.

A few minutes later, Roll's and Milo's huddle was over, and they were all on their way inside.

Milo entered first. He was carrying a cloth bag. Roll held open the door for everyone, and Wolf streamed in last.

"Need a hand in the interrogation room?" Wolf asked on the way by.

Roll stepped next to him as they walked down a long hallway toward a waiting room.

"No, I don't need your help, detective. You just remember this isn't your case. If it weren't for you being such a scumbag and blackmailing me, you'd be on your ass up in Rocky Points."

"You're not being blackmailed," Wolf said.

Roll looked at him. "The hell I'm not."

"You can't blackmail somebody with information that everyone already knows."

Roll went quiet.

"If you think you're hiding anything from anybody the way you're acting with Cassandra Windell, then you're mistaken."

Roll studied the hallway floor as they walked.

"Sorry to break the news."

Roll slowed to a stop. "Okay, smart guy. Then if you're so sure everyone knows, then why don't I just kick your ass out of here now?"

Wolf shrugged. "Because, once a cheater, always a cheater."

"The hell are you talking about now?"

"I'm saying, you met your second wife by cheating on your first wife. You said she was married at the time, too? That she left her current husband for you?"

Roll nodded. "Yeah. And?"

"And I'm saying once a cheater, always a cheater. It goes for everyone. You. And Helen."

Roll's eyes went blank.

Wolf slapped him on the arm and continued down the hall. "Glad I could help."

They all gathered in the reception room. Roll was last to join them, his face looking redder than usual. Sobeck announced their presence to the man on duty and the warden appeared a few minutes later.

They were led through a pair of locked doors, and down a set of corridors to a darkened room with a single window looking into an interrogation room beyond. The building was as arctic as the morgue had been but smelled like chemical cleaner instead of embalming fluid.

"Here they are," the warden said, gesturing through the tinted window to a table where Jesse sat with his lawyer. They were on the right of a table, facing left. Two empty chairs sat opposite them, waiting for interrogators. "He gives you any trouble in there, just shout."

Wolf eyed the warden, wondering if he was joking. Jesse was slouched in his plastic chair with his hands cuffed in his lap. The only part of him that showed any sign of life was his hair, which stood up at all angles. Next to him sat his lawyer, dressed in a three-piece suit and tie.

A man in uniform sitting behind a desktop computer introduced himself as Sergeant Conroy. "We're rolling camera and audio. You can head in whenever you're ready."

Roll and Milo entered. Milo sat, placing the cloth bag in front of him while Roll rested in the other chair. Rachette and Wolf took up next to Sobeck and Triplett at the one-way glass looking in.

Rachette sidled up next to Triplett, accentuating his below-average height next to the tall lanky man.

"Jesse," Sheriff Roll said. "We heard—"

"My client chooses to not answer your questions at this time."

Their voices were tinny, coming out of a pair of speakers

mounted on the wall on either side of the observation window.

Roll ignored the lawyer. "Jesse. We found Kyle's body yesterday."

"My client chooses to not answer your questions at this time," he repeated. "And we demand you either charge him or let him go."

"It was our understanding you wanted to talk to us, Jesse," Roll said.

"You were mistaken," the lawyer said. "I want you to charge my client or let him go."

"We found Kyle's body, Jesse," Roll said. "We found what you left with him, too. You wanted us to find it, right?"

Jesse raised his head. Tears escaped his eyes and streaked down his cheeks. "He's dead?"

Milo and Roll eyed each other. "Yes, Jesse. He's dead. But you already knew that, didn't you?"

"What are you talking about?"

"Jesse, you don't need to engage these men."

Wolf noticed for the first time the tattoos creeping out of the collar of the white t-shirt underneath Jesse's orange jumpsuit. Flames licking his neck. Apparently, his hair was the tip of the fire.

"We found what you left in his hand," Milo said.

Jesse shook his head and said something unintelligible.

"What?" Rachette leaned into the glass. "Hey, can you turn this up?"

Sergeant Conroy held up a thumb and the hiss of the speakers increased in volume.

"—client chooses to not answer your questions. Jesse, I advise you to not speak."

"I know. I heard you the first time," Jesse said. "I didn't do anything. I didn't kill Kyle, and whatever you're finding was planted. This is crazy. Something's going on. What did you find? What are you talking about?"

"Jesse," his lawyer pleaded.

"No. I want to hear." Jesse put his cuffed hands on the table. They seemed calm and steady. "Come on, I want to know."

Roll and Milo eyed each other.

"Jesse, why don't you tell us what we want to know, and then we'll tell you what you want to know," Milo said. "Like these lawyers say, quid pro quo."

Jesse raised an eyebrow. "What do you want to know?"

The lawyer sat back and put a hand to his forehead. "Jesse, you realize anything you say can be used against you in the court?"

"Yes. I know my rights. Thanks, Chip. I appreciate it. Don't worry, you'll get your payment."

That seemed to be enough to satisfy, or offend, the man, because he sat back, crossed his legs, and looked at his watch.

Roll nodded to Milo.

Milo reached into the cloth bag on the table and produced the evidence bag containing the bracelet. He pushed it across the table in front of Jesse. "You recognize this, Jesse?"

Jesse frowned and studied it. "Yeah. It's my bracelet. Where did you find that?"

"This is your bracelet?"

"Yes. I lost it the other night, the night Kyle and I got in a fight. It ripped off my wrist. I've been wondering what happened to it."

Milo pulled it back slowly. "You lost this during the fight."

"Yeah. I mean, I think. That's the only place I can figure. It would make sense."

"Where did you get this bracelet, Jesse?" Milo asked.

"From my dad. I took it from his stuff when he died."

Milo nodded. He reached in and got a second evidence bag, this one containing the headlamp. "Do you recognize this, Jesse?"

Jesse made a face and studied it, then shook his head. "No, sir."

Milo stared at him for a beat, then pulled it back.

"And how about the cell phone battery, Jesse?" Milo asked.

"What about it?"

"Why was it removed from your phone when your uncle and Detective Wolf came to get you down in Canyon of the Ancients."

"Isn't it obvious?"

"No, Jesse. It's not."

"I didn't want you guys to track where I was."

Milo nodded. "Is that the same reason you took your cell phone battery out of your phone on Friday night?"

Jesse stared at the desk for a full ten seconds. "I never took my battery out of my phone Friday night."

"We think you did, Jesse," Roll said.

"Why would you think that?"

They stared at each other across the table. Jesse didn't blink.

"It was in my pocket that whole time during the fight. I

noticed it was acting up after that. Kyle slammed me hard on the ground. Ask Jimmy." He glanced at the window.

Milo sat back, a mirthless smile on his lips.

"Little bastard," Triplett said under his breath.

"What happened to your father, Jesse?" Milo asked.

The question pulled Jesse's lower eyelids up. "He had an aneurism. Died in his sleep. You know that."

"And you know we're being recorded. Gotta be thorough."

"What's that got to do with anything?"

"Just trying to understand what this bracelet is all about, Jesse. Did you love your father?"

Jesse remained silent.

"Jesse, your father was never around, right?" Milo asked.

"What does this have to do with anything?" the lawyer asked.

"That's a good question, Chip," Jesse said.

"Even though we're friends, Jesse, I gotta ask the questions like this for the recording."

Jesse scoffed. "Friends. With a question like that? The way you guys harass me and Kyle all the time? That's friends?"

Milo tapped a finger on the table. "Harassing? How?"

"You guys have been all over us lately."

"You two were posting videos online that specifically said you wanted to kill Alexander Guild. You don't think that's a valid reason for us to come check on you two? See what you're up to? That's not harassment, Jesse. That's good police work."

"I never said I wanted to kill Alexander Guild." Jesse leaned forward. "Check that video. Kyle said that, I didn't."

"You guys pulled the video from the web, but I seem to remember you exploding a watermelon perched on top of a dummy dressed in a suit and tie with a sign pinned to his chest that read 'Alexander Guild.' That was you pulling that trigger in that video."

Jesse's eyes darted and squinted. "I didn't..."

Rachette looked at Wolf. "You heard of that video before?"

"Shhh." Triplett put a finger to his lips.

"Yeah, yeah."

Milo continued. "You can see why we're talking to you, Jesse. Right? You can see why you would be a person of interest for Kyle and Alexander Guild's deaths, right?"

"Jesse, I advise you to not answer that question."

"I have nothing to hide."

"It doesn't matter," the lawyer said. "They're baiting you into saying things that will be used against you."

"Just please be quiet."

The lawyer held up his hands and re-crossed his legs.

"I know it looks like I did it," Jesse said. "I was dating Hettie behind Kyle's back, and I would have been pissed off at Guild for killing Hettie's father."

"One could look at it like you were avenging her father," Roll said. "A chivalrous act."

"Whatever. Call it what you want. I didn't do it." He nodded at the bag. "So, what's with the bracelet?"

Milo picked up the bag. "When we found Kyle's body, we found this wrapped around one of his fingers."

Tears poured out of Jesse's eyes, and the suddenness and severity of his crying made everyone behind the glass exchange glances.

"Why are you crying, Jesse?" Milo asked.

"Because I miss my friend."

"You miss Kyle."

Jesse wiped his eyes, and then they erupted in more tears. The wracking sobs twisted his face. "I'm such an asshole. I was such an asshole to him. He was so nice to me."

"What do you mean, Jesse? Tell us what you mean," Roll said.

Jesse waited for the tears to stop, then he spoke with his eyes shut. "You know what I mean. I was screwing his lady behind his back. I was a bad friend." His voice was a whisper now. "I'm so terrible."

"Can you tell us about what happened at the bar, please Jesse?" Milo asked.

Jesse opened his eyes and sat back. "I had enough of sneaking around Kyle's back. Me and Hettie had been talking, and I decided I wanted to tell him the truth. It wasn't like Hettie and Kyle were that close, anyway. They were like barely ever spending the night at each other's houses and stuff. He was ..."

"He was what?"

"He was kind of an asshole to her. I didn't like it. She didn't like it. She wanted to break up with him, but then when Hettie's dad was killed a few months ago, she just checked out. She didn't have the strength to break up with him on top of burying her dad and all that."

"Why don't you tell us about you and Hettie," Roll said. "When did you two start dating? Just recently?"

"We've been dating like six or seven months now. She and I...we've always been good friends growing up. We were in the same classes in middle school, and then in high school. But, never, you know, boyfriend-girlfriend. And then, after we graduated, we kind of lost touch. We weren't really friends at all.

"But then, some time last year Kyle started dating her. They hooked up at some party, and she started hanging out with us."

"Who's us?" Milo asked. "You and Kyle? Or do you guys also hang out with other friends?"

Jesse shook his head. "You know it's just me and Kyle hanging out. She became the third. And, from the beginning, we both realized that we were attracted to each other."

"So, from the beginning you started dating Hettie behind his back," Roll said.

"No. Not from the beginning. But, like some months later...yeah...we hooked up one day and talked about it."

"But you never talked to Kyle about it," Milo said.

"No. We didn't."

"Did he suspect anything?"

"I don't think so. I think he was oblivious. He didn't pay much attention to Hettie. Treated her like a thing."

"And that made you angry," Roll said.

Jesse's eyes flashed. "No. It didn't make me angry."

Roll nodded. "My mistake."

"It made me want to tell Kyle that I was dating her. That I was going to take care of her from now on. Like I said, he didn't even like her anyway. Treated her like garbage."

Roll and Milo nodded. Said nothing.

"Anyway, we talked about telling Kyle the truth, and we were going to. But then Hettie's father was shot by Alex

Guild, and that threw a wrench in our plans. She was really broken up about her father's death, obviously. We kind of took a break after that. Hettie didn't really hang out with me or Kyle for a couple months. She was too shaken up, you know?"

"But she started spending time with you two again, right?" Roll asked.

Jesse nodded. "Yeah. And we started hanging out more."

"You and her," Roll said.

"Yeah. And this time, I was pushing to tell Kyle everything. He deserved to know, and we deserved to be together without hiding."

"And what did she say?" Roll asked. "Was she on board with that? Did she want to tell Kyle, too?"

"Yeah. She did. But she was scared."

"Why? Did she think Kyle would hurt her?"

Jesse shrugged. "Maybe. He can...could be pretty mean. I mean, you guys know."

They sat in silence for a beat.

"And, finally, we decided we were going to tell him," Jesse said. "And so we did."

"So, you two told Kyle," Milo said. "The night of the fight. At the bar."

"Yeah."

"And then what?"

Jesse scowled. "He was real pissed, that's what happened. Punched me across the table. Started swinging at Hettie, trying to slap her. Then I punched him, and he came after me. I led him outside, and I turned and faced him, and he gave me this." Jesse pointed to his still-black eye. "And the lip. He threw me down, kept hitting me until Jimmy came out and broke it up. Thanks Jimmy." Jesse nodded at the window again.

Wolf looked over and saw Sobeck narrow his eyes.

"And then what happened?" Roll asked. "You got in the fight, and where did you go?"

"Kyle got in his truck and sped off. And me and Hettie hung out for a minute or two, and then we left."

After a moment of silence, Milo opened his notebook and flipped to a page. "You went straight home?"

"That's right." Jesse looked at Milo's notebook. "Well, technically I dropped Hettie off at her house and then I went home."

"So, you dropped Hettie off and then went home."

"My client—"

"I dropped her off and went home."

"And what did Hettie do?"

Jesse shrugged. "She was home for a bit and she came over to my house."

"What's a bit? Two hours? Two minutes?"

"I don't remember."

Milo jotted something down.

"It was like an hour. I was pretty upset. I went home and smoked some weed, had a beer. Then she showed up. Whatever time that took. I wasn't staring at the clock."

"Okay, understood," Milo said.

"He said he was going to kill me," Jesse said.

Milo raised his chin. "Who?"

"Kyle. During the fight. He said he was going to kill me."

Milo stared at him for a beat, and then scribbled in his notes some more. "Okay."

Jesse sat back with a huff.

"And what about Hettie?" Roll asked. "What did he say to her?"

"He said he was going to beat the shit out of her. That he'd kill her. Make her pay. That kind of stuff."

"And what did you say?"

"I don't remember. He was freaking out. He was coming after me and telling me I'm dead. That we're both dead. That's why Hettie came over. She was scared. She wanted to be with me, and not at home with her mom. She thought Kyle might come after her."

Milo scribbled some more. "We checked Hettie's phone records, Jesse."

Jesse shrugged.

"She called you twice after you dropped her off at home. We can tell she made the first call at her house, and the second call outside your house."

"Is that a question?"

"No, Jesse. But we are confused. Why would she call you at your house?"

Jesse shook his head slowly, staring at the table. "I don't know why she did that."

"Did you talk to her on the phone?" Milo asked.

Jesse looked at him. "The battery was screwed up on my phone. How could I have done that?"

"Okay." Milo nodded and put down the pen. "Jesse, what clothing were you wearing the night you were at the bar?"

"A pair of jeans. A t-shirt. A Browning t-shirt."

"Browning firearms?" Milo asked.

"Yeah."

"You mind if we go into your house and take a look at that clothing?"

"You want to get into my client's house you can get a warrant."

Jesse seemed to like that remark from his lawyer because he nodded.

"We're working on that, Jesse. Today. Just so you know, we will be searching your house. Probably right after our talk here. Later this afternoon"

Jesse sat still, his face calm.

"Are we going to find a .45 caliber handgun?"

"Nope."

"Are we going to find Kyle's blood on the clothing you wore Friday night?"

"No."

"Are we going to find gunshot residue from that fifty-caliber rifle that shot Alexander Guild?"

"Nope."

"Did you kill Alexander Guild?" Roll asked.

"No."

"Did you kill Kyle Farmer?"

"No."

"Do you know who did?"

"I don't know." Jesse chuckled to himself. "Maybe."

Milo leaned forward. "What do you mean by that, Jesse? Maybe."

"Well, somebody trying to make it look like me, right? I've had a lot of time to think about all this sitting here. And I'm thinking maybe it's one of those two deputies of yours."

"What two deputies?" Roll asked.

"Rod Triplett. Jimmy Sobeck. Jimmy was in the PTSD group with Hettie's dad, wasn't he? He has a pretty good motive to be shooting Alexander Guild."

Wolf, Rachette, and Triplett looked down the window at Sobeck.

The man's face had gone white. He was blinking rapidly and pointedly not turning to face them.

"And, I don't know," Jesse continued. "You don't know those two, sheriff."

Roll's lips peeled back. "I don't?"

"I mean, they hate us. Frickin' hate us. Pulled me over for DUI a while back, made me eat dirt while they searched my car. I wasn't even drunk."

"Had you been drinking when they pulled you over?" Roll asked.

"I had, like, a beer. I wasn't even driving funny. It was way over the top the way they were treating us."

"Did they find anything in your car?" Roll sounded like he already knew the answer.

Jesse exhaled.

"Did they?"

Jesse said nothing.

"Because they told me they found some marijuana, a gun under your seat, and an open beer."

Jesse fluttered his lips. "That was Kyle's beer. I wasn't drunk. It was over the top."

They sat in silence for a good minute.

The lawyer cleared his throat. "If you three are done, I'd like to discuss dismissal of my client from this holding facility. You clearly have nothing on him."

"We're not ready to discuss that yet," Roll said.

"Then you'll need to charge him."

Roll stood up. "We'll be in touch soon."

"That's not good enough, Sheriff." The lawyer stood, buttoning his jacket with a flourish.

"Thank you, Jesse," Roll said, making for the door.

Milo got up slower and followed his superior out.

"How's that warrant coming?" Roll asked his deputies.

They both seemed shell-shocked. Wolf and Rachette remained silent.

"Well?" Roll asked.

"We've been watching the interrogation, sir," Triplett said.

Sobeck was still staring through the glass, eyes locked on Jesse.

"Let's get out of here," Roll said. "He's not giving us shit. The way I see it, we can remedy all that easily enough. First, we get inside his house. We have the body, we have the slugs. We get into his house and we can maybe find that weapons. We can get that clothing he was wearing Friday night. If he shot Kyle, and then wrestled around with the body, wrapping him like a burrito with that tarp, then he'll have blood on those jeans and t-shirt. He'll have GSR all over it. Maybe we'll find the boots he trudged around in."

Triplett gave his partner a sideways glance and straightened. "Yeah."

"Let's go." Roll left for the door.

"You believe what that shit bag just said in there?" Sobeck said.

They all stopped and looked at him. Sobeck's skin was red, his mouth turned down. His eyes bore into the sheriff's.

"Nope. Let's go." The sheriff walked out.

The rest of them followed, and Sobeck passed Wolf and

Rachette as they marched down the hall, beating them out to the parking lot, Triplett following in stunned-looking silence.

On the way to the car, Rachette spoke under his breath. "That was weird, right?"

Wolf watched Sobeck and Triplett climbing in their vehicle, not looking at or speaking with one another. "Yeah."

CHAPTER 28

"WHAT ARE they doing without a search warrant this late?"
Rachette asked. "You want to drive?"

"Sure." Wolf took the keys and climbed in. He had to
slide the seat back to get his legs under the steering wheel.
"You heard them, they're working on it. The judge was probably out fishing all weekend. Who knows?"

Outside, Roll paced the parking lot and spoke heatedly
into his phone. Wolf knew the feeling. The sheriff was
getting pushed on and pulled at from all sides. Wolf didn't
envy him, but at the same time Wolf couldn't help wishing he
held the reins of the investigation.

Come to think of it, he probably needed to get used to
this feeling—sitting in the car with Rachette, looking out on a
job that used to be his. Waiting on orders rather than doling
them out.

"What if Jesse's right?" Rachette asked. "And Sobeck
took the bracelet off Jesse during the fight? Or it could have
fallen off and he pocketed it. Do you know what Sobeck did
after the fight?"

"According to the bartender, he closed his bar tab and left, too."

Rachette popped his eyebrows. "Seriously?"

Wolf eyed the tinted glass of Triplett's cruiser.

"And in the same PTSD group as Hettie's father?" Rachette continued. "If he was close to Hettie's father, he'd be pissed as hell after that shooting, maybe more than the average person in town since he'd been sharing intimate secrets with the man, getting to know him. You know, buddy-buddy. You know how it is with those groups."

Outside, Roll hung up his phone and walked to Sobeck and Triplett's car. After a quick conversation with the sheriff, Triplett rolled up his window and drove away.

"How about you stay here." Wolf popped open the door and got out.

Roll walked over and met Wolf at the front of his SUV.

"What's the word?" Wolf asked.

"We're still trying to get that warrant. I can't get a straight answer." Roll sighed heavily. "But they're saying no more than two hours. So we wait."

"Do we know where Hettie Winkle is right now?" Wolf asked.

Roll eyed him. "Why's that?"

"Because I'd like to talk to her."

Roll blinked. "This isn't your investigation, detective."

"What did it look like the first time you spoke to her? Like she was lying?"

Roll thought about it. "I didn't get the impression she was lying."

"When you talked to her, did you tell her about the blood you found up at Kyle's house?"

"No. I didn't."

Milo climbed out of the FJ and walked over to them. "What's happening?"

"We're discussing Hettie Winkle," Roll said.

"I think we should talk to her again," Milo said.

Roll nodded. "Okay, why don't you give her a call. See if she's home or at the diner, or what."

"The diner?" Wolf asked.

"She works at Lucille's. The diner in town," Roll said.

"With Jill Sobeck?"

Roll nodded. "Yeah. So what?"

"Just curious, I guess."

Milo hesitated.

"What is it, detective?" Roll asked.

"Sir."

Roll waved a hand. "I know. We have to talk to Sobeck about where he was after that bar fight. I said call Hettie Winkle."

Milo pulled his phone out of his pocket and walked away.

Wolf and Roll stood gazing at landscape in silence. Wolf could feel the energy coiled around the sheriff.

"She's home!" Milo pocketed his phone. "I told her we're coming over to talk."

Roll nodded and Milo got back in the FJ.

"See?" Roll eyed Wolf. "I don't need you on this investigation."

Wolf nodded. "Yeah. I know."

They stared at one another. "But I've decided you might be useful."

"Oh yeah? What changed your mind?"

"Because I've figured out who's screwing my wife.

There's been this guy at her office I've seen with her too much lately."

Wolf raised an eyebrow. "Glad I could help?"

Roll walked away. "Try and keep up."

The trip back down to Ridgway took twenty-six minutes, which was record time. The tailwind helped, but so did the flashers and Roll's mood. The sheriff passed every vehicle he came upon, and Wolf's forearms ached from gripping the wheel.

Up ahead, Roll's cruiser turned right into the town of Ridgway, past the motel, and hung a left onto an oiled dirt road. After traveling two blocks they were out in green pasture, among modern houses and cows.

"Nice places," Rachette said, whistling softly.

They parked in front of a two-story house on a few acres of grassland, dotted with the occasional tree. Wolf had little knowledge of the real estate market in Ridgway, but the place would have fetched over a million, maybe two, up in Rocky Points.

"Is this Hettie's place?" Rachette asked Roll as they met at the top of a walkway to the front door.

Milo had his cloth bag dangling from his hand.

"Ray Winkle was a developer," Roll said. "He did a lot of projects in Telluride. Big, multi-million-dollar homes. Hettie lives here."

"Ah."

The place had metal siding interspersed with multi-colored wood, and white stucco faces, and many windows—

artistic touches that showed Ray Winkle had been good at what he did.

The heavy wooden front door opened, and a young woman stood just inside. She had long blond hair that reached past her shoulders, framing a pretty face and big, coffee-colored eyes. She wore a turquoise checked flannel and jeans and stood barefoot on the wooden porch.

Wolf's first impression was that she was way too good for Kyle Farmer or Jesse Burton, and he wondered what the hell she was doing hanging out with a couple of misfits like them.

"Hi Hettie," Roll said, taking off his hat and stopping a few feet from the front door. "This is Detective Wolf from Rocky Points, and Tom Rachette."

Wolf and Rachette took off their caps and nodded.

Hettie stood silent, staring at them. She fidgeted with the hem of her shirt.

"Could we come inside?" Roll asked.

She looked over her shoulder.

"Is your mother here?" Roll asked.

She nodded. "Yeah. But she's sleeping."

Wolf recalled the dash clock saying it was almost noon when they'd arrived.

"How's she doing?" Roll asked.

Hettie shook her head. That seemed to be answer enough for Roll, who nodded.

"We all deal with grief in different ways," Roll said.

"Yeah. Well I'm pretty sure getting pissed drunk twenty-four-seven is a way to not deal with grief." She stepped out and shut the door. Then she sat on the step. "We can talk here."

Roll put his cap back on. "Right." He folded his arms and

eyed the monolithic peaks on the horizon. "Such a great view you guys have here."

"You have the same one from your house," she said. "What do you want to talk about, sheriff?"

Roll cleared his throat. "Hettie. We've had some developments in our case. Have you heard about them?"

She picked up a pebble and twirled it in her fingers. Wolf noticed her bare nails were bitten to the quick.

"You found Kyle," she said.

"That's right."

"He was killed. And we think it was Friday night."

She threw the pebble. Picked up another one.

"Hettie. Can you tell me about what happened after that fight at the bar again, please?" Roll asked.

"I told you. Jesse dropped me off here. I got in my car and went over to his house. Stayed there all night. Came home the next morning. Went to my shift at Lucille's."

"And, from your phone, we were able to figure out that you called Jesse twice Friday night. Can you please tell us about that?" Roll asked.

She shrugged. "I called him twice."

"Why did you call him?"

"I called to tell him I was coming over."

"Did he answer?" Roll asked.

"No."

"So, you called him. He didn't answer. So what did you do?"

"I went over to his house."

"And then what?"

She shrugged, picked up another pebble, twirled it in her fingers. "I went inside. We hung out."

"But your cell phone says you called him again. Did you do that?"

She tossed the pebble. It rolled up and stopped next to Wolf's foot.

"I called him again, yes."

"Did you talk to him at that point?" Roll asked.

"No. He didn't answer."

"Was he home?"

She nodded.

"Hettie. Can you look at me please?"

Hettie took her time, then looked up.

"Was he home when you went over there? Or was he not home, and that's why you called him?"

She put up a hand as a visor against the sun, dropping her face in shadow. "He was there. I just wanted to let him know I was there. But he wasn't answering. So I went inside."

"And then you two did what?"

She shrugged. "Had a beer. We talked. Watched television. Went to bed."

"Are you telling me the truth right now?" Roll asked.

She looked around at them in turn, then dropped her hand and picked up another pebble. "I'm not sure what you want me to say, Sheriff."

"I'm asking...was he really there? Or he wasn't, and now you're lying to me, because you're trying to cover for him?"

She said nothing.

"Because," Roll continued, "the cellular data shows that he might have taken his battery out of his cell phone."

"Maybe that's why he didn't answer then." Hettie looked up at him.

Roll smiled. "But, why would he take out the battery, Hettie?"

"I don't know."

Milo cleared his throat. "Hettie, have you seen this before?" He bent down and dangled the bag with the bracelet in front of her face.

She looked at it. "That's Jesse's bracelet."

Milo stepped back and put it in his cloth bag "We found that wrapped around Kyle's fingers. It was placed in Kyle's hand. Kyle was then wrapped in two tarps. Then he was drug down the mountain behind his house and buried in the ground."

Hettie sniffed, and wiped her cheeks.

"How about this?" Milo pulled out the second bag containing the headlamp. "How about this, Hettie. Do you recognize this?"

She looked at it and shook her head. "No."

Milo kept it in front of her. "You sure?"

"Yes. I'm sure. Are you guys through with your questions now?"

Milo stepped back and slipped the bag back into his satchel. "We're just trying to get to the bottom of what happened, Hettie. We're trying to bring justice to whoever did this to Kyle."

"Like you tried to bring justice to Alexander Guild when he killed my father?"

An icy silence took over.

Wolf cleared his throat. "What did you and Jesse talk about over at his house that night?"

She looked up at him. "Who are you?"

"I'm David Wolf. I'm a detective up in Rocky Points."

"Yeah. I heard." She shrugged. "I don't know. We talked about us."

"How did you feel after Jesse told Kyle about you two cheating behind his back?" Wolf asked.

"I felt great. It was a nice feeling. Thanks for asking."

Wolf nodded. "Why didn't you go straight over to Jesse's house that night? He was hurt, right? You could have gone with him to help him clean up. Maybe tend to his wounds?"

She frowned. "I don't know."

"He dropped you off here," Wolf said. "I just find that odd that he would drop you off here. And then you called him and went over to his house."

She picked up a pebble.

He ignored Roll and Milo's glances and continued. "Did you two get in an argument after the fight at the bar?"

She said nothing.

"He was the one who told Kyle about you two cheating behind his back, right?"

She flicked the rock into the grass.

"You had been hesitating to tell him, right?" Wolf asked. "You were probably, understandably, upset at Jesse for telling Kyle, if you weren't ready to tell him yet."

Hettie sniffed and looked at Wolf. Her eyes fell back to the ground. "We got in an argument on the way home. I told him to drop me off."

"Jesse dropped you off," Wolf said. "And then what? Later you started feeling bad and wanted to talk it out with him?"

She nodded. "Yeah. I called him. He didn't answer, so I went over there."

"But he wasn't there, right?" Wolf asked.

She shook her head. "No. He was there. He was just not answering his phone."

"I don't think he was there," Wolf said. "I think he was very upset with what happened, and then, on top of it all, he was devastated that you had rejected him after fighting for you at the bar. He fought, gallantly, for you. And you rejected him. You told him to drop you off at home. Did you break up with him?"

When she looked up her eyes were filled with hate. "You don't know what the fuck you're talking about." She got up. "I'm through talking."

"Hettie," Roll said.

"Bye, sheriff." She opened the door, slipped inside, and shut it.

Roll looked at Wolf. "You have a way with people, detective."

They turned and walked to their vehicles.

"Yeah," Milo said. "But that was highly informative. Jesse's a hothead to begin with."

"The kind of hothead who tries to stab a teacher when things don't go his way," Wolf said.

"You've heard about that."

Wolf nodded. "From his uncle."

"Heard about what?" Rachette asked. "He tried to stab a teacher?"

Roll's phone chimed in his pocket and he pulled it out. "Yeah, we're on our way." He poked the screen and stepped faster. "We have the warrant, boys. Let's move."

CHAPTER 29

THE DEVELOPMENT where Jesse's house lay was a ten-minute drive away on the other side of the valley.

A handful of boxy earth-toned modern houses stood among the low junipers and sage. Cleared lots on either side of the road without foundations or any signs of construction told of a slow real estate market, and a developer not doing as well as Hettie Winkle's father before he'd been gunned down by Alexander Guild.

The CBI van and Triplett's vehicle were already parked in front of a decent-sized house. Roll and Milo pulled up behind them and stopped, and Wolf took up end position and shut off the engine.

"Decent spread for a single male, early twenties. I have to start growing recreational marijuana."

Wolf shut his door and they walked to the gathering of men at the head of the driveway.

"We gonna be able to help with the search or what?" Rachette spat a lump of Copenhagen onto the road.

"Probably," Wolf said.

"What were you and Roll talking about back at the station this morning when you sent me out of the room?"

"Women."

"Aha. I have no idea what you're talking about."

Roll stood at the top of the driveway. "Special Agents Rushing and Jackson, Milo, and I will head in and do the search."

"I'd like to join you if you don't mind," Wolf said.

Roll took a breath to consider it and nodded. "Okay. Sobeck, Triplett." He nodded. "Rachette. Please keep the scene secure."

Wolf ignored the resentment on Rachette's face and walked down the driveway toward the house.

Rachette stood with Sobeck and Triplett, watching the men don booties and gloves and immediately get stuck at Jesse's locked front door.

"They gonna bust the door down?" Rachette asked.

Sobeck and Triplett said nothing in response.

Rachette had grown up back in Nebraska with an annoying little sister and had spent the bulk of his life ignoring her. He felt a tinge of empathy now.

Back at the house, they had pushed open the window and Sheriff Roll was climbing his way inside.

"Whoa, easy," Triplett said.

The old man disappeared into the blackened opening, and a few seconds later opened the front door. The others streamed in and disappeared into the doorway.

"There they go," Rachette said.

The two deputies ignored him again. Fine. Screw them. Rachette pulled his can, took a dip, and closed his eyes toward the sun.

CHAPTER 30

THE INSIDE of Jesse Burton's house was cool and smelled of air freshener.

The floors were brand new, as were the counters, the kitchen appliances, and the paint on the walls. And it was all covered in a thin veil of dust. Discarded microwave meal boxes littered the countertops. The trash bin on the kitchen floor was overflowing, pushing up its lid. There was a definite bachelor scent behind the air freshener.

"I'll take the bedroom," Special Agent Rushing said. "Agent Jackson will check the drains."

Roll sidled up next to Wolf. "Me, you, and Milo—let's split up and look for anything interesting."

Wolf watched Roll and Milo follow after the two CBI agents and took the opposite direction. The first door he came to was open, revealing a laundry room within. The washer and dryer were the kind with glass doors and touch screen technology, bulky and powerful looking.

He pulled open the top of the washer and looked inside.

Pieces of clothing were pressed to the edges by a spin cycle that had finished days ago.

Reaching in with his gloved hand, careful to not touch the edges of the machine in case of unseen blood smears, he picked through the clothing and found the Browning t-shirt Jesse had worn Friday night. There were a pair of jeans, as well as socks and underwear. One outfit.

"Got something?" Milo stood in the doorway behind him. Wolf showed him.

"There's a full load of laundry, and then some, waiting on the floor in his room. Interesting he decided to wash only these clothes," Milo said.

Leaving the garments for the forensics team, Wolf and Milo walked down the hallway to another door that led to a garage.

They stepped down two stairs into a two-car space, which was illuminated and warmed by a parallelogram of sunlight streaming in through a window. One spot stood vacant; in the other stood a Yamaha YZ 450 F that looked like it had seen plenty of action hitting the ground at speed.

"There's a shovel." Milo walked to a yellow-handled shovel hanging on the wall.

The detective bent down and stared close at the blade. "Well used. But clean as a whistle. If there's any dirt from up there at that campsite, they'll be able to find it and trace it back."

A rake hung next to the shovel. A push-broom. There were two tool boxes on the ground along one wall, a riding lawnmower parked under the window. Other than dirt, dust, and old leaves, there wasn't much of anything else.

"No tarps," Wolf said.

Milo nodded.

The door opened and Agent Jackson bent down and studied the knob in the glow of a powerful pen light.

"You got something?"

"Blood."

The man set down a kit and began to work.

Wolf and Milo pushed past him and moved back down the hallway, and joined Sheriff Roll and Agent Rushing in the master bedroom.

The space yawned wide and tall. An unmade king-sized bed dominated the center. At odds with the room's adult dimensions was the juvenile wall décor – a ratty poster of a woman holding a beer, an American flag, and an absurdly wide flat screen TV.

Just as Milo had reported, a pile of clothing mounded in the corner, filling the room with musty stench.

"You guys find anything?" Roll asked.

Milo reported the clothing in the washer, the shovel on the wall of the garage, and Agent Jackson's discovery of blood on the doorknob. "How about you guys?"

"Luminol's showing blood in the shower drain and the sink." Special Agent Rushing pointed to the master bathroom.

"I'm sure we'll find some more blood on that clothing in that washer," Roll said. "Or will we?"

Rushing shrugged. "We'll find out with analysis."

"Kyle beat him up pretty good," Wolf said. "He had a split lip. He would have been bleeding when he got home. It follows he would have prints on his steering wheel and door, the outside knob of his garage, in the sink, in the shower if he decided to clean off."

"Beer and weed." Roll scoffed. "Must have been some good marijuana. Made him forget to tell us about the shower he took when he got home."

Milo folded his arms. "Again, from a defense-attorney's point of view, maybe he was getting the blood off. Concerned about stains."

"Yeah," Roll said. "Or, that could be Kyle's blood he washed off his hands. Could be Kyle's blood all over the clothing in that washer." Roll rubbed the side of his neck. "Fifty-caliber GSR on his clothing and skin."

"Did you find any firearms?" Wolf asked.

Agent Rushing pointed toward the closet. "We have a Glock 17 Gen 5, nine-millimeter, and a Kimber 1911, also nine-millimeter inside there. Add that to the Kimber nine-mil you took off him down in Canyon of the Ancients."

"No forty-five," Wolf said.

"No."

Wolf walked out the bedroom and down the hallway toward the kitchen. A living room sat off to the left, where a leather couch and lounge chair wrapped around a wooden coffee table. A lipstick-smeared glass stood on an end table next to the couch.

"What do you have?" Roll appeared behind Wolf.

He gestured. "Looks like Hettie's lipstick on the glass."

"What does that tell us?"

Wolf shook his head. "Nothing."

"All right," Roll said. "Let's head outside."

They went back to the kitchen, where a sliding glass door led out to the back yard.

Outside, the sun beat down on the rear of the property, baking the air to oven temperatures.

The lawn was flat and spacious, leading toward a view of the mountains to the distant southwest. The behemoths rose up into the sky, sunlight shining off the strips of snow. Luckily, a breeze slid down from the heights, cooling the sweat beading around Wolf's cap.

Two horseshoe pits were cut into the lawn to the right, and to the left stood a tall dirt berm, which was littered with shattered glass and shot-through aluminum.

Crushed beer cans were strewn on the porch, near a well-used barbecue. The grass was over a foot long, striped with motorcycle tire gouges. Dozens of brass shells sparkled on the lawn.

Must have been a fun neighbor to have. Wolf eyed the nearest house, which gleamed to the north. Thankfully for the people living inside it they were a good quarter-mile away.

Wolf went to the lawn and picked through the brass.

Roll knelt next to him. "What you got?"

He handed over a shell. "Nine-millimeter."

Roll flicked it away and picked up another casing.

They sifted through for a few minutes, and Wolf paused as he picked up a thicker spent casing. "Got one."

"A what?"

"A Federal forty-five ACP."

"Forty-five?" Roll took the shell from Wolf and twirled it in his fingers. "Well I'll be. The bastard has one after all."

"Could be Kyle's," Wolf said. "Or someone else who brought their gun over to shoot."

Roll stared at him.

Wolf shrugged. "Defense attorney said it, not me."

Roll sighed. "And of course, those bullets were too

mangled inside Kyle to trace to a gun, a gun we still don't have."

The sheriff dropped the shell.

"You're going to need some patience to see this case through, sheriff."

Roll turned to face the mountains. "Yeah. I know. Tell that to the United States senator that called me again this morning. Or the calls from three different television stations I avoided."

Wolf picked up the forty-five shell again. "Alexander Guild's dead. There's nothing you can do about that, and all the outside interest and pressure's not going to change that. Pretty soon all this evidence is going to mount, and you'll have your answers. Other people can wait for justice to be done, the right way."

"Tell that to Jed Farmer."

Rachette took out his can again and packed another dip. His lip was getting beaten up by all the chewing. He'd been really going after it hard lately, knowing he was going to quit pretty soon. The only problem was he'd been doing that for over a year now.

"Hey, you mind if I get one of those?" Triplett asked.

Sobeck and Triplett sat in the open rear of Triplett's SUV.

"Yeah. No problem." Rachette walked over and handed over his can, happy to have a companion in his vice. "You want one too?" he asked Sobeck when Triplett handed it back.

"No, thanks. Quit that shit after the army."

Rachette suddenly realized there was a good chance he was stuck out here for a reason. Wolf hadn't fought to get Rachette involved in that search, which meant maybe he was out here to talk to these two and get some intel.

They stood in awkward silence, and Rachette mentally fanned through some lines that would make them friends.

"Met your wife," he said. "She works at Lucille's Diner, too. Right? With Hettie?"

Sobeck nodded.

"She's a good-looking gal."

Sobeck raised his eyebrows.

"I mean your wife. Not Hettie. Well, she's good-looking, too. Shit. Sorry." Rachette quit talking.

"How many deputies you guys have up in Rocky Points?" Triplett asked, thankfully changing the subject.

"Twenty-three. Then all the brass."

"Got that fancy new county building up there." Triplett had chew grains all over his thin lips. "I was up there last year. Nice place."

"Wipe your mouth, dumbass," Sobeck said.

Triplett used the sleeve of his shirt, unperturbed by his partner's scolding. The two were close, obviously.

"Yeah. Not bad, I guess," Rachette said. "We used to be in a tiny building with just a few of us. We've grown a lot, and fast. How about you guys? How many you have?"

"Me, Sobeck, Milo, and Roll."

Rachette shook his head. "You serious?"

"We have a few volunteers out there," Sobeck said. "But yeah, just the four of us on the payroll."

"You guys grow up together?" Rachette asked.

"Yep," Triplett said. "Known each other since elementary school."

"Right here? Or down in Ouray."

"Here. Ridgway."

They stood nodding their heads. Or maybe it was just Rachette. He surveyed the house, noting the professionally landscaped yard, full of shimmering aspen trees and well-maintained grass. The house was prettier than his own up in Points. Majestic Peaks rose in the distance.

"Pretty nice place for a rat-looking twenty-three-year-old kid like Jesse Burton," Rachette said.

Sobeck fluttered his lips. "Kid's got dough. You saw Kyle's house. Too much dough for the amount of brains those two have, you ask me."

"Weed," Rachette said.

Triplett spat. "Weed."

That got him some affirmative grunts and nods. He was doing better. The wife thing was probably coming right back to the forefront of Sobeck's mind right now, though.

"You two had some run-ins with them, huh? Jesse and Kyle?"

It was getting awkward again. He had to push through, there was no getting around it.

"I mean, I heard what he said. And believe me, I know what it's like to chase around the same little shits running around Rocky Points. Some of them deserve a smack to the back of the head every once in a while. Maybe more, you ask me." He spat on the ground for effect.

Silence took hold again.

"You trying to interrogate us now?" Triplett added his own spit to the ground.

Rachette frowned, insulted. "Just wondering what he was talking about back in that interrogation room. I mean, he all but flat-out accused you of framing him. I know that would piss me off. I'm not looking for answers or anything...I don't know." He was floundering.

Sobeck's face hardened and he stood up from the rear of his vehicle. "As far as I'm concerned, you and your anxiety-ridden detective buddy can go back to Rocky Points. And you can step right over there and stop talking to us right now."

Triplett stood up, too, looming over Rachette.

Rachette stepped toward them. A few inches shorter or not, a foot in the case of Triplett, he never backed down when it came to somebody insulting his family. And Wolf was, by all definitions, family.

"You'd better watch how you talk about my boss, there, Jimmy."

"Oh, really." Sobeck squared his block-like body.

The man's pecs and arms had some girth, but Rachette had experience with rumbling underneath his belt.

"Yup." Rachette raised his chin and put his own pecs into the ring.

"Hey!"

They turned to see Roll walking quickly out of the doorway, a cell phone held up in the air.

The three of them broke like a football huddle and watched as Milo and Wolf came outside after the sheriff.

"What's going on?" Triplett asked.

"Just got a call from Cassandra, who just got a call from Hettie's mother. Hettie's gone from the house and left her phone. She's freaking out, I guess."

"Weren't you just over there?" Triplett asked.

"Yeah, we were."

"You sure her mom's not drunk again?" Triplett asked.

"Of course she's drunk," Roll said. "Just go see what she wants. We'll meet back at the station."

"Yes, sir," Triplett said. The two of them shut the rear of their SUV and climbed behind the driver's seat.

Rachette took his time moving out of the way as the car backed up and almost ran him over. They were gone in a cloud of dust.

Wolf came up the driveway and watched the vehicle disappear into the distance.

"What was going on here?" Roll asked Rachette.

Rachette gave him a puzzled look. "What do you mean?"

"I mean you two looking like you were going to come to blows."

"He said something I didn't like."

Roll looked between Wolf and Rachette, then walked back toward the house with a quick stride.

Wolf lingered and came over to him. "What was that?"

"I was trying to get Sobeck to talk."

"And?"

"And he got real touchy about it. Told me you and I needed to go home and not come back."

"You got in his face."

"It got out of hand quick." Rachette sucked in a few breaths, feeling the adrenaline tightening his chest. "Sorry. I figured you wanted me to talk to him."

"I did."

"There's something about those two guys, I'm telling you. I don't trust them."

Wolf looked back toward the house with that noncommittal ice-stare he got when he was thinking hard about some angle Rachette had never considered.

"You guys find anything?"

Rachette listened while Wolf told about the clothing in the washer, the blood on the exterior handle of the garage, and the .45 shells lying in the back yard.

"Did you find the gun?"

Wolf shook his head. "No gun, no boots, no tarps, no shovel."

Rachette turned the opposite way and stretched out his back, catching a sight of a figure in the distance. "Who is that?"

Wolf turned around.

"It's her." A woman had just climbed out of a red Jeep. Rachette recognized those heart-shaped buttocks and long blonde curls hanging on a slender back from earlier that morning. "It's Sobeck's wife."

They watched in silence as she walked without hesitation to the door of the house and disappeared inside.

"That was her, right?" he asked, already knowing the answer. Her walk was distinct.

"Mmhmm," Wolf said.

"Looks like her house. You don't just walk into a house if it's not yours...wait, here she comes again."

To put a pin on the point, she came out of the door, went back to her Jeep, opened the back, and pulled out two grocery bags. A boy came skipping outside and climbed up inside the vehicle.

After she shooed him out, the boy ran around the back of the house and disappeared.

Then Jill Sobeck put a hand up as a visor and stared

down at them, her gaze undoubtedly drawn by the line of law enforcement vehicles. After a brief stare-down with the two of them she shut her Jeep and went back inside.

"Well, that's a development," he said, turning back to Wolf.

Wolf had that glare again, now pointed back down at Jesse Burton's house.

"What are you thinking?"

Wolf snapped out of it. "I'm thinking if Sobeck lives right there, then you're right. That's certainly an interesting development."

CHAPTER 31

TOWN HALL in downtown Rocky Points had not changed much since 1903. With each quick step she took, the worn pine flooring creaked under Patterson's feet. The window glass was warped and looking at the pines outside was like looking through a rain-soaked windshield. Or a deranged man's eyes.

A circle of wooden chairs sat in the middle of the room. Apparently, they were having a kumbaya session. A tray of donuts sat next to a full-to-the-brim pot of coffee on a folding card table. Could they be so out of touch that they catered the event? And who eats a donut and coffee at eleven a.m.?

Margaret nodded her greeting, and when Patterson ignored her, she returned to a sober conversation with the County Treasurer, Leopold Helms, a blowhard lawyer Patterson had met during her stint working at the law firm.

DA White, dressed crisply for a city man and over-dressed for a Rocky Mountain district DA, stood with two members of his staff. She ignored him, too.

Margaret came over. "Hey."

"Hey," she said. "Wolf's not coming."

Margaret nodded. "I know. I heard."

"I don't see how this is going to go down without him. I mean, obviously this has to do with Wolf." She looked at her aunt and shrugged. "You're just going to seal his fate behind his back?"

"Well, we don't have much choice," Margaret said. "And, as you'll see in a few minutes, it's not my choice. None of this is."

She turned away from Margaret and sat down in one of the chairs.

Over the next five minutes, she crossed her legs and toyed with her phone, radiating an air that repelled everyone except Yates, who sat down next to her with a powdered donut and a brimming coffee.

Though they had agreed to carpool there, they ended up driving separately after the scene in the squad room. She looked at him and he looked at her. He nodded, she nodded back, and he took a bite of his donut. They were good. And now she wanted a cup of coffee and a donut. But she stayed where she was and stared at her phone some more.

After another few minutes, it looked like all eight members of the council were there, along with MacLean, Wilson, and DA White.

"All right, everyone let's get started," Margaret said. "Please be seated."

All eyes went to the mayor, but she sat and folded her arms. MacLean cleared his throat and stood up.

"Thank you all for coming here today." MacLean ran a palm over his mustache and hiked up his jeans. "I first want to thank all of you for your patience."

He looked directly at Patterson after that comment.

She must have looked utterly unamused, because that's what she was trying to do.

"Right." MacLean stopped and looked down at the floor.

When he spoke next, it was blunt. To the point. The words hit Patterson with the force of a Mack truck.

Yates spilled his coffee as he set it on the floor and leaned onto his knees.

It was clear everyone but Patterson and Yates already knew. Her aunt burst into tears, which instantly added to the pools already gathering in Patterson's eyes. The more MacLean spoke, the more the group slumped in their chairs, the more they sniffed and wiped their eyes.

When the sheriff was done, he looked at Patterson. "So how about you? Are you ready to do your duty?"

She spoke but no sound came out.

"What was that, Heather?"

She cleared her throat. "Yes. Of course I am."

CHAPTER 32

"You KNOW who lives up in that house?" Wolf asked.

Milo was lining up the evidence bags outside the CBI vehicle. He stopped and looked where Wolf was pointing. "Yep. Deputy Sobeck."

They stared at one another for a beat, until Milo went back to straightening the line of bags.

Rushing, Jackson, and Roll came out of the house carrying bags of their own and brought them over.

Milo stepped aside and stood next to Wolf. "Why?"

"I think it's interesting."

"Why's that interesting?"

"I would have to know more about the history between Sobeck and Jesse Burton first. Right now, it's just a general interest in the fact that two people involved in the action Friday night live right next to one another."

Milo hitched up his pants.

"We'll meet back at the Marshal's office in thirty minutes," Roll said, walking past. "I don't care what you do, but I'm grabbing some food in the meantime."

Wolf stepped in front of Milo. "We'll drive you back."

Milo considered the offer as Roll got into his FJ and fired it up.

"I don't like where your thoughts are going."

"Who said anything about the direction of my thoughts?"

Milo eyed him. "You heard Jesse say what he said this morning, and now you're starting to consider Sobeck a suspect."

"And you've seen all this evidence turning up. Two sets of prints. A partial that doesn't match Kyle or Jesse on that headlamp." Wolf shrugged. "You have Sobeck's prints on file from when he applied to the sheriff's department."

Milo rolled his neck. "Yeah. We do."

"Well?"

Milo shook his head. "And they don't match, or else they would have come up in the IAFIS search."

"But you didn't check the partial specifically, manually, with Sobeck's prints."

Milo let out a breath. "Just a second." He walked over to Roll's driver's side window and spoke to the sheriff. They spoke for a while, then Roll drove forward, and flipped a U-turn around Milo, leaving Milo standing in the dirt road.

"All right," Milo said. "Let's go. We have twenty-five minutes, and the Burger King drive-thru down the street is slow as shit."

Wolf walked to the car. Rachette took the back seat. Milo sat down in front, saying, "And you guys are buying."

Wolf fired up the engine and followed Roll's dust trail back toward the highway.

"So," Wolf said.

"So what? What do you want to hear? We'll check the partial against Sobeck's prints."

"How about the history between Sobeck and Jesse Burton."

Milo stared out his window. "Let's see ... history. Jesse grew up here. We all did, including Sobeck. Jesse used to live in town but moved in over here like a year ago. That was after Sobeck and his family already lived here."

"Is there any bad blood between the two of them?"

"Like, was Jesse telling the truth back there in the interrogation room?"

Wolf nodded.

"They deserved what they got that night, as far as I can tell. Jesse, Kyle, and Hettie were joyriding on the back roads, hauling ass around a corner and almost went head-on with Sobeck. Jesse was driving. Sobeck and Triplett were in Sobeck's cruiser. They pulled them over, found open containers, a gun, that Kimber 1911 nine-millimeter you took off him down in Canyon of the Ancients, marijuana, a pipe."

"When did that happen?" Wolf asked.

"A couple months ago."

"And do you think that was enough to make them hate each other from that point on?"

Milo shrugged. "I do get the sense Sobeck might have roughed them up a bit that night. I don't know. Apparently Jesse mouthed off and Sobeck put him on the ground. I heard about it from Triplett."

"He put Jesse on the ground in front of his girl," Wolf said. "In front of Hettie."

Milo said nothing.

"And what about Hettie?" Wolf asked.

"What about her?"

"What's her story? She seemed angry. Does she get along with everyone in town?"

Milo shrugged. "She's a good girl. Kind of an idiot for hanging out with these two, but overall she's a good cookie. As far as seeming angry—it's a shame what happened to her dad. I don't blame her."

They sat in silence while Wolf turned onto Highway 550 toward town.

"What else?" Wolf asked.

"Well, you saw that setup Jesse has in the backyard."

"What setup?" Rachette asked.

"A shooting berm," Milo said.

"Ah. Pretty standard around here, isn't it?" Rachette asked.

"Yeah, but I guess Jesse was shooting at all hours when he moved in," Milo said. "All around a disrespectful move to begin with, especially if you're new in the neighborhood. So Sobeck went over and told him to back it down. Sobeck had his kid up there at his house trying to sleep. And it's just a little creepy having a neighbor blasting off so many shots."

"Looks like he's still doing plenty of shooting to me," Wolf said.

"Yeah, but not like he was. Believe me. They were firing at ten at night. That type of stuff."

"Okay," Wolf said.

"Anyway, Jesse and Kyle moved their parties up to Kyle's most of the time after that."

"And how did that scene play out?" Wolf asked. "I mean, was Jesse respectful? Did they have an argument? Or did he just stop?"

Milo shrugged. "Knowing Sobeck he was probably forceful."

"Forceful," Wolf echoed. "Meaning?"

"Meaning...ever since Sobeck came back from the war he's had a bit of a short fuse."

They rode in silence for another beat, and Wolf caught Rachette's eye in the rearview.

"What about Sobeck's wife and Triplett?" Wolf asked.

Milo turned toward him with a sour look. "What of it?"

"We saw Sobeck's wife coming out of Triplett's vehicle this morning, behind the diner," Rachette said from the back seat. "They were hugging. Looking pretty friendly."

Milo waved a dismissive hand. "You guys are barking up the wrong tree there. Jill Sobeck isn't screwing around with Rod Triplett. You've seen her and you've seen him, right? She's a looker, he's a chimpanzee with a voice box. I mean, they're good friends, but he's always been in the friend zone with her. You know how it is living in a small town. You know things. And Jill and Triplett? Not happening. Take a right."

Wolf turned and they eased back up the hill into town, toward Lucille's Diner on the right, the motel, and from this distance they could see the back of the Soaring Eagle Bar shining in the midday sun.

"Drive-thru all right with you guys?"

"Does a bear claw you to death if you punch it in the nads?" Rachette laughed to himself. "Yeah. It sounds good to me."

Wolf drove through and put the meal on his Visa. To Milo's credit, he fought to pay his own portion by handing over a ten, but Wolf waved it off—a move that made him think about the state of his job.

The clock read 12:15. The County Council meeting was probably already over. His fate was already determined.

They drove back to the Ridgway Marshal's office.

"Just park here." Milo pointed to a spot in the shade of an oak across the street.

"You mind if we eat here?" Wolf asked, eyeing the clock which told him they had fifteen minutes to go before Roll's rendezvous time. "I'd rather not stare at dead body pictures while I eat my hamburgers."

"Amen to that," Milo said, digging into the bag and divvying up the meals.

With the windows open to let in a fresh breeze, they ate in silence like they were in a contest.

Wolf won, with Rachette in a close second.

"Why's Sobeck not home lately?" Wolf asked.

Milo exhaled and rubbed his forehead, like he was fighting the urge to go to sleep. "He's been fighting with his wife, or something. He's not exactly an open book."

Rachette put a dip in his lip, sending a blast of Copenhagen swirling through the cabin.

"You're the detective," Wolf said to Milo. "What do you think? Is it that short fuse you're talking about?"

Milo looked around.

Roll's FJ was parked across the street from the building, but Sobeck and Triplett's vehicle was missing.

"Okay. The story going around is that Sobeck punched his kid."

"Whoa," Rachette said. "What the hell?"

"Not, like, out of anger. Not the short fuse I was talking about. And, you know what? I misspoke. He doesn't have a short fuse at all. He's just having issues separating the past from the present...or something."

The news made Wolf sit back hard. He thought back on the happy looking kid running around Sobeck's house a few minutes ago. "What happened?"

"Supposedly his boy came into his room and woke him up. He freaked out and punched him. You know, was having one of the dreams. Thinking he was back in the war."

Wolf did know. "What other problems is Sobeck having? Anything at work?"

Milo looked like he was holding his tongue.

"You think he might have gone overboard that night with putting Jesse on the ground?" Wolf asked.

Milo shook his head. "No. It's not that. I mean, he might have roughed him up a little, I don't know. I wasn't there and haven't looked at the dash footage. And I'm not about to. I'm just saying that he acts strange sometimes. It's hard to explain. He gets this far-away look. Like a deer in headlights. And then he kind of...just gets confused. Like, one time I was gassing up the cruiser and asked him to get me a coffee inside the store. He heard me, nodded with that look I'm talking about, and he came out with a flippin' cheese Danish for me. I was like 'What's this? I asked for a coffee.' And he freaked out, saying I asked for a cheese Danish. He was pissed. Like I was messing with him or had insulted his mother or something." Milo shrugged. "Just little stuff like that."

Wolf and Rachette eyed each other in the rearview.

"Check me if I'm wrong," Rachette leaned up between them, "but all this sounds like a pretty big motive for Sobeck killing Alexander Guild. I mean, I only know what I've read in a couple news articles, but the guy sold ammunition to the

US military, right? The big stuff. Bombs. Bunker busters and the like, right? The guy was the god of war. He profited on killing people. He sits in his big mansions, I'm assuming he has multiple, and he cuts off the locals who want to walk past his property to get to the local hunting grounds. He shoots them dead. Meanwhile, Sobeck is out in the field, killing people for his country, getting screwed up in the head, coming back and punching his kid."

Rachette sat back.

Milo rubbed his forehead again, his eyes clamped shut.

"You've been thinking the same," Wolf said. "That's why you're sitting here right now."

Milo sat forward and looked out the windshield with vacant eyes. "It's not something I've been wanting to think about. But yeah. He's not looking too good in my mind. He was at the bar. I can't verify his whereabouts after he left."

"Where's he staying if he's not home?" Wolf asked.

"The Timber Ridge down in Ouray. Just on the north edge of town."

"And have you talked to them to see when he showed up Friday night?"

"No. Not yet. Been kind of busy. And I'm telling you, it's been little stuff with Sobeck. Not major character changes or anything, and he's always been a good guy who's looking out for his fellow man. It's a big leap from cheese Danish to double murder."

Was it? Wolf wondered. "And how about Roll? Is he suspicious of Sobeck, too?"

"We haven't talked about it. I asked what he thought and he didn't answer. He went dead silent on the way down from Montrose. But, yeah. He's suspicious of him, too."

"And what about that PTSD group that Jesse was talking about?" Rachette asked. "Was he really in there with Hettie Winkle's dad?"

Milo nodded.

"Which adds to that giant motive I was just talking about. Guild shoots Hettie's father, which pisses off Sobeck to no end. He probably became good friends with her dad after sharing all those war stories and such, I mean, I wouldn't know. I didn't serve." Rachette spat out the rear window.

Milo was staring at his phone. "This isn't good."

"What's wrong?" Wolf asked.

"We gotta get inside." Milo got out, slammed the door, and ran across the road.

"What was that?" Rachette asked, climbing outside.

Wolf shut his door and watched Milo disappear into the Marshal's office. "Let's go."

Wolf and Rachette jogged after him. Inside, Cassandra stood with the phone pressed to her bosom. "He's already out!" she yelled over her shoulder.

Roll came out of the murder room with an incredulous look. "What did you say?"

"They released him a few minutes ago."

"Give me that." Roll took the phone from her hands. "Why the hell wasn't I told about this?" Roll's face seemed to melt as he handed the phone back to Cassandra.

She put the phone to her ear, then lowered it and dropped it to the cradle.

"They let Jesse out?" Milo asked.

Roll nodded. "Thirty minutes ago. His lawyer's driving him down now."

"What are you going to do?" Milo asked.

"It's not that big a deal, is it?" Wolf said. "You could put somebody on surveillance to make sure he doesn't flee again."

When nobody answered him, Wolf looked at the phone still clutched in Milo's hand. "Wait. What's that message you just got?"

"It was from me," Roll said. "They have Hettie."

"Who?" Wolf realized and he answered himself. "The Farmers."

CHAPTER 33

"Damn it!" Roll paced in front of the gruesome photos at the front of the room.

"What did they say?" Milo asked. "How long did they give? Where?"

"Two hours. He didn't say where. He said he'd be back in touch, and I'd better have Jesse when he called back."

"Does he know that Jesse's been released?" Wolf asked.

"I don't know. I don't see how he would."

"Maybe Jed Farmer has friends up in Montrose," Wolf said.

Roll walked to the window and looked through the blinds.

"Sir," Milo said.

"What?"

"We have to put him under arrest," Milo said. "We have to question Sobeck."

Roll turned and stared into nothing. "You really think he's got anything to do with this? It's Jesse. It's Hettie lying and covering for his ass."

"We can't skip over the signs," Milo said. "He has motive to kill Guild. We don't know where he was after the bar Friday night. He was there, and Jesse's right—he could have taken Jesse's bracelet during that fight. There are two sets of boot prints. There's the headlamp with a partial that doesn't match Jesse or Hettie. There's—"

Roll waved his hand like a bee was attacking him. "I know, I know. And Kyle? Why kill Kyle?"

Milo spoke in a low, calm voice. "I don't know why, sir. Maybe to make it look like it was Jesse."

"That's psychotic," Roll said. "That's not Sobeck. He may have had a rough time returning to civilian life, but..." Roll's voice faded away.

Milo said nothing.

"Rachette and I could go down there and take a look at the place he's staying," Wolf said. "What's it called?"

"The Timber Ridge Lodge," Milo said.

Roll scowled. "And search his room?"

Wolf nodded.

"So, an illegal search of his property. That's what you want to do."

"We have probable cause," Wolf said.

"Oh, really."

"Seems like we're erring on the side of probable cause, sir," Milo said. "A woman's life is at stake."

"Shhh," Cassandra held up a finger and looked toward the entrance. "Never mind. Sorry. It's not them."

"How about you just call Sobeck and Triplett and see where they're at," Wolf said.

Roll nodded and pulled out his phone.

Roll paced. "Hey, where are you guys? ... okay," he

turned toward the rest of them and spoke for their benefit, "you're still at Hettie's house, talking to her mother. Okay, I need you to step outside to talk. Okay, listen, I just got a call from the Farmers. They have Hettie and they're demanding we release Jesse and bring him to them or else she dies. I need you two to head back here ASAP... Bring her down to the station here and tell her the truth... Cassandra can keep her company...okay, then just leave her. Just come back!"

He hung up. His chest heaved.

"Hettie's mother is falling over drunk. It's one in the afternoon on a Tuesday, for Chrissakes." Roll pocketed his phone and folded his arms. His eyes bore through the commercial carpet.

Rachette cleared his throat. "So the issue is that we need to get Jesse up there, to wherever the Farmers tell you they are?"

Roll pulled his eyebrows together. "You employ this man?"

Rachette ignored him. "And you obviously don't want Hettie to die, which will happen if you don't bring Jesse to them. And if you bring Jesse up, that puts him in danger. Seems to me, the only way you could stall them is by telling them you figured out it wasn't Jesse."

"Then they're going to want to know who did it," Roll said.

"But you could tell them it's a trade. Hettie for the truth."

"This isn't poker. I'm not gambling for a woman's life with a three-six off-suit."

Rachette folded his arms. "Just trying to brainstorm."

"We're wasting time," Wolf said. "Let's go. You make a call to the Timber Ridge Lodge."

"And if you don't find anything?"

"Then we deal with that, then."

Roll snorted. "And what do I do about Sobeck?"

"I think it's time you ask him what he did after that bar fight."

"And if you do find something at Sobeck's?" Roll asked.

"Then we have something to gamble with."

"Probable cause, huh?" Roll nodded. "All right. Go. I'll call. Go fast."

Wolf and Rachette jogged out.

CHAPTER 34

THE MANAGER of the Timber Ridge Lodge looked between Wolf and Rachette, eyed their badges again. "What's going on, anyway?"

"We just need to get into that room, please," Wolf said. "Time's ticking."

"Time's ticking." The manager scoffed. "And you have no warrant."

"We have probable cause."

"Yeah, that's what the sheriff told me over the phone. Probable cause for what?"

Rachette slapped a hand on the counter. "Probable cause for me shoving my foot so far up your—"

Wolf pulled him away. "Sir. We have a young woman in danger, and we have probable cause to believe her life depends on us getting inside that room."

The manager turned his back as he fetched a key from a hook. "Sounds like bullshit, and next time tell Roll to come here himself and not send his lackies."

"Lack—"

Wolf put a finger in Rachette's face. Rachette clenched his mouth shut.

"Okay, follow me."

They trailed the manager outside and walked down the rear of the building along a wooden walkway. They passed balls of fragrant pink flowers hanging from hooks, and the whistling hummingbirds feeding on them. A column of steam rose from a pool in back. Two elderly women sat sipping wine, their bared breasts floating in the water in front of them.

Rachette nodded and gave a salute. "Afternoon, ladies."

They waved back with smiles.

Wolf gave him a look and Rachette's face went sullen.

The cliffs behind the building rose hundreds of feet. Wolf had been to Ouray many times, but usually just passed through. It was known as the Switzerland of America due to the jagged peaks surrounding the town. Thermal hot springs leaked out of the rocks, filling clothing-optional pools all over the valley.

The manager went straight to a first-floor room.

"Please don't touch the doorknob," Wolf said.

The manager backed away and handed over the key. "You open it then."

Wolf and Rachette put on latex gloves and bent down to study the doorknob. Bright afternoon light reflected just so off the stained wooden walkway, illuminating the entire knob clearly. Wolf saw nothing out of the ordinary but knew without a proper dusting by the forensics team there was no way to know with the naked eye.

Gingerly, he inserted the key and twisted the knob. The

door opened with a creak. Inside, the room was littered with dirty clothes. The bed was unmade.

"When is the last time the cleaning staff was in this room?" Wolf asked.

The manager shrugged, keeping his distance. "Not for a few days."

"Can you get more specific than that?"

"I don't know. I guess it was last Friday morning."

Wolf stared at him. "The staff doesn't come in to clean every day?"

"Not this weekend. She had an emergency down in Durango. I didn't get to it. Last cleaning was Friday morning." The manager's face said take it or leave it.

"I'd appreciate it if you didn't touch the room from now on unless Sheriff Roll tells you otherwise, okay?"

The manager nodded and left.

"Bye now," Rachette said.

Wolf went inside first. The queen-sized bed stood along the right wall, flanked by two nightstands, both littered with beer cans.

"Check that inside knob, will you?"

"On it."

Beyond the bed, a mirrored closet stood halfway open, revealing a pile of dirty clothing on the floor inside.

Wolf went to the closet and picked through the clothing with a pen from his shirt pocket. Holding his breath, he found a pair of jeans and checked every square inch for signs of blood.

There were none as far as his macroscopic vision was concerned. Not even on the inside of the legs, where murderers who stood over bodies and finished their victims off were often hit by spatter.

"I'm not seeing anything on the knob," Rachette said.

The shirts piled on top of the jeans looked clean, minus normal wear and tear of a man thrust into bachelorhood and whose sole piece of furniture was a queen bed. Food stains on the front—red, but most likely ketchup looking at the downward strike angle below the chin. Pizza smears from hands without napkins.

Wolf left the pile as it was and walked to the bathroom.

Rachette stood inside. "Not much here."

A toothbrush sat on the counter, next to it a travel-sized tube of toothpaste. A boxy wooden framed shower had a bottle of men's bath wash sitting on the plastic basin.

A towel hung on a hook behind the door. Wolf plucked it off and looked on both sides. Nothing obvious.

"We need Luminol," Rachette said, bending over the sink.

"Yeah."

"I don't know what we thought we were going to be able to find. But without that CBI forensics-mobile, it's not gonna be squat."

Wolf eyed his watch. It had taken them twenty-nine minutes from the Marshal's office to where they were now. "We have to go to Sobeck's house."

"And do what?"

"If Sobeck did all that to Kyle Farmer, he'd need a tarp and a shovel." Wolf thought back on the design of Sobeck's house. "He had a detached garage."

"Yeah," Rachette said. "He did."

"Back to Ridgway."

They left the room and shut the door behind them, Wolf dialing Roll as he walked.

"What do you have?" the sheriff asked.

"There was nothing here."

Roll exhaled into the phone.

"How about you?" Wolf asked. "Did you talk to Sobeck?"

Roll paused for a moment and when he spoke again, his voice was quiet. "I did."

"And?"

"And he's understandably upset, and he's saying what I thought he would say. That he had nothing to do with any of this. That he went straight back to the Timber Ridge Lodge after the Soaring Eagle Bar. That he thinks Jesse was just lying, trying to pull the wool over our eyes."

Wolf sat back behind the wheel of his SUV and fired up the engine. Rachette was already inside. "We're on our way back up. But we're going to stop by Sobeck's house."

"His house? Why?"

"Because if he did do any of this, he would need a shovel and two tarps, right?"

Roll said nothing.

"You there?"

"Yeah. Yeah. Fine. You keep me posted as soon as possible."

Wolf hung up.

CHAPTER 35

"You two again." Jill Sobeck leaned against the door jamb and crossed her arms. "What do you want?"

Wolf stood on the front deck of the house, Rachette behind him at the base of the stairs. "Ma'am, we're—"

"Who's that?" A woman in her sixties came up behind Jill.

"It's just some men who work with Jimmy."

The woman pushed her head out. "What's going on?"

"Hello, ma'am."

She stared at Wolf expectantly.

"Mom. Please head back inside. Okay?"

After a suspicious glare she ducked back in. Jill's kid was asking questions in the background now, and grandma told him to get back to playing.

"Sorry to bother you."

"Are you?" she asked.

The corner of Wolf's mouth rose. "Yes. But it's important. Could we please talk to you outside?"

She looked utterly annoyed but stepped out and shut the door behind her. "What?"

"We're hoping we could have a quick look inside your garage."

Her eyes narrowed. "Why?"

"You know about Kyle Farmer's murder, right?"

"Of course. Everyone knows about it."

The door opened and her mother stepped out, shut the door behind her. "Why do you want to see inside the garage?"

"Mom. Go back inside."

Wolf looked between Jill and her mother. "It has to do with the case."

"You have to have a warrant for that." Jill's face was an ice mask, but the crease between her eyebrows exposed concern.

"That's right. We need a warrant. Or we have to have your permission. I'm asking your permission."

"What are you looking for in there?" her mother asked, nodding toward the outbuilding.

Wolf kept his eyes on Jill. She was wavering, thinking it over. "Jill. A woman's life hangs in the balance here."

"Whose life?"

"Hettie Winkle's."

Jill's face fell. "Why? What's going on?"

"He was here Friday night," her mother said. "Told you, Jilly. He was inside that garage."

"Mom." Jill closed her eyes.

"Who was here?" Wolf asked.

"Jimmy," her mother said.

"Jill, your husband was here Friday night?"

"My mom says he came over and was inside the garage. I never saw it. I was sleeping on the other side of the house. She told me the next day. Now what's going on with Hettie?"

"You're friends with Hettie?"

"Yeah. She works at the diner with me. She's younger, but we're close. Now what's happening? You tell me or you're not getting anywhere near that garage." Her lips quivered.

"Kyle's family is threatening her," Wolf said.

"Why?"

"They want to know what happened to their son," Wolf said. "We need to figure that out. And we think looking inside your garage might help us."

"My room's right there," her mother was down off the porch and pointing at a wide-open window on the ground floor. "I heard some clanking Friday night, thought it was raccoons or maybe a bear. I saw him come out carrying a bunch of stuff."

"What kind of stuff?" Rachette asked.

She pantomimed by pitching out her arm. "Held a bundle of blankets under one arm, and a shovel in his hand. Something else. Boots, I think."

Wolf and Rachette eyed each other.

"What time was that?" Wolf asked.

"Middle of the night. Just after midnight. He parked down the street. Or must have, because he walked away down the road. Went around the bend, around those trees and out of sight."

Jill's mother pointed at a berm landscaped with pine trees.

"I saw his headlights come on, swivel away, and he drove

off. I went to the kitchen and watched his taillights go all the way down to the highway."

"Then where?"

She frowned. "I don't know. He went out of sight."

"Did you see if he turned north, or south toward town?"

"North. Away from town."

Wolf eyed his watch. "Could we please take that look now?"

Jill nodded, wiping her eyes. "Mom, go back inside."

"You gonna show them?"

"Yes! Go inside!"

Her mother climbed the stairs and went back inside.

Wolf stayed silent, trying not to push Jill. She looked like she was still wavering, but then she walked toward the garage.

Wolf and Rachette followed.

"After my mom told me what she saw, I looked in here."

She went to the side of the two-car garage, inserted a key, and opened the door, revealing a space that had been decorated with an anal-retentive touch. She went in first and they followed. The afternoon light illuminated boxes with little plastic screw drawers atop a clean workbench. Tools hung on the pegboard walls. A table saw stood opposite on a smooth concrete floor that Wolf would have been comfortable eating off of.

The first car spot was vacant, serving as a workshop space, while a motorcycle, a four-wheeler, and a riding lawn-mower filled the second spot. Behind them, a tic-tac-toe board design of shelves stood against the far wall. A wet-dry vacuum, tires, and large plastic bins were neatly stored in their proper places, including a pile of folded moving blankets and a stack of black tarps.

Jill hooked her thumbs on her jeans, facing a shovel that stood in the corner. "He usually hangs everything up in its place. So it was a little strange to see he left the shovel here," she said. A rake, spade, hoe, and a few other implements of the same matching brand hung neatly on the wall, proving her point.

Wolf pulled out his cell phone and turned on the flashlight, then bent down and put it on the blade of the shovel. Dirt clung to the metal, but he saw no obvious signs of blood on it or the handle.

"Did you touch this?" Wolf asked.

"Yes. I hung it up. But...then I got a feeling and I put it back where I found it."

Wolf stood and took a cell phone picture.

"A feeling?"

She nodded. "Because there're also boots over there. Over on the ground by the shelves."

Rachette and Wolf moved toward the shelving on the other side of the garage and saw a pair of boots sitting on the concrete. Dried mud was crusted on the sides of the soles. Using his shirt sleeve, Wolf tipped one over, exposing the bottom.

He flashed the bright beam of his phone, illuminating the familiar tread pattern that had stomped through the blood, and had left the single, perfect print in the mud behind Kyle's gun shed.

He snapped some more cell phone photos as Rachette bent down next to him and studied the upturned boot.

"Looks like that could be blood in there," he said under his breath.

Wolf looked up and met Jill Sobeck's now watery gaze.

"Please explain to me. You said you got a feeling. Did the sight of these two things make you suspect some sort of foul play?"

She wiped her nose. "Well, no. Not like, right away. I got a bad feeling when we heard about you guys finding Kyle Farmer yesterday. And then, when I learned more about the Alexander Guild shooting, this just...I realized this looked all wrong in here. On Saturday, I came in and put the shovel back and ignored the boots. But once I heard about the investigation, and Kyle, I... came back in and got that bad feeling. So I put the shovel back where I originally found it.

"I'm telling you, it's not like Jimmy to leave a shovel sitting in the corner like this. Or his boots muddied and sitting out. The military ingrained some organizational habits in him, you know? And...my mom saw him. Friday night. Saw him come in here for this stuff. I started wondering if... something might have been wrong."

"With him?" Wolf asked.

She nodded, almost imperceptibly.

"Have you told anyone about this?" Wolf asked.

She looked at Wolf desperately. "That's why I was talking to Deputy Triplett earlier this morning. I usually have my mom take me to work, but I asked him to come pick me up today."

"You told him?" Wolf asked. "He saw this?"

Her face dropped. "No. I chickened out. I ended up just asking about the case."

They stood in silence, and Jill started crying. "I was so scared."

"But you suspected that Jimmy might have had something to do with the two murders we're investigating," Rachette said gently.

She shook her head emphatically. "No. I mean, I don't know."

"We heard about what happened with your son," Wolf said.

She looked at him.

"About how he hit him, and that's why he's not staying here right now."

"It was a total accident. Zachary just came into the room in the middle of the night and caught him at the wrong time. He lashed out because of his condition, he wasn't trying to hit Zachary. He was having a nightmare, and just pushed out." Tears streamed down her face. "But Jimmy didn't mean to do it."

"I served in Afghanistan, too. It's not easy to come back and forget."

She wiped her eyes. "When I came in here and saw all this, I could see what he'd done. I could see why he would want to kill Alexander Guild for what he did. We all wanted to kill the bastard for shooting Hettie's father. Hettie's father was Jimmy's friend, and Hettie works with me at Lucille's. She was so devastated, and the way Guild got off without a single thing happening to him? Just a slap on the wrist for supposedly protecting his property? And Jimmy had been in a support group with Hettie's father. They'd become close." Her voice became a whisper. "And there's more. More reason for Jimmy to want to kill that bastard."

"What's that?" Wolf asked.

"There was a time when Alexander Guild came into the diner. He was totally inappropriate. Put his hand on my arm, then the next time I came back to the table he caressed my leg. I slapped him in the head and walked away from the table. It was a big deal. You've seen Lucille, she saw me and came over apologizing. He wasn't as nice as you two, though. He almost got me fired. Stormed out. Made a big scene.

"That was something that traveled around town. I never told Jimmy about it, and he never said anything to me. But I'm sure he knew about it. Hettie probably told Kyle and Jesse. Rod knew about it."

"Rod Triplett?" Wolf asked.

"Yes."

Silence took over.

"And what about your husband and Kyle Farmer and Jesse Burton?" Wolf asked. "Was there some animosity there?"

She frowned. "No. I mean, they were little shits, but they've always been little shits and Jimmy's dealt with them. They're always shooting off their guns and riding dirt bikes, but they've kept it to respectable times nowadays."

"Because Jimmy told Jesse to cut it out, right?" Wolf asked.

"Yeah. Exactly."

"And that didn't cause any animosity?"

"No."

Wolf nodded. "Can I ask you a personal question?"

"What?"

"Are you and Deputy Triplett seeing one another?"

She snorted. "No. We're just good friends. We all grew

up together. I'm not dumb. I know Rod's always had a thing for me. But me and Jimmy have always had a thing for each other."

"You didn't tell Rod about any of this when you saw him this morning?"

"No. Like I said, I chickened out. I just turned the subject to Jimmy, and how I was upset about him still being gone."

"And why is he still gone?" Wolf asked.

"Because he's beating himself up. I've told him to come back. But my mom also opened her fat mouth and told him the opposite—that he needs to stay away and get better. She freaked out and got into a big shouting match with him. You know how in-laws can rile a person up. Jimmy left and hasn't been back. I'm gonna have to kick her out if I want him back. But..." She put a hand over her mouth. "But if Jimmy...it looks like he's not coming back if he did all this horrible stuff."

"We're going to have to get a team over here," Wolf said.

"I know." She sniffed. "That's why I locked the place up. So Zachary or my mom couldn't get in to disturb anything."

Wolf narrowed his eyes. "It was unlocked in the first place?"

She matched his expression. "Yes. We don't lock our doors around here. Nobody does."

Wolf said nothing.

"What?" she asked. "Is that important? Tell me. You think this was somebody else? Because it would make sense. He parked all the way down the street. Didn't pull up. I've been wondering why not? Maybe it's because the person wanted to hide their car."

Her face fell. "If he didn't want to wake us up, he would have decided to park far away, I guess. And my mom says she saw him." Her expression hardened. "But her eyesight is shit. She's completely blind in one eye and she wears glasses she hasn't updated for years."

They descended into silence again.

Wolf checked his watch and saw the Farmers' ultimatum clock had thirty minutes left.

Rachette was over by the boots, bending down again. "Hey, Wolf."

Wolf walked over. "What is it?"

Rachette backed away and pointed down.

He saw Rachette had tipped the other boot over on its side, revealing a wadded piece of paper stuck in the mud that clung to the boot's sole. The piece of paper looked pristine compared to the rest of the boot—shiny white and free of mud.

"You have some gloves?" Wolf asked.

"No. They're in the car."

Wolf pulled his sleeve over his hand and plucked the piece of paper. He flipped it over and dropped it on the concrete.

It was a crumpled receipt, but with a little angling of his head he could easily read the printing. The bottom of the paper was ripped along a perforation, but the top was torn haphazardly, removing the pertinent store info.

"There's no store name or time stamp," Wolf said.

"Damn," Rachette said.

They both knew that with a time stamp and store name, they could easily go to the store and check security footage for the said time, thus seeing who purchased the items listed below.

As for the items, a portion of the list had been torn off,

but there were three products listed in itemized fashion, and a cash total.

The items were written in some convenience store accounting system shorthand, with abbreviations for products and then the cost. The first read GTRD for $2.99, the second, LYPC for $2.35. The third item read JCFG, for a dollar and change.

"GTRD," Rachette said. "Looks like Gatorade to me. About the price point you'd expect. LYPC? No clue. What do you think?"

Wolf snapped another cell phone photo and stood, leaving the receipt on the ground. "I'm not sure."

"What is it?" Jill Sobeck was standing next to them, looking down.

"Listen, Jill. We have to make a phone call." Wolf ushered her out of the garage, Rachette behind them.

"Please lock it again," Wolf said.

Jill did. "Are you going to arrest Jimmy?" she asked, turning around.

Wolf said nothing. He scrolled on his phone for Roll's number.

"I texted Jimmy pictures of the shovel and the boots."

Wolf lowered the phone. "What?"

Now she had puppy-dog eyes. "Right when you guys got here. I texted him photos of the garage I took earlier. I've been thinking about sending them to Jimmy and asking him what gives. And then when we saw you two pulling up and coming to talk to us, my mom was freaking out, saying you guys would think we were holding back information. I sent it off before you guys came to the door."

Tears spilled out of her eyes. "I wasn't trying to hide what my husband had done or anything. I just ... I was confused. I ..." She stopped talking and stood shaking her head.

Wolf raised his phone. "I have to make a call, okay?"

She stood mute, staring at the ground.

He walked away from her and Rachette, the digital tone trilling in his ear. The phone rang five, ten, then fifteen times, with no answer, so he hung up.

"What's going on?" Rachette asked, appearing next to him.

"I just called Roll and I'm getting nothing. Not even voicemail."

"How about Milo?"

"I don't have any of the other phone numbers." He pulled up the Ridgway Marshal's office on Google Maps and tapped the phone number.

"Ridgway Marshal's Office."

"Hi, Cassandra. This is Detective Wolf. I'm trying to get hold of Sheriff Roll. It's very important."

"You just missed him," she sounded frantic. "They headed up to Kyle's house with Jesse. Did you hear they have Jesse with them now? The Farmers have Hettie and they're threatening to kill—"

"Can you give me Detective Milo's phone number please?" Wolf asked, cutting her off.

She gave the number and Wolf relayed it to Rachette. Rachette pulled his own phone and punched it in.

"And what's the radio channel they're using?"

"Seventeen."

"Thanks."

He hung up and Rachette handed him an already ringing phone. "Milo's number."

"Detective—"

The voice clipped off and was covered in static.

"Milo, this is Wolf. Can you hear me?"

"Hey," Milo said. "Yeah, but probably not for long. We're up at Kyle's."

"What's going on?" Wolf asked.

The connection cut in and out. "The Farmers have... now...Jesse..."

"Hello? You there?"

A blast of static answered him, and then the call disconnected.

CHAPTER 36

THE TOPS of Wolf's thighs hit on the bottom of the steering wheel as the SUV bounced over a rock jutting out of the road.

"Ah!" Rachette bounced hard in his seat, hitting his head on the ceiling. "Damn good this seatbelt's doing. This road's shit!"

Wolf steered with one hand, grabbing the ceiling bar with the other, while his foot continued to press hard on the gas. The wheel twisted back and forth as they lurched over more ruts and stones.

"Any response yet?"

Rachette had both their cell phones in his lap. He plucked Wolf's and looked at the screen, then his own. "Still no reply. I'm down to one bar here." Rachette pulled the radio from its hook. "This is Detective Rachette, calling for Sheriff Roll, do you copy? Detective Milo, do you copy? Deputy Sobeck, do you copy?"

No answer.

"Sobeck has reception," Wolf said. "His phone was the

only one last time we were up here."

Rachette looked at him. "You want me to get his number from Cassandra? And then what? Tell him 'Hey, Jimmy, we found your boots and shovel?'"

Wolf gripped the wheel and concentrated on the road. "We're almost there, anyway."

Rachette looked at his cell phone, pinching his fingers on the screen. "Looks like less than a mile. And what are we going to do when we get there?"

Wolf was wondering the same thing.

When Rachette raised the radio to his lips again, Wolf put a hand on his arm. "Wait. They might not be answering for a reason."

Rachette hooked the hand-piece back on the radio. "So, really. What's the plan?"

"The plan is: keep your eyes and ears open, and stay out of danger."

Rachette sputtered his lips. "That never works."

"We'll have to work with what the situation gives us."

"I'm not sure I'm gonna like what these Farmer guys give us."

They rounded a corner and there was a long straight-away. Wolf pressed the gas and got it up to sixty miles per hour.

They passed a road that cut up into the woods on the right. Wolf saw crime scene tape was hanging off two trees, broken and strewn on the ground in the middle.

"Wait! Stop! Back there!"

Wolf had already jammed the brakes and they halted in a ball of dust. He turned the SUV around and turned up the road.

"There it is," Rachette said, leaning into the windshield.

Kyle Farmer's house was visible through the pines ahead, along with a lot of vehicles.

Wolf stopped behind Roll's FJ Cruiser. Sobeck's cruiser was parked in front of that, which was parked behind Jed Farmer's hulking black pickup truck.

They got out into eerie silence and both drew their guns.

Roll's vehicle gave off heat and the engine ticked. Sobeck's smelled like burnt rubber.

They stood now in the center of the asphalt-paved driveway, at the shadow's edge of Kyle's house. The door to the shed-arsenal was shut. The crime scene tape across the stairway to the front door fluttered on a breeze. The front door to the house was now closed.

A shout came from ahead, down in the valley, too faint to make out the words.

"You hear that?" Rachette asked.

Wolf nodded and walked to the edge of the driveway. "Down."

They ducked behind some trees and looked.

Far below, they saw Sobeck, Triplett, Milo, and Roll standing in a line on the valley floor. Behind them, protected by the human barrier before him, stood Jesse, his shock of orange hair a spark among the grass. Roll and Triplett held rifles across their chests. Roll was talking, and his voice echoed up as a murmur.

Fifty or so yards away, at the edge of the grove of aspens near the exposed hole where they'd unearthed Kyle stood Jed Farmer, his two sons, and a blonde woman—Hettie—on her knees, a gun pressed to her head.

Jed was shouting, holding a rifle pointed at the ground

between them. His eldest son stood next to him, his rifle aimed loosely between the two groups as well. The youngest Farmer, Gabriel, was in charge of their hostage.

Rachette's eyes were wide open. "What do you want to do?"

His detective's ready, willing, and able tone sent a spike of adrenaline into Wolf's veins. Bringing Rachette here was a mistake. Wolf was putting a young father of two little boys in danger.

"What's up? Speak to me."

"I don't have a plan," Wolf said.

"So what?"

Wolf shook his head. "I'm not putting you in danger."

"I'm not putting you in danger by leaving you, if that's what you're getting at."

"Yes. You are. I want you to get back to the SUV and—"

"Screw that."

Wolf opened his mouth to speak again.

Rachette cut him off. "Nope."

Wolf looked back down through the trees. Roll was talking again, sounding like he was pleading. Jed Farmer was clearly having none of it.

"Your plan is to get down there and stop hell from breaking loose," Rachette said. "The Farmers think it's Jesse that killed their son. Now we know that's not true. But we don't have to tell them it was Sobeck. We can be vague."

"First of all, I'm not so sure about what we just found out. Second, we're gambling with that woman's life down there."

Rachette shrugged. "Those boys are forcing our hand. You want to fold? You want to just sit here and watch it play out without doing anything?"

Wolf stared at him. That's exactly what he wanted his detective to do, but he knew wishing something that was impossible was a waste of time.

"No."

"Neither do I."

Wolf narrowed his eyes. "They don't know about you."

"Yeah? So?"

"So, maybe we can use that." He nodded to the radio on Rachette's belt. "I'm heading down, I want you to stay here and keep that radio on."

"No. I'm not—"

Wolf cut him off. "Listen to me, they don't know you even exist. We might be able to bluff them into thinking you have a sniper rifle aimed on them. You keep that radio on, and you wait for my signal. When I give you the word, you fire in the air to let them know you're real."

"What if they—"

Wolf cut him off again. "Just keep that radio on. Fire in the air when I tell you. Trust me."

Rachette swallowed, looked down the hill, then back at Wolf. "I don't like this."

"It's the only way." *The only way to keep your stubborn ass out of danger*, Wolf thought.

Rachette eyed him suspiciously, then nodded. "Okay. I'll be ready."

Wolf nodded. "You have your backup piece on you?"

Rachette lifted his pantleg, revealing his ankle holster. "Of course."

"Good. Hand it over."

313

CHAPTER 37

"Mr. Farmer!" Wolf called out.

Jed Farmer's rifle swung up and aimed at Wolf. "Freeze right there!"

Wolf already had his hands raised high above his head. He stood a good half a football field away at the forest edge, but he had no doubt if he moved wrong his heart would explode from Jed Farmer's well-placed round. The man pressed his eye to a scope, and Wolf could only assume the optics were sighted perfectly. "I'm just here to talk!"

"You trying to get yourself shot?" Jed asked.

"No, sir. I'm just here to talk."

"What are you doing here, Wolf?" Roll asked.

"Shut up!" Jed walked through the tall grass toward Wolf, the black hole of his barrel leading the way. "Keep your positions," he told his sons.

Hettie Winkle squealed as Gabriel Farmer jerked her head. Seymour remained motionless.

Jed marched over, his cheek pressed up against the stock of his rifle as he swished through the foliage. He stopped, his aim unwavering. "Take off your gun and throw it away."

Wolf unclipped his paddle holster and threw it in the grass.

"And your backup piece."

Wolf bent over, pulled the backup piece from under his right pant leg and threw it into the grass next to his Glock.

"Now get over here. Walk in front of me."

Wolf followed Jed's orders, walking toward Roll and his posse.

"Nope. Over there, next to the girl."

Wolf veered toward Hettie Winkle.

She looked thoroughly beaten, physically and mentally. Her head was cocked sideways from Gabriel's clamp on her frizzed hair. Her eyes were wide, red-rimmed and smeared with eyeliner. Her lip was cracked, a stream of blood running down her chin. Her t-shirt was ripped around the neck and her jeans were covered in mud. Despite the warmth of the afternoon, she shivered uncontrollably as she knelt at Gabriel Farmer's feet.

"Stand right there." Jed pointed to a spot in front of Seymour.

Wolf stopped and faced Roll and his group. Out of the corner of his eye he saw the shadow of Seymour's rifle move positions, and Wolf could feel the invisible aim on his back.

"I was wondering where you went," Jed said. "They told me you went back home up to Rocky Points. Now I know the sheriff was lying to me."

Jed walked up to Wolf's other side. The barrel of his rifle came up inches from Wolf's face. "Where's that old bastard? Jesse's uncle?"

"He's in the hospital up in Montrose."

Jed's barrel rested, none too gently, on Wolf's cheek. "Tell him to come out of those trees or I'll shoot you in the head."

"He's in the hospital up in Montrose. Had a heart attack."

Jed went silent.

Roll, Milo, Sobeck, and Triplett now stared at Wolf. They were ten paces away. A first down. Jesse was behind them, kneeling, his eyes locked on Hettie.

"What the hell are you doing here, Wolf?" Roll asked, not looking or sounding too pleased.

Jed lowered his barrel, keeping his aim between the two groups.

"You heard the sheriff," Jed said. "Why are you here? Why are you stumbling out of the trees twenty minutes after these assholes?"

"I'm late because I was searching a person of interest's house."

"Oh? So what?" Jed spat at Wolf's feet.

"I found some new evidence that suggests this person was involved in your son's murder."

"Whose house were you at?" Jed raised his barrel to Wolf's face again. "Jesse's?"

Wolf shook his head. "No, sir."

"I told you, Jed!" Jesse said. "I didn't do this! It was somebody making it look like I did it. I swear to you."

"Shut up!"

Jesse did.

"Sir," Wolf said. "I have a son of my own. I have a son of my own. Twenty-two years old."

Jed walked in front of Wolf, his eyes locked on the hillside, as if he'd seen movement.

Wolf continued talking, trying to keep his attention. "I'm not sure what I would do if what happened to your son happened to mine."

Jed raised his rifle and aimed it at the hillside.

The wind whipped up, and the aspen trees hissed and swayed behind them.

Wolf continued. "I can't imagine what I'd do if someone did something to my son. I supposed I'd want to shoot them right in the head. Get it over with."

Jed lowered his gun. "That's the idea. That's the idea, right on the nose."

"The problem is," Wolf said, "we're not sure who killed your son yet. So, this isn't doing anyone any good here."

"But you just said you have new evidence. Tell me about this, or you're dead." Jed raised the gun on him again. "Whose house were you at? What did you find?"

Everyone watched Wolf.

"I found the pair of boots that left the tracks in your son's blood up there on the porch. And I found the shovel that buried your son." Wolf nodded toward the hole in the ground.

"Who was it!" The end of Jed's barrel slammed into Wolf's temple. "Where were you? Whose house?"

"Let the girl go. Let her get up and walk, and I'll tell you. You don't need her now. You have me."

"You're not giving me orders, you piece of shit." Jed knocked him on the head. A warm river of blood ran off his scalp and down his back. "Tell me!"

"If you shoot me, you'll never know," Wolf said. "And it's not who you think it is."

Jed's nostrils huffed. The barrel rested on Wolf's temple.

"Please," Wolf said. "I have a son I want to see again, too. I know you want to see justice for your boy. And I don't blame you one bit. But you have to let it happen the right way. And we're almost there."

"I'm through with pig-justice," Jed said. "You know where this man just was, sheriff?"

Roll said nothing.

"I think the sheriff does. I think I don't need you anymore, Mr. Wolf. Goodbye."

"They're looking into me." Sobeck's voice was low, but he might as well have shouted it through a bull horn.

Jed whipped his gun and aimed at Sobeck. "What was that?"

"I said, they're looking into me. That's where you were just now, right?" Sobeck looked at Wolf. "My house?"

"Why don't you lower the weapon, Mr. Farmer," Roll said. "And we'll talk it out."

"Why don't you answer the question, Mr. Wolf." Jed's gaze was now locked on Sobeck.

Wolf saw the look in Sobeck's eyes that Milo must have been talking about. But instead of a deer in headlights, he saw a cat on the hunt. His pupils were pinpoints, his eyelids wide open. His expression blank.

"I just got a text from my wife when we pulled up," Sobeck said. "She sent me some pictures from my garage. Somebody came over and used my shovel out of my garage to bury your son, then returned it. Somebody used my boots, stomped around in your son's blood, and returned them to my garage. Somebody took my headlamp and left it down here, next to your son's grave. Those were my tarps wrapped around your son when we dug him up." Sobeck's voice was calm and ice cold. "Somebody's making me look like I did this. But I didn't do it. And that's the truth."

"Is that true?" Jed's eyes whipped to Wolf, then back on Sobeck. "Did you find those things at his house?"

When Wolf didn't answer, Jed backtracked and stepped behind Wolf.

"I said, is that true?"

"We found those things at Deputy Sobeck's house. Yes. And it appears like someone might have put them there."

"Might have? Who might have put them there?"

"We don't know that," Wolf said.

For a long, drawn out moment, Jed went silent. Then he kicked Wolf in the back, sending him stumbling forward. "Get over there with your friends."

Wolf walked the gap between them. Time seemed to slow to a halt, and a flash of his grandson's smile filled his vision. He stopped next to Milo and turned around to face Jed's gun which was now pointed at Sobeck.

"We're still early in this investigation, Jed," Roll said. "You have to let us do our job. We're doing our job. We're making progress."

"No. We're not early in this. We're late. I can't take another damned second that my son's death goes unsolved by you good-for-nothing pigs. Pig-justice isn't gonna do us any good. We're gonna squeeze the truth out of this group, right here, right now."

Jed leaned into his aim at Sobeck. "Did you kill my son?"

With steady deliberation, Triplett raised his gun and aimed at Jed.

"Guys," Wolf said under his breath.

Seymour Farmer aimed his gun at Triplett.

"No," Sobeck said. "I didn't kill your son. And I didn't kill Alexander Guild. Now that guy? I wish I would have. But your son? No, Jed. I didn't do it."

"Stand up here, Jesse," Jed said.

Jesse held frozen behind the line of men.

"Stand up here next to the sheriff or I shoot my way to you."

Jesse squeezed between Roll and Sobeck.

Jed swiveled the barrel to Jesse. "Did you kill my son?"

"No, sir."

Jed aimed at Triplett.

"Come on, man," Triplett said. "Just lower your gun."

"Did you kill my son?"

"No. I didn't."

"You didn't?" Sobeck asked, looking up at his partner.

Jed paused.

Triplett looked down at Sobeck. "What?"

Jed stepped forward, barrel locked on Triplett. "What was that, deputy?"

"Are you serious right now?" Triplett asked. "Me? What the hell are you talking about?"

"Yeah, what are you talking about, Jimmy?" Jed asked. "Did you just figure something out about your partner here?"

"Jed," Wolf said. "We have new evidence being analyzed. Evidence that will prove beyond a doubt who killed your son. But we need a little more time."

"Shut. Up." Jed's eyes bounced back and forth between Sobeck and Triplett.

"You've been after my wife for years," Sobeck said. "You knew I was gone every night down at the motel. You know I leave my garage unlocked. You could have come in and taken my stuff. Made it look like I did it."

"Yeah, and you know someone else here who would have known that stuff? This orange-haired asshole right here! I wouldn't do that to you. What are you talking about?"

"You do love my wife, though. Don't you?" Sobeck asked.

"I love your wife? I don't love your wife."

"You love my wife."

"Of course I love your wife. I'd do anything for your wife. Just like I'd do anything for you!"

"You've always loved Jill. You go talk to her at the house sometimes, don't you? You go inside my house, and you eat my food, and drink my beer, and sit there with my son, and you talk with my wife, and her mother. Don't you, Rod?"

"You two need to stop talking," Roll said.

"No, no, no." Jed's rifle lurched in his grip. "Keep going, Deputy Sobeck. I want to hear more of this. I want to watch the guilty look on this guy's face some more."

"Guilty look? No." Triplett shook his head. "Listen. Why the hell would I kill Kyle? And Guild? Why would I do that? That's crazy!"

"And make me look like I did it?" Sobeck bared his teeth. "I don't know. You tell me."

"Shit, Sobeck. You're not making sense. Jed, Jimmy's not doing well after the war. He's—"

"You shut up," Jed said. "I want to hear what Jimmy has to say. Go ahead, Jimmy."

"You go to my wife's place of work and talk to her in your car out back in the alley, don't you?" Sobeck asked. "Just like you did this morning?"

Triplett swallowed, looking like a caught man.

"You watch her ass as she walks back inside, and you wish you were the one married to her, don't you? You wish I was out of the picture."

Triplett looked at Wolf. "You told him?"

Wolf's eyes were on Jed's trigger finger, which was flicking back and forth like a spider's leg.

"Told me what?" Sobeck asked.

"That...that I was talking to her. I was just talking to her. And we were talking about you!"

"No. He didn't tell me anything. I know because I was there this morning. I've seen you talking to her three times now. It's a thing for you two now, right?"

"Nothing's going on. We're just talking. She asked me to pick her up this morning from home. She needed a ride to work. She said she wanted to talk. She was upset."

"Is that what you two do now?" Sobeck asked. "You guys talk?"

Triplett shook his head. "This is crazy. This is crazy."

"She doesn't love you." Sobeck bared his teeth. "She's my wife. *My* wife!"

The air hummed, like the moment before a lightning strike.

And then there was a flash, and a blast of thunder coming out of Jed Farmer's rifle. And then Triplett fell backwards.

"No!" somebody yelled.

Sobeck dropped to a knee, aimed, and shot Jed. A fountain of blood spewed from the man's throat. He dropped his rifle and clutched at it while falling backwards.

At that moment, Wolf saw Rachette come out at a full sprint from the grove of aspen trees behind the Farmers, gun raised.

Wolf knelt and lifted his other pant leg, groping for Rachette's backup piece. His hands felt like blocks of ice from the surging adrenaline.

Seymour Farmer shot next, hitting Sobeck. Sobeck bent over and clutched his stomach, but before he hit the ground he aimed and fired.

Hettie made a noise and went limp in Gabriel Farmer's grip. Blood blossomed on her chest.

Gabriel stood up from behind his fallen human shield and raised his weapon. More fire—a staccato burst of three that came from three different directions almost simultaneously—and Gabriel convulsed wildly, blood spurting out of him as he fell to the ground.

"Cease fire!" somebody yelled.

But Seymour shot, and more shots rang out, stinging discharge particles hitting Wolf in the face. He raised Rachette's backup piece from the ankle holster and aimed it at the spot where Seymour disappeared into the grass. But even from such a short distance, the gun had no reliable accuracy and Hettie lay slumped beyond. As Wolf realized he had no shot, Seymour rose, locked eyes on him and fired.

Wolf dove onto his back, and the sky split above him as the bullet passed over his face.

And then there two more quick shots, and all that remained was a high-pitched whine in Wolf's ears.

"Clear! All clear!" Rachette's voice echoed through the valley.

He stood up, taking in the scene.

Seymour Farmer was slumped on the ground. Behind him, Rachette was lowering his Glock.

Next to Wolf, Sobeck and Triplett lay motionless, Sobeck's eyes closed and his partner's staring into nothing. Jed gargled, laying still in the grass, eyes open and staring up. Gabriel was next to him, looking dead from multiple gunshots. Roll stood over them both, keeping his rifle trained on them as he kicked their guns away.

Jesse crawled through the grass and reached Hettie. "Hettie! Hettie!" He rolled her onto her back, revealing a lot of blood.

Wolf moved to her quickly and put his fingers on her neck, finding a weak pulse. "We need a helicopter!"

Milo was over Sobeck. "Yeah we do. I've got a pulse." He dug into Sobeck's pocket and pulled out Sobeck's cell phone. "I'll call."

"Hettie!" Jesse's face was twisted. "Hold on! You're gonna be okay!"

But she was unconscious, barely alive.

Wolf took off his shirt, wadded it up, and put it on the hole spitting blood on her left breast.

"Helicopter's on its way!" Milo said.

Roll put his jacket over Triplett's body.

Wolf stared at the carnage, smelling the blood and gunpowder as it swirled on the wind.

Jesse bent close to Hettie, whispering in her ear.

"You all right?" Rachette appeared over him.

"Yeah."

"You son of a bitch. You never called me on the radio. You were lying to me. There was no plan."

He looked up and saw Rachette was waiting for a response. "Thanks for shooting him before he shot me."

"Yeah, yeah. You're welcome." Rachette walked away.

Wolf adjusted the shirt over Hettie's wound. The blood flowing out had not slowed down. The fabric was soaked all the way through.

"I told you," Jesse said.

Wolf met Jesse's wild-eyed stare. "You told me what?"

"That I didn't do it. I told you."

"I know you did, Jesse." Wolf nodded. "You told everyone that. I just wish I could believe you."

Jesse flinched like he'd been slapped in the face. But he said nothing. He just put his head on the ground, put his mouth next to Hettie's ear, and whispered.

CHAPTER 38

As WOLF TRAVELED north over Williams Pass, struggling to keep the vehicle between the lines in the wind, he fought to keep his thoughts in the present moment. He knew firsthand how worrying too much about a nonexistent future could bring a man to his knees. Especially when that future involved letting somebody else down.

"What is the worst that could happen?" Dr. Hawkwood would have asked him, had the psychiatrist answered Wolf's call earlier that morning.

I could lose my job. I could no longer have an income. I could let them all down.

But he wasn't letting anyone down, was he? They would have their jobs. They'd have their futures. They weren't the ones on the chopping block. And him? He could sell his ranch, probably for millions, if Margaret's real estate rants over the last couple years held any truth.

Everyone was safe, if he really thought about it.

Or were they? What happened when MacLean was done with his current term? There would be a new election. And

Margaret had mentioned she knew of two outsiders who were showing interest in running. Was there any truth there? Would either of the outsiders be able to take down Undersheriff Wilson in an election? And if they did, would they fire everyone in their wake and bring in their own crew? That kind of thing happened more often than not.

No. He would be just fine. It was the rest of them that would be left swinging in the wind without him there.

Summiting Williams Pass and coasting down into the mouth of the Chautauqua Valley, the uncertainty flooded back in on him.

What's the worst that could happen?

Twenty minutes later he rolled into downtown Rocky Points. A line of cars choked Main Street, moving slowly along the rows of shops. He turned into a side road and took the back way to the county building.

Once parked, he got out into the warm late-morning air and stretched his arms overhead. His muscles were knotted from sleeping in his SUV in the Montrose Hospital parking lot the night before. After the Armageddon shootout at Kyle's house, Wolf and Rachette had accompanied Roll and Milo to the Montrose hospital, where Sobeck and Hettie went straight into emergency surgeries.

Deputy Triplett had needed no medical attention, as he was dead, along with the Farmers, though Jed had somehow survived his neck wound for another half an hour before dying on the medevac helicopter ride.

Hours later, and after receiving the promising news that Sobeck and Hettie had made it through their surgeries, Rachette headed home. Wolf had planned on following, but the second he'd sat in his car he had hit the proverbial wall.

He could have checked into a motel, but he had been too tired even for that, and instead he fell asleep in his seat, not moving a muscle until morning.

Now, as he stifled a yawn, he stared at the mountains reflected in the windows of the Sluice-Byron County Building. A breeze tickled past his face, smelling of pine trees and food cooking on Main. And in that moment a wave of calm washed over him. He pictured Sarah's smiling face. She always showed up right when he needed her.

"I know," he said to no one.

He jogged through the rear entrance and up the stairs to the third floor. Out in the terrazzo hallway, he passed his own office, his eyes focused on MacLean's aquarium. The blinds were wide open, revealing no one inside, which was surprising, since they were set to meet three minutes ago.

"Wolf!"

He followed MacLean's voice back to his own office. He ducked in and saw Rachette, Patterson, and Yates, along with MacLean and Wilson.

Rachette and Patterson sat on the synthetic leather couch, Yates and Wilson in the chairs in front of his desk. MacLean sat in Wolf's chair and made no move to get up. Instead he motioned to a single chair against the wall. "Sit."

Patterson and Yates looked at him with unreadable expressions. Rachette nodded, looking like a kid in the principal's office.

"What's up?"

"Sit." MacLean said again.

Wolf sat, and Wilson and Yates turned in their chairs to face him.

"We heard all about what happened down there from Rachette," MacLean said.

Wolf nodded.

"We're glad you're okay."

Wolf held out his hands. "A little bruised, but alive, thanks to Rachette."

"How's the girl doing? And that deputy?"

"They're both stable after surgery last night," Wolf said. "But one deputy is dead, along with all three of the Farmers."

"How about Burton?" MacLean asked. "How's he doing?"

"I haven't seen him yet. I'm planning on heading down to the hospital after we're done here. But according to Cheryl, he's doing fine."

Wolf felt suddenly hot. He took off his jacket and draped it over the back of his chair. "Now that the small talk's done, how about we get this over with."

"Sounds like a good plan," MacLean said.

Rachette cleared his throat. "If I could just say something first, sir?"

MacLean looked at him. "Sure. Go ahead."

"I just want to say that I've not approved of the way you and the council have gone about dealing with the situation at hand. All this subterfuge, this, behind the back." He looked at Wolf. "Sir. I just want you to know that you've always been the best boss I've ever had, and that's what I told the council members who interviewed me. I just...no matter what happens, I want you to know that."

Patterson and Yates said nothing. Patterson kept her eyes down. Not that Wolf felt he was owed anything by her, but it caught his attention.

"Thanks," Wolf said.

MacLean looked bored. "You guys done?"

All eyes moved back to MacLean.

"Good. So, I'm sick. Pancreatic cancer, stage three. And the doctors have told me it's most likely terminal."

Wolf blinked. He uncrossed his legs and sat forward.

"We've been scrambling with the news behind the scenes ever since I got the diagnosis. Personally, I'm not taking this laying down. They've given me shit odds, basically told me to sit back and die, so I've said screw them and I've decided to treat the cancer with alternative methods, which means I'll be leaving the country ASAP. Or, as soon as I figure out who's going to succeed me in office. The way I see it, Patterson is the most qualified to do your job, Wolf. No offense meant to Detective Rachette and Yates, but you guys couldn't organize your way out of a paper bag."

"No offense taken, sir," Rachette said.

They laughed.

MacLean stood and stared out the window with his back turned.

They sat in silence, waiting.

Wolf looked at Patterson and saw she was staring at him intently, her eyes liquid and full of sorrow.

When MacLean finally turned around, his own eyes shimmered. "I had to tell everyone at the meeting yesterday, even without you two there. I apologize, but, like Detective Rachette pointed out, the subterfuge was getting to be too much. Undersheriff Wilson, perhaps you could explain to Wolf what you're thinking."

Wilson looked at Wolf. "Sir. Dave. I took this job as undersheriff when you refused. I wouldn't have taken the job, no offense, Sheriff MacLean, if Dave hadn't encouraged me to do so."

"No offense taken, sir," MacLean said, mimicking Rachette's tone.

They paused, letting the moment pass. This time, they all held their somber expressions.

"We need somebody to step in as interim sheriff," Wilson said. "And we want you to do the job."

Wilson opened a folder he'd been carrying on his lap. He spoke quickly, as if to cut Wolf off before he could speak. "MacLean and I gave our recommendation to the council, and they wanted confirmation that the rest of the department would be on board."

Wilson picked up the papers and flipped through them, keeping a hard grip on the stack.

"Every single person they asked in this department, from the receptionist downstairs to the squad members down in that room, to the detectives in this room."

"And the sheriff," MacLean said.

"And the sheriff. Everyone thinks that you're the most qualified for this job. That's what the council meeting was about this week. They wanted the data before they made the official nomination, and, of course, with your recent history they wanted to cover all their bases." Wilson shook the papers in his hand, then set them back in the folder. "The nomination became official yesterday. So what do you think?"

Wolf raised his eyebrows. "I think you're much more qualified for the job."

Wilson shook his head. "No. I'm not, Dave. You are. The people of this department look up to you, not me."

"If the council would have interviewed everyone about

you, I'm sure the answers would have been unanimously the same," Wolf said.

Wilson took a breath and leaned back. "The alternatives are we bring in an outsider to run the department as interim Sheriff. Or I step up and take the job, and we bring in an outsider to take my position as undersheriff, effectively grooming the outsider for the Sheriff job when it becomes available in two years."

"What about you?" Wolf asked. "You could be the sheriff in two years."

Wilson sucked in a breath. "Dave. You're better for the job. I don't want it knowing you're right there on the bench. It's like, you know, if a quarterback gets hurt, and the second-string guy gets passed over for the third string guy. Only, the second-string guy should have been in the game the whole time to begin with! No offense, sheriff."

MacLean frowned at the back of Wilson's head.

"Dave," Wilson continued. "We need you. We need you in the game."

Wolf looked at Patterson. She looked like she was holding her breath. "Okay," he said.

Wilson froze with his hands outstretched. "Okay?"

"Yeah. Okay. I'll do it. As long as you promise to ride out the term with me."

"Of course. Yeah."

Wolf looked at MacLean. "So that's that?"

MacLean nodded. "That's that."

The others sat in stunned looking silence.

Patterson stood up and walked to Wolf. She bent over and embraced him in an awkward hug. "I'm sorry," she said.

"For what?"

"For not telling you about the interviews."

Wolf stood up. "I'm not worried about it. You shouldn't be."

"Congratulations, sir," Rachette said, shaking his hand.

"On what?" He chuckled, eyeing MacLean. "The way I see it, I just got demoted to the bottom."

MacLean's somber expression evaporated, and he smiled that way he had been lately—and now Wolf saw it for what it was—like a man who'd come face to face with his mortality and had completely accepted it.

Wolf stepped to the man and embraced him.

Reluctantly, MacLean raised his arms and hugged him back. After a few seconds he slapped Wolf on the shoulder blades and pushed him away. "Okay, enough. I'm not gonna start crying again. I'm done with that."

The others crowded the sheriff.

"Get back. Everyone back."

Patterson ignored him and dove in for a hug. Yates, Rachette, and Wilson piled on, and when the huddle broke, MacLean's cheeks were streaked with tears. "Thanks people. Thank you."

Wolf broke the silence. "When is my interim position official?"

"Right now. I've cleared out my office. Patterson's ready to move in here. I'll help you get on your feet in the next couple days, but I'm leaving this weekend." He shrugged. "Sorry for the trial by fire, but I have to go."

"I understand, sir. And I wish you luck."

"I don't need luck. I'm gonna kick this disease's ass. You watch."

Wolf nodded. "I can't wait to see that, sir. Okay, since this is official—"

"Actually," MacLean held up a finger, "You have to accept the Council's nomination. Margaret will get in touch with you on that. They'll swear you in, and then it's official."

"Right. Well, we'll pretend it's now, and as my first official order of business I'd like to require everyone to attend a barbecue at my house."

"Hells yeah," Rachette said. "Party time."

"Sounds good to me," Yates said. "We need to blow off some steam after all this. It was getting pretty tense in here."

"When?" Patterson asked.

"Tonight."

She made a pained face. "Your detectives are on duty until ten P.M. on Wednesdays. You know that, right?"

He looked down his nose at her. "Right. Okay, fine, tomorrow. Or Friday."

"Saturday would be better. There's the smooth jazz festival at the base village Friday night. We'll be stretched as it is. And then we have the rest of the weekend off. If you have it any other night, nobody will show up."

He sucked in a breath. "Saturday it is."

"Good choice. And besides, this way you have proper time to invite everyone."

"Yes, all good points. Thank you, Chief Detective."

"And then you'll have time to prepare. You know, something better than a bring your own booze get together."

"Are you done yet?" Rachette asked. "And she's wrong. You can have it whenever you want."

They looked at Wolf.

MacLean held up his hands and walked between them. "Aaand I'm out of here."

"Wait a minute," Wolf said. "Are you still here Saturday?"

MacLean nodded. "I'm leaving Sunday morning."

"Can you make it?"

"Wouldn't miss it for the world."

"All right, then Saturday it is."

"See you guys then," MacLean said. "I'm going home." He left the room.

Wolf looked at his squad—Patterson's squad, he corrected himself. "And I'm heading down to County to see Burton."

"I would come along," Rachette said, "but I'm sure Burton would rather see syphilis."

"You're probably right," Wolf said.

"Hey, that's not nice." Rachette made a pained face, then dropped it. "The guy never liked me. I'm not sure how I even got hired by him in the first place."

"There was probably very little competition?" Patterson asked. "Maybe nobody else had applied?"

"Ha. Shut up." Rachette's face went serious. "What are they doing with Jesse down there in Ridgway?"

Wolf shrugged. "They're putting twenty-four-seven surveillance on him. But ... he's a free man."

Yates and Patterson looked at each other.

"And that's bad?" Patterson asked.

"The whole thing's still up in the air," Rachette said. "It's a mess of a case. Glad it's not ours."

Wolf picked his jacket off the plastic chair. Something shiny fell from the inside pocket as he slipped his arm in.

Rachette bent over and picked it up. "Gum."

When Wolf reached out for it, Rachette pulled it back and sniffed it. "Mmmm, Juicy Fruit. Can I have a piece?"

"Please," Yates said. "Your breath's like a dog took—"

"Boys, please," Patterson said. "How about you get out of my office."

Wolf stared at the piece of gum as Rachette unwrapped it and put it in his mouth. And then realization slapped his mind into gear. "Wait, no!"

Rachette spit it out. It bounced off Patterson's leg before it hit the ground. "What? What!"

"I took some pieces of gum off of Jesse when we picked him up in Canyon of the Ancients. I must have missed pulling one out of my pocket when I handed them over to Roll."

"Okay. So...you want to return it to him?"

Wolf pulled out his phone and scrolled through his photographs from Sobeck's garage.

"What is it?"

He dialed Sheriff Roll's number and walked to the window, the phone pressed to his ear.

"Roll here," the sheriff answered.

"It's Wolf."

"Yeah. How's it going?"

"I need to talk to you. About Jesse."

"Oh yeah?"

"Where is he?"

"We just pulled into the parking lot of Sluice-Byron County Hospital."

"He's with you right now?"

"I'm escorting him to visit his uncle." The sheriff grunted

and wind hit his microphone, like he'd just climbed out of his car. "We're headed inside now."

"Keep a close eye on him."

"That's the plan. Why? What's going on?"

"I'll be there in thirty minutes." Wolf hung up.

CHAPTER 39

WOLF KNOCKED on Burton's hospital room door and pushed it open without waiting for a response.

Inside, Jesse stood off one side of Burton's bed. He watched Wolf come in and nodded.

Roll stood a few paces behind Jesse. The sheriff nodded, turning slightly to show that his hand rested on his gun.

"Wolf," Burton said, a wan smile stretching his lips. "What's my sergeant deputy doing here?"

Wolf smiled at the reference to the last rank Wolf had held under Burton's command. The drugged look on Burton's face made it hard to know if the man was kidding or if he really had no concept of when or where he was.

"How's he doing?" Wolf asked Jesse.

Jesse's electric orange hair was slicked back, stuck to his head. He wore ripped jeans and a long-sleeved motocross jersey with the number six-six-six on the back.

"I'm doing fine," Burton said. But his face twisted in pain, and he pulled a pillow onto his chest, hugged it tightly with both hands, and coughed with his eyes clamped shut.

Wolf winced as he watched Burton's body constrict in agony.

When he had finished expelling his lungs, Burton released the pillow and let his arms flop to his sides. "Just fine. Just had a doctor saw open my chest, and now there's a tickle in there that won't go away so I keep coughing every two minutes. I'm still hung over, I want a drink, and I'm pretty sure the worst is yet to come on that front. But..." he put up a finger and nodded contentedly, "but ... I am taking some pretty strong pain pills. So that is good."

Wolf nodded. "How's Hettie?"

Jesse nodded. "She's okay. Still sleeping. But she'll fully recover."

"Good to hear. What do you think she'll tell us when she wakes up?"

Jesse raised an eyebrow. "What do you mean?"

"I remember that day we went down to get you down in Canyon of the Ancients. You were despondent. I didn't know you, but to me it looked like you'd given up on life."

Jesse straightened. "I was pretty depressed about the situation, I guess."

Wolf nodded. "Until we got you into the car, and we told you that Hettie said you two were together the night of the murders."

Jesse made a sour face. "What are you talking about?"

"Once we told you Hettie said she was with you all Friday night, I remember looking at you in the mirror, you perked right up. Now I know why. Because it was a surprise. Because you suddenly had an alibi, from the one person you were sure was going to give you up to the cops."

"I have no clue what you're talking about right now." Jesse shook his head as if he felt sorry for Wolf.

Burton wrapped his arms around the pillow and coughed again, his eyes locked on Jesse.

The machines next to Burton beeped, and a long sheet of paper rolled out.

There was a knock on the door, and then a nurse entered. "Excuse me," she said, putting two hands on Jesse's shoulders as she pushed past him. "I just have to get this. Are you finished with your lunch, Mr. Burton? Would you like me to take your plate?"

"No, darling. I'm still working on my Jello."

She snapped off the piece of paper and read it. "Looking good. I'll be back to check on you in a bit." The air swirled with the scent of flowers as she left the room, the door closing behind her.

"You got into an argument with Hettie on the way home from the bar, right?" Wolf said.

Jesse stared into nothing.

"She was upset with you for confessing everything to Kyle. That's what she told us when we talked to her. She had put off telling Kyle for months. In fact, she probably would have kept the secret going had it not been for you. But like you said, you were sick of hiding the truth. And you fought for her. And you got beat up for her. It's never fun getting whooped by another man. But to make things worse, she was mad at you for what you did."

Jesse barely shook his head.

"I think I'm right," Wolf said. "She told us you two got into an argument and you dropped her off at home. And when you did that, you were devastated, weren't you? You were bleeding, you were broken. I can only imagine how hard that must have been. That kind of thing will make your blood boil. You were rejected."

Jesse shook his head harder now.

"Just like your father did to you all over again, right?"

Jesse's head swiveled smoothly over to Wolf. His eyes were like a cat's just before pouncing.

"You had a .45 in your Jeep, under the seat. You always have a gun there, right? Like you did that night you were pulled over by Sobeck and Triplett. You were enraged, and in the heat of the moment, all you could think about was lashing out. Lashing out at Kyle, who, even after you fessed up to him and got your clock cleaned, was still standing in between you and Hettie."

"No," Jesse said.

Wolf continued. "You went up there, knocked on the door, and you shot him twice. Dead. And then what? You weren't done. You decided you were going to avenge Hettie's father, right?"

"No," Jesse said. "I didn't do any of this. It was Sobeck. He was trying to make it look like I did it."

Wolf nodded. "That's why you called us up to jail in Montrose, so we'd start thinking it might be Sobeck. My detective and I went to his house. We found a pair of boots in his garage. They had blood on the soles, and mud from where Kyle was buried."

"See?" Jesse said. "He did it."

"No, Jesse. You did it. You shot Kyle, and then you got the fifty-caliber from the shed, went down to Alexander Guild's and shot him. And then you came back. And then you pinned it on Sobeck. He lives right there next to you, as you painfully know. You two have a history, right? Back in that interrogation room you said Triplett and Sobeck were always hassling you and Kyle, but you meant Sobeck was harassing you, right? He's the one hard on you. The way he came over and roughed you up for shooting guns at all hours. Then there was that time you three were out joyriding, when he pulled you over. He put you right into the dirt in front of Hettie."

Jesse lowered his eyes. Shook his head again.

"Must have been humiliating."

Jesse said nothing. Burton's monitoring machines hummed gently.

Wolf continued. "You knew Sobeck had been gone from his house, because Hettie and Jill are friends from working at the diner together, and you heard all about Sobeck's troubles from Hettie. So you got into your Jeep and you drove down to the Sobecks', and you went into the garage and found the shovel, the tarps, the boots, and a headlamp. You parked far away and snuck inside, but Jill Sobeck's mother saw you coming out of the garage with the stuff."

Jesse narrowed his eyes.

Wolf nodded. "She saw you. And you walked back down the road, got back into your Jeep and went back up to Kyle's. Then you made it look like Sobeck did it. You stomped around in Kyle's blood. You even decided to put your bracelet in Kyle's hand to make it look like somebody was framing you." Wolf shook his head. "That was a hedge, because you realized it was really going to look like you did everything, right? So, why not make it over-the-top looking like you did it? It worked on me, I must admit. I thought it looked so nice and tidy like you did it that I started looking for other suspects."

"Me too," said Burton.

"No." Jesse's voice was a whisper.

"Brilliant stuff," Wolf said. "And then you wrapped up Kyle and dragged him down, buried him, and left the head-lamp in the grass, for a blunt clue for us to follow."

"No." Jesse's voice had more force. "It wasn't me. There's no proof."

"When you climbed back up the hill after burying Kyle," Wolf said, "you had Sobeck's boots on. You had been step-ping in Kyle's blood, and there was mud on the soles of the boots. You're smart, you've proven that, so you knew that if you got into your Jeep, you'd leave traces of all that blood and mud on your foot pedals, and then you'd be tied to the scene. But you had to transport the boots and shovel back to Sobeck's garage, right? You had to plant the evidence there. The shovel was clean enough, no blood on that, but the boots were a different story. So you took them off, and you took a plastic bag from the rear of your car."

The corners of Jesse's mouth dropped down.

"And you shoved the boots in there to transport back to Sobeck's."

Jesse stared blankly.

"But there's one problem," Wolf said, pausing.

Jesse's eyes focused on Wolf.

"There was a receipt in the bag, and it stuck to the mud on the boot." Wolf pulled his phone and showed the picture of the receipt.

Jesse made no move to look closer.

"This item here. It says GTRD. Which I'm assuming is

Gatorade. And this third item? JCFG. What's that stand for, Jesse?"

Jesse said nothing.

"Juicy Fruit gum," Wolf said. "That's the brand of gum I pulled from your pockets when I frisked you down in Canyon of the Ancients."

Roll walked over to Wolf and stepped close. "Listen, there's no time stamp or address of the store on that receipt," Roll whispered. "No way of getting surveillance footage."

Wolf ignored him. "Did you kill Kyle and Alexander Guild, Jesse?"

Jesse shut his eyes.

"Answer the question," Burton said.

Jesse said nothing. A tear slid down his cheek.

"I know why you ran, Jesse," Wolf said. "Because when you got home after doing all that, murdering Kyle, murdering Guild, burying Kyle and making it look like an innocent cop did it all, she was there. Hettie was waiting for you at your house. And you felt shame for what you did. Because it was all for nothing. Hettie had come back to you anyway. All you needed to do was stand up to Kyle, like you had done. You didn't have to act out that fantasy you'd been thinking about, planning, for who knows how many months. You didn't have to kill them and ruin a good cop's life."

Jesse shook his head more.

"And she probably wondered where you had been all night, right?" Wolf asked. "And you had no answers for her. Then over the next couple days, everything unfolded, and you knew that the cops were going to talk to you and Hettie. You knew she would figure out that you did it. You knew

Hettie would reject you again and you knew that Hettie would tell the cops that you were out all night. So you ran."

Jesse blinked and another tear raced down his skin.

"I remember the moment we told you that Hettie said you were with her all night. I remember looking at you in the rearview mirror and seeing the light return to your eyes. You ran because you thought she was going to tell everyone you did it. But then she lied for you. She gave you an alibi. And you felt like you'd been given a second life."

Jesse wiped his eyes.

"So, I ask you again. What do you think she's going to say now when she wakes up? You think that after four more deaths she's going to continue to lie for you? Are you going to make her do that for you? Are you going to keep kicking and screaming? Or are you going to be a man and 'fess up?"

Jesse moved with lightning speed, picking up something from the lunch tray and darting behind the hospital bed. A machine crashed to the floor as Jesse pulled it off its mounts by getting tangled in its wires. He wrapped his muscular arm around his uncle and lifted him clean up.

"Freeze, Jesse!" Wolf pulled his gun and aimed.

Roll pulled his, too.

Burton grunted in ultimate pain.

Jesse, ducking behind his uncle, let go of the headlock and clamped his hand over Burton's mouth. He twisted Burton's head to expose the neck and put a fork to his jugular vein.

The hospital room door flew open and the nurse came in. "Is everything—oh my God!"

"Get out!" Jesse screamed at the top of his lungs. "Now!"

She did, and the door clicked shut.

Wolf held his aim out the window behind Jesse. There was no shot.

"Jesse," Wolf said.

"He wasn't a good cop," Jesse said.

"What?" Roll asked.

"Sobeck! He's an asshole piece of shit. He hit his kid and ditched out on his family. He's a piece of shit."

Roll nodded. "Okay, okay, Jesse."

"Just shut up ... just shut up." It looked like Jesse was trying to destroy reality with each blink. Finally, his gaze landed on Wolf. "None of this would have happened if you hadn't shown up."

"What do you mean, Jesse?" Wolf asked.

"I mean I was going to shoot my uncle and shoot myself." Jesse's voice bounced with emotion. "Down there in Canyon of the Ancients I was going to blow his head off and then my own. None of any of this would have happened."

Wolf lowered his gun. "Please, Sheriff. Lower your weapon."

Roll eyed him. "I don't know about that, detective."

"Please." Wolf holstered his gun. "Jesse. Please. Your uncle's really hurting right now."

"I don't care! I've been hurting my whole life and he didn't care!"

Burton clawed at Jesse's arm, struggling for breath, his eyes wide. He was trying to get his legs underneath him, probably to alleviate the stretching of his chest.

"Please, Jesse." Wolf watched Burton struggle. "Jesse, I don't think that's what you were going to do. I mean, that's what it seems like, but ... sometimes things aren't what they seem, you know?"

Jesse sobbed. "What are you talking about!"

"I mean, to me, it looks like you called your uncle down there to help. To help you. You knew the jig was up, you knew you'd messed up, and that you'd made a big mistake. And you wanted your uncle's help. You wanted him to be there for you while you confessed everything."

Jesse's head was down, so Wolf was unable to see his face, but it looked like Jesse's grip was letting up.

Burton's eyes were like a trapped animal's, tracking Wolf as he walked slowly toward the bed.

"Jesse. You didn't want a bunch of lawmen you didn't know to bring you in. You wanted your uncle. You wanted him by your side while you told them all exactly what happened. That it was all a big mistake, and that you were sorry."

Jesse relaxed the fork's pressure on Burton's neck.

"That's what it looks like to me," Wolf said.

He reached out, and he pulled Jesse's hand away from Burton's skin. Jesse let go of the fork, and then his uncle's face.

CHAPTER 40

"Dah! Dah!" The tiny hand gripped Wolf's upper lip and twisted.

"Ahh!" Despite the sharp pain, he resisted pulling the appendage away.

After an agonizing few seconds, the hand released and slapped Wolf's forehead.

"What are you doing? You're beating me up!"

Ryan giggled until he was breathless, and then slapped Wolf again on the head. "Dah!"

Wolf laughed just as intensely, taking the beating. As he stared at the boy's beautiful green eyes, Wolf could see why they were so often called windows to the soul. He couldn't shake the feeling of déjà vu he got with this kid, like they'd known each other for a long time.

"You guys having a battle of wits?" Jack walked up with a heaping plate of food.

"He can't get enough of you, I swear," Cassidy said as she joined them.

"That's cause I'm his gram-pa! Gram-pa!"

Ryan giggled some more and put his head on Wolf's shoulder, a simple gesture that instantly melted his heart.

Then Ryan grunted. And vibrated a little.

"Oh." Cassidy wrinkled her nose and put down her meal. "Poopies. Here, I'll take him."

Wolf gladly handed him over and picked up his soda from off the deck. "My God I love that kid."

Jack smiled, watching Cassidy swish into the house with a now crying boy over her shoulder. "I know the feeling."

They stood watching the crowd gathered on Wolf's front lawn. Bluegrass music streamed from speakers on his front deck, just audible beneath the excited chatter of three dozen people.

Smoke rose from two barbecues, the one nearest the keg manned by Rachette, who was laughing hard as Yates grabbed his crotch and screamed the punchline to a story, one that made Patterson bust out laughing as well.

The mayor was there, playing cornhole with three children and a dog who pranced after the beanbags.

"This is great," Jack said.

Great was not the word. There were no words for the mist of gratitude, relaxation, elation, and fulfillment swirling in his body.

"How's it going in Carbondale?" Wolf asked.

"Oh, yeah. That." Jack sipped his beer. "I haven't told you yet."

Wolf eyed his son. "What's that?"

"I've decided to become a fireman."

"Really. What about the job in Carbondale? I thought mineral exploration was treating you well."

Jack shrugged. "It's just not me, you know? I've figured

out I need to be helping people. Not helping companies. But people."

Wolf slapped his son's back. "That's great."

"I mean, I still have the job. I've just been working hard in my off time. I got my EMT cert from the Carbondale Fire Department, and they know I'm gunning to be part of their team. Or wherever I can get. As long as it's in the mountains, I guess. Cassidy's on board with this."

Wolf smiled. "That's really great."

"The chief there's a cool guy. He says there's going to be some openings in the next year, and I think he likes me. So we'll see."

"Who's the chief?"

"A guy named John Lassiter."

"I know him."

"I'd rather you not talk to him," Jack said. "I think it would be weird."

Wolf nodded and gripped his son's shoulder. "That's great."

"You've said that a few times already."

There was a commotion as Rachette dropped a hamburger on the lawn.

"Okay, I'm getting a beer," Jack said, and left.

Wolf smiled, musing at the adult conversation with his son. It was only minutes ago Jack was a floppy-haired ten-year-old sneaking sodas from the cooler at events like this.

"Where's Ryan?" Patterson appeared at Wolf's side. "And why's Rachette eating meat off the ground?"

"He's inside getting a diaper change, and because he's Rachette."

Patterson looked up at Wolf. "I'm really glad you're going to be sheriff." She slurred just a tad.

"Yeah. We'll see about grooming the next person to take over after me. Because that's the last job I want in the world."

"Really?" She sipped her beer. "I guess that makes sense. You're an investigator at heart, right?"

"Something like that."

"Who would you groom? Wilson's pretty adamant about not taking the job. Not sure what his problem is on that."

Wolf nodded, looking her in the eye. "We'll figure it out."

She crinkled her forehead and lowered her beer.

"Speaking of sheriff," Wolf said, eyeing the crowd. "Where's MacLean?"

"I saw him earlier," she said. "But I don't remember where. Damn, I'm getting drunk. But we have the babysitter tonight, I'm off tomorrow, and Scott's driving, so I'm getting another beer."

Wolf watched her swerve away toward the keg. He turned to the house, walked up onto the deck, and went inside.

The door to his study was closed and he popped it open. There was no one in the room, but he walked to the window and looked out onto the back lawn.

MacLean was out in the fading light by himself, lounging on a padded lawn chair.

Wolf walked through the house to the kitchen, and out the rear entrance. The door hissed shut, the silence deafening compared to what was happening out front. Crickets sang nearby, while an owl hooted somewhere in the woods.

"Hello, sheriff," MacLean said, hidden by the chair's high back.

Wolf padded on the grass and found MacLean staring up at the night sky.

"Hello, sheriff," he said back. "You're not out front."

"Nah."

Wolf sat down on the vacant seat next to him, facing the darkened forest. The mountain above was still glowing faintly.

MacLean was wrapped in blankets taken off of Wolf's couch, a disturbing reminder of Kyle Farmer bound in the black tarps under that Ridgway earth. He raised his eyes to the sky and saw what MacLean was staring at—a spray of stars growing brighter with each second the sun set further behind them.

"Is Bonnie okay?" MacLean asked.

"Yeah." Wolf recalled seeing MacLean's wife chatting in a circle out front a few minutes earlier. She had seemed subdued, not okay.

MacLean grunted and looked up again.

Wolf sat in the chair and felt the tension in his back melt away, the coolness of the padding penetrating through his fleece.

They sat like that for a while, until MacLean said, "I didn't want to come, but Bonnie thought it was a good idea. I didn't want to talk to a bunch of people."

"I understand."

The owl hooted again.

"It's such a strange feeling, knowing you're gonna die," MacLean said. "I mean, really, when you think about it, there's absolutely no difference in my life now than from a month ago. Back then, I was oblivious, but there was still a hundred percent chance I was going to die. There's no change today. Still a whopping sure bet I'll be leaving this world soon. Only now I've got odds it's going to be the cancer that takes me down." MacLean sighed. "What are you thinking about?"

Wolf pulled down the corners of his mouth. "I guess now I'm thinking about when I'm going to die."

"Shoot, I'd say sooner than later. You have a grandchild now. You're an old man."

Wolf grinned.

"Are you feeling up for the job ahead?" MacLean asked.

Wolf considered the question as he stared at Orion's belt. The rest of the week at the station had gone smoothly. As far as the physical move from Wolf's office to MacLean's went, he'd had to carry two cardboard boxes worth of material down the hallway.

The official swearing in with the County Council had been quick and easy. Wolf got the sense that some members were less enthused by the change than others, and that the unanimous sentiments within the department had won out over opinions within the council.

MacLean had spent two days relaying enough behind the scenes action from the last few years to fill a book and had walked Wolf through some of the new duties he'd be account-able for. From what Wolf could gather, he could decide for himself how he'd run the department, which was good, because the detail of MacLean's day-to-day routine, sitting behind his desk and making phone calls, was less than inspir-ing. Wolf planned on being out in the field more, where his father had done most of his sheriff's work, and where Wolf had done his during his short stint as sheriff years ago.

Then again, in those days he and his father had run a

much smaller ship than the behemoth behind the glass walls in Rocky Points today.

"If I have to be honest," Wolf said, "I've spent a few hours staring at the ceiling of my bedroom the last few nights."

MacLean chuckled. "That's part of the job description."

"So I remember."

"If you're not worried, you're not the right man for the job." MacLean sat up and scooted to the end of the chair. He turned and looked at Wolf. His eyes were dollops of oil in the moonless night. "You're the best cop I've ever known. Don't let that get to your head, now. Mind you, I haven't known that many cops. Well, a building or two full of them...but it's the truth."

Wolf nodded. "Thank you, sir."

"And you'll do just fine."

"I hope so."

"I know so."

Wolf scooted forward and joined him at the edge of the chair. "You could have waited until I accepted the position before you gave away mine."

"If I thought you would have refused, I wouldn't have done it."

"I could have. Wilson did."

"Wilson's not a dumbass."

Wolf smiled. "You've been talking to Burton."

MacLean's mustache curled up. "Saw the old man at his house earlier today. Shit, I thought I was in bad shape. That guy's a mess." He straightened and pulled the blankets tight around his shoulders. "We made a pact. We're going to survive. We even made a fishing date—June seventeenth, next year."

An inhale shook in MacLean's chest.

Wolf looked toward the house. Bonnie MacLean stood in the window of his kitchen looking out. She turned and disappeared back inside.

"I want you to promise me something," MacLean said.

"What's that?"

"Take care of her if I don't make it. I mean, she's a strong woman and can take care of herself. Just...make sure she remembers that."

Wolf nodded. "Of course. I promise."

MacLean nodded, and then he tilted his face to the sky. "You head back in. I think I'll stay out here with the stars. And can you send Bonnie out? I think we'll sneak around the house and go quietly."

Wolf stood up. "Sure thing."

"See ya."

Wolf squeezed his shoulder. He tried to come up with something profound to say but drew a blank. "Later, old man," he said, and he turned to walk across the lawn towards the kitchen.

"June seventeenth!" MacLean yelled.

He stopped and turned around.

MacLean was standing, almost invisible in the darkness beyond the house's glow. "You mark that day on the calendar. I'll come see you too. If I'm not there in person, I'll be there in spirit. If you feel a sudden urge to go to the bathroom, that's me working my magic."

Wolf laughed. "I'll look forward to seeing you in person, then."

They waved at one another, and MacLean sat back down, disappearing into the darkness.

Wolf turned back to the house. He paused at the door, and then he stepped through, back into the melody of a bluegrass song.

Thank you for reading Divided Sky. I hope you enjoyed the story, and if you did, thank you for taking a few moments to leave a review. As an independent author exposure is everything, and if you'd consider leaving a review, which helps me so much with that exposure, I'd be very grateful.

CLICK HERE TO LEAVE A REVIEW

I love interacting with readers so please feel free to email me at jeff@jeffcarson.co so I can thank you personally. Otherwise, thanks for your support via other means, such as sharing the books with your friends/family/book clubs/the weird guy who wears tight women's yoga pants sitting next to you right now, or anyone else you think might be interested in reading the David Wolf series. Thanks again for spending time in Wolf's world.

Would you like to know about future David Wolf books the moment they are published? You can visit my blog and sign up for the New Release Newsletter at this link – http://www.jeffcarson.co/p/newsletter.html.

. . .

As a gift for signing up you'll receive a complimentary copy of Gut Decision—A David Wolf Short Story, which is a harrowing tale that takes place years ago during David Wolf's first days in the Sluice County Sheriff's Department.

Gut Decision (A David Wolf Short Story)– Sign up for the new release newsletter at http://www.jeffcarson.co/p/newsletter.html and receive a complimentary copy.